ARROW TO HIS
HEART
A STRIPLING WARRIOR NOVEL

.

ARROW TO HIS
HEART

A STRIPLING WARRIOR NOVEL

MISTY MONCUR

BOOKS

STANSBURY PARK, UTAH

Published by Eden Books, Stansbury Park, UT

ISBN-10: 0-9898959-2-0
ISBN-13: 978-0-9898959-2-7

Moncur, Misty Leigh, 1978-
Arrow to His Heart / Misty Moncur
Summary: Isabel falls in love with Kenai while helping him learn to live again after he returns from the Lamanite war.

ISBN: 978-0-9898959-2-7

Library of Congress Catalog Control Number

2014937472

For Dave

CHAPTER 1

The sun was just clearing the tops of the pines, and already I was sloshing a deer hide around in the large basin with a wooden paddle. Father had skinned the animal and was expertly wrapping up the meat to haul home.

I glanced at Jarom. My brother was waiting for the hide, tapping his knife idly against the scraping log. If no one else showed up with more work for us to do, Father would let us go home before the midday meal, with the rest of the day free to do as we wished.

Normally, I preferred work at the tannery with my father and brother to anything else, but I had plans for the afternoon, a little bit of spy work I could only get to if we were finished here.

But as I plunged my hands into the basin to wring murky water through the skin, I noticed someone come into the clearing. Because I hadn't seen him since I was eight years old, it took me a few moments to realize it was my eldest brother, Zeke, who ambled into the clearing, shaded his eyes, and found my father.

"Jarom," I said to get his attention, and when he glanced over at me, I nodded in Zeke's direction.

Jarom stood up straight, his knife falling idle in his hand.

Zeke gave me a little wave, but called out, "Father!"

Our father looked up, and when he saw Zeke, he grinned, dropped the bundle he was wrapping on the table, and jogged out to meet his son. They clasped arms as men do, but then my father embraced Zeke joyfully, lifting him off his feet.

I laughed with them and looked to Jarom. But Jarom didn't even smile, just raised a brow and tossed his scraper aside. He ran his hands through his hair as if he expected it to be long, but he had been keeping it cropped short since returning from the war several months ago, and there was nothing for his fingers to grasp onto.

I looked back at my father and Zeke. Zeke's hair was still long, just as I remembered it, and he looked much the same to me as he had when he had marched out of the village with Helaman's army.

"Isabel?" he asked as he came toward me.

I nodded.

"You grew up."

I grinned and glanced down at myself. At fourteen, I wasn't exactly a woman grown, but I certainly wasn't the eight year old girl he remembered.

He put his hand on my shoulder, greeting me formally, and he laughed when I blushed. Then he turned back to Father.

"Have the Lamanites retreated then?" Father asked him.

"We've been reconstructing the towns for many months now," Zeke said with a sideways glance at Jarom, who was standing back a pace with his arms folded tightly over his chest.

Jarom had not stayed in Judea to rebuild the southern cities. He had gone with Kenai, a family friend who was all but a brother to mine, to fight in the east with the armies of Captain Moroni. It had surprised everyone when he and Kenai had returned before Zeke and some of the others.

"But we can talk of that later," he continued. "I need to speak to you first..." He glanced at Jarom and me. "About Keturah."

2

Father glanced at us too and then at the ground. He was quiet for a moment, as if he knew bad news was coming. But what bad news could there be? Surely Zeke wanted to make official what had been all but official for most of his life—his betrothal to the girl he loved. Surely he wanted to see it done as soon as was possible.

"Izz, let that skin soak overnight."

I looked from my father to the basin. "It doesn't need to..."

But I trailed off when I looked back and saw his face. I bit my lip and turned to Jarom to see if he knew what was wrong. He was already gathering his things, slinging his satchel over his chest.

"Alright," I said and obediently followed Jarom out of the clearing. Father was meeting a friend here early tomorrow. It wouldn't harm the skin to soak until then.

"Jarom." I had to jog to catch up to him. "Wait up. What was that?"

He grunted but slowed his pace.

"Do you know what's wrong? Something's wrong."

"Probably."

"What is it? What has it to do with Keturah?"

Keturah was Kenai's sister. She was promised to Zeke, and I had always thought of her as a sister. Our mothers had been best friends since their childhoods, and though Leah's children were not of our blood, they were our family in all other ways that mattered.

"Zeke doesn't want to marry her."

"What?" It was unthinkable.

"It's why he stayed in Judea so long. There's a girl there."

"A girl?" What could he mean by that? "What kind of girl?"

"A girl he—" He cleared his throat. "A girl he loves."

I laughed. "No he doesn't." Zeke and Keturah had been inseparable before he had left. And even if he had met another girl, I didn't think putting Keturah aside was really an option. Too many people were counting on it.

Keturah had gone to the war too, but she had been home for the past year, and she had told me herself she was going to marry Zeke. It really was as good as done.

"Yes he does," Jarom insisted flatly.

"Even if that's true, it doesn't matter."

"It matters because he's the eldest and he gets his pick."

His pick? What did that have to do with anything? He was picking Keturah. Everyone knew that.

"I don't see how that affects you," I said. I couldn't see Jarom with Keturah. It nearly gave me the giggles.

"Nobody does," he said quietly.

When we got back to the house in the village, Jarom hefted one of the big axes and, without a word to anyone, went into the forest behind the yard. He wanted Mother to think he was going to cut wood, and he would probably come back with some, but I knew he wanted to be alone. I just didn't know why. I didn't understand what he had been saying. None of it made any sense to me.

"Please tie Abigail to the post out back."

I watched Jarom go and sighed as I put my tools down, but I did as my mother asked because we couldn't have that crazy old goat wandering around the yard during the celebration.

My parents' eldest son was home from the war. Mother and Sarai, even Chloe, were already rushing to prepare the celebratory dishes to give him a proper welcome home. I was of no use to them in this, and I tried to stay out of their way. They didn't even ask me to help.

When the goat was secure, I wandered across the road. I thought I might talk to Keturah, ask her outright what was going on, but she was nowhere to be seen. The place was quiet. Even Leah was not at home.

It was a good time to go.

Glancing furtively at my mother and sisters, I slipped from the village and set out for the maize fields, but halfway there I stopped in my tracks when I saw Kenai coming down the trail toward me. I turned and darted into the trees, and feeling ridiculous, I hid behind a thick trunk. I didn't know if he had seen me, but he would have been blind to miss me.

Not that I expected him to, but I was disappointed that he didn't chase me down or call out to me. I waited with a pounding heart. When I judged him to have passed, I peered out from behind the tree, eased away from it, and followed him back to the village.

I was glad to see he was talking to a group of men outside his gate when I passed it. Hopefully, he didn't notice me slip through my own gate and into my family's yard.

What Jarom said turned out to be true. No sooner had we sat down to eat than Zeke stood to address the crowd and all eyes turned to him.

"I have decided to withdraw from courting Keturah." He swallowed hard. "A marriage won't suit either of us. Keturah is in full agreement. We wish to make it clear immediately so there will be no false hopes." He looked to Leah, Keturah's mother, and Micah, her eldest brother. "I'm sorry to you both. I will make restitution to your family if you should want it."

Micah gave his head a slight but definitive shake.

If Keturah was in agreement, it wasn't really necessary, the restitution. But being promised to Zeke had kept other suitors away, and if no other men offered to marry her, Micah could still seek the bride price from Zeke. He wouldn't though.

That was why I was alone at my father's tannery, stretching the deer skin so it could dry overnight, fuming that Jarom had been right, fuming that I always had to do what my parents wanted and Zeke didn't.

When I began to hear shouts and noises I couldn't identify in the forest surrounding me, I looked up and noticed the twilight had begun to wane into darkness. I decided I better hurry home, so I swiftly stowed my things in the small tanning hut and started for the village.

A group of men came through the trees in front of me, five or six of them, and I knew immediately by their clothing and their shaved heads they were not Ammonite like me. I had walked directly into their path. There was no avoiding them. I froze, but they had already noticed me.

One of them, a short one with greasy ointment on his skin to ward off bugs, grinned and swept me along with them, forcing me back along the path into the clearing. I might have gone peaceably, as there seemed to be no other choice. I might have tried to run later when a better opportunity presented itself. It's what my mother would have done. But the man's hands skimmed my body, and I reacted, rearing back and kicking out. I screamed as I twisted in his arms, pulled his hair, scratched at his face.

His grip broke and I started to run from him, but where I had been alone only minutes before, the clearing was filled now. It teemed with coarse men and other women and girls. My eyes caught on girls I knew, girls I had known my whole life, and my conscience pricked. I knew I should run. I should run as fast as I could to the village and get my brothers. Zeke was home tonight. There was a celebration. He and Jarom were there, and many of their friends. But when I started to run, I heard a child's cry.

I turned back. Running away was not the answer. The

men had made short work of tying their captives into a long line—women, girls, and even little children—and were already herding them from the clearing, one big man tugging on the rope.

The man who had grabbed me before growled and lunged for me. His friends were laughing at him, at the scratches on his face. I would have too, but he caught me and got my arms pinned behind me, yanking them hard. When the leather thong cut into my wrists, I winced and stilled.

The man sneered something I did not understand into my ear. The other captives were disappearing through the trees. I started to follow them, but the man tugged me back against his body, tight, and let his hands roam over me again.

I sucked in a breath. I had never been manhandled in such a manner. Mustering all my strength, I shoved my shoulder back into his chest, shrugging him off of me, and I ran toward the others. Before I entered the trees, the sneering man and his laughing friends behind me, I turned toward the village and let out the loudest scream I could.

The wildcat. The call my brothers used to communicate over distances in the woods. I hoped they would hear it amidst their celebrations. They had to. Or I would have to rescue these girls on my own.

It was dark in the forest now, but I could tell we cut a path through the trees toward the West Road. I had never traveled far from my village, and when we emerged onto the road, I was farther south than I had ever been on it. The strange men, some manner of Lamanites I thought, all had weapons at the ready, and even the young children among us knew to stay quiet.

I had my good tanning knife tied securely around my waist, but I couldn't get to it, tied the way I was, so I followed along swiftly in the line without drawing attention to myself. When at last we stopped and I was sitting apart from my captors, the darkness shielding me from them, I was able to slip my legs through so my arms were in front of me. They burned from being behind my back, but slowly the feeling came back into them. After long moments, I was able to ease my knife out, but it wasn't a simple matter to slice through my bonds. I couldn't hold the knife the right way to put pressure on the cords.

"What are you doing?"

I turned at the sound of Abish's whispered words, no louder than the breeze.

I scooted closer to her and held out the knife.

When she saw it, her eyes shot to mine for a brief second, but she took it in her tied hands and turned it toward my bonds.

In silence, she cut me free. I winced when she sliced into my skin, but feared to make a sound. Then I took the knife and did the same for her. I had turned to cut Rachel free when one of the men called out.

I looked up in time to see Jarom wrestling with one of the guards near the small fire.

My kinsmen were here! They had heard the call of the wildcat and come for me!

I saw Kenai take another of the guards to the ground. I saw them struggle, saw both of their bodies go stiff, but when Kenai retreated back into a crouch, the Lamanite man did not get up.

Others were moving in the firelight now, boys I knew. Zeke was there and Micah and Muloki, and with the strength of my kinsmen around me, my eyes found the man who had grabbed me. No one was fighting him, and he was sliding back into the darkness like a snake. In a moment he would be gone, running free through the forest.

I thought of the way he had touched me, of what these men intended for us. He would not get away. I gripped my knife

8

and lunged for him. I wasn't sure how I managed it—adrenaline, fear, anger, humiliation—but I found myself standing over him as he bled into the earth.

"Isabel."

I knew the voice, but I couldn't take my eyes from the man on the ground, his hand clutched over his bleeding wound, to turn toward it.

"Izz."

I felt his hand on my shoulder. It brought me from my shock, and I turned to look up at him.

"It's me," he said cautiously when he saw my eyes. "Kenai."

I nodded, jerkily moving my chin up and down, because I couldn't speak.

He looked at me for another moment and then pulled me into his chest. *He's protecting me*, I thought, but I could sense the fighting around us had diminished. I knew my kinsmen had won, too. They had the clear advantage over their sleeping enemy. I would be safe now.

Then why were Kenai's arms around me if they were not warding off some immediate danger? I wanted to pull away, to look up and find the answer in his face, but I had already seen it.

I just didn't believe it.

Suddenly, I saw the man at our feet rise up on his elbows, and just as suddenly, he fell, sprawled back on the ground.

Kenai's hand covered the back of my head, and he turned my face into his chest. "Don't look."

After a moment, his grip loosened. "Are you okay?" he murmured into my hair.

I nodded, more sure this time, but I said, "My hand is cut."

He eased back and inspected the hand I held out to him.

9

I thought the cut had been small, but my hand was covered in blood and clutching my knife. My hand fell open and the knife fell to the ground with a dull thud.

"Here," Kenai said, and he took my other hand and positioned them together between us. Slowly, he tipped water from his own water skin over them, rubbing them between his thumb and fingers to clean off the blood, which I realized then was not mine.

Suddenly, Kenai stepped back.

I felt dizzy for a moment, looking up to see Kenai turn and replace his water skin at his belt. He put his hands on his hips and avoided my eyes as if I had not just been nestled in his arms. But then Zeke was there, running his hands over my arms, drawing my attention to him.

"Izz! Are you okay? Are you hurt?"

I looked beyond him. The fighting seemed to be done. "I'm..." I swallowed hard. "I'm not hurt."

He surprised me with a hug of his own, but it was nothing like Kenai's had been. His hands did not linger in my hair and his chest did not rumble with murmured words.

"You heard the wildcat," I said in relief. "You heard it."

"Kenai did, and then Jarom ran in from the forest. He said he had seen Lamanites near the West Road. No one knew where you were." His eyes pierced through me in the darkness. "But Chloe said she had seen you go toward the tannery."

"I had work to finish," I said lamely.

He snorted and passed me a piece of venison from his satchel. "It's a long walk home," he said and turned to Kenai. "Can you keep an eye on her?"

I didn't hear Kenai's answer, and I didn't dare look at him to see his response, but when Zeke stalked away to help dig shallow graves for the Lamanite dead, Kenai stayed awkwardly near my side. Would he rather be digging graves with the other men than stand next to me?

I didn't think I could eat, but Zeke was right. I would need the energy to return home. While I ate the venison, I watched Keturah move among the men, watched as she spoke gently to the children and helped loose the bonds of the other captives and give them food. *I should help her*, I thought, but I didn't want to find that Kenai would not follow me, so I stayed where I was.

Kenai bent and picked up my knife. He wiped it clean on his tunic and passed it to me without a word.

"Were any of the men hurt?" I asked as I put it away at my belt.

He scrubbed at the back of his head and glanced around. "No." Then he jerked his hand down to his satchel as if he just remembered he carried it. "Here." He dug through it and pulled out a small jar and a bandage.

I reached for the bandage, but he shook his head and stepped closer.

His hands were steady as he expertly applied the salve and administered to my wound. It was no deeper than the skin, but it did sting. He gently smoothed some of the salve over the chafing at my wrists.

"Thank you," I said when he was done, and neither of us said any more until Keturah made her way over to us.

"Come on," she said, glancing between us, schooling her expression. "We're going to get moving. The other girls are anxious to get home."

CHAPTER 2

I traveled through the dark night between Keturah and Kenai, hardly believing what had happened, what I had just done. The reality was starting to sink in. I pulled in a slow breath and assured myself it wasn't anything Keturah and the others hadn't done.

Zeke and Jarom glided quietly through the night ahead of us. And though my heart was still pounding from the danger and excitement, stalking Lamanites through the forest was probably very routine for them.

I cast a secret glance to my side, where Kenai walked protectively near me.

He hadn't left my side since the fighting started. He had shielded me from the death of the man whose escape I had prevented. He had helped me wash the blood off my hands, pouring water on them and rubbing them with his own. He had watched me eat the venison. He had bandaged my hand, given it a little squeeze when it was wrapped up tight.

I wondered what had happened to him in the war to make him the way he was—melancholy, disinterested, violent at random times. I wondered if time would heal his heart.

And mostly, I wondered why he had held me so tenderly after I had stabbed that terrible Lamanite man.

I wasn't discreet enough. Kenai must have felt me

watching him because he deliberately looked down to catch my eye. He didn't smile at me, not even a little, before he turned his eyes back to the path, but he glanced at me now and then. I could feel it.

It was noticeably lighter, but I stumbled over a stone in the path.

Zeke and Jarom were talking in low tones ahead of us, but Zeke turned to ask, "You okay, Izz?"

I tossed my hair back. "Perfectly fine."

Jarom turned back too, and I saw him roll his eyes at my snippy comment before he turned to take a long, hard look at Kenai.

My brothers had been gone so long I hardly knew them anymore. When Jarom had strolled into the village a few months ago, I hadn't even recognized the man hugging my mother, with his hair cut short and his thick arms wrapped around her. He was taller than I remembered too. And Zeke had said only a few words to me since he had arrived home yesterday—he was too busy bowing out of his responsibilities as the firstborn son. We were all three like strangers.

Zeke turned to Keturah next but only looked her over briefly before turning forward again—like it wasn't his duty to ask after her welfare, like it wasn't his privilege to know she was okay, like he wasn't her intended husband.

It wasn't that I felt Keturah should have to marry my brother if she didn't want to. I was heartily against that. But she was supposed to want to. All the other girls in the village wanted to. She was refusing him just because she could. She was spoiled and selfish and heartless, and most importantly, she got everything her way, and I never did.

My fingers slid to the tanning knife at my belt, and I remembered the day after Zeke and Jarom had left for the war. I had acquired a new chore that day. Not only did I have to milk Sachemai, my family's little goat, but I had the new responsibility of milking Mui while Keturah was away with the army. I liked that her family had entrusted me with this responsibility, but I hated milking the goats.

"Steady now," I said to Sachemai as I patted her side. But she wasn't steady, or I wasn't, and what milk I had gotten into the bowl went everywhere.

I ground my teeth and stared at the mess. Chloe giggled and Sarai gave me a sad smile as she righted the bowl and wiped away the drips. The stupid goat was happily cropping the grasses at the edge of the yard.

I might have started to cry if Father hadn't come from the hut then, surveyed the scene, and decided he had too much work to accomplish alone. He said he had given all his skins to the militia for scabbards, tents, leggings, kilts, water skins, and satchels, and he needed my help.

That one moment, that one decision had changed my life.

Or, at least, it had changed my chores. After that day, Sarai cared for the goats, and I went with my father to the tannery.

It smelled at the tannery—that was my first impression—and I was sure I smelled of animal carcass when I went home that evening because Father and my brothers always did. But I didn't care.

It was nearly dawn and we had come quite a ways while my mind had been wandering. At the pace we were traveling, we would be home in the village in a quarter of an hour.

Keturah squeezed my arm and gave me a smile before jogging ahead to talk to Muloki. She slugged him in the arm, and he laughed heartily, his laughter contrasting the soft footfalls and quiet murmurs of the other travelers.

Most of the other captives travelled ahead of us in a group led by the man called Jashon and his brother. The rest travelled in smaller groups, interspersed with the men who had come to rescue us.

Keturah was furtively watching Jashon, or perhaps his brother, as she walked beside Muloki. I noticed because I was doing the same thing. But why was she pining after that strange warrior when she was supposed to be pining after my brother?

"You think she's crazy," Kenai broke into my thoughts.

"Oh," I said, surprised. I had never been shy around Kenai, but I felt a blush rise on my cheeks. "I...no. I don't. I don't think that, I mean."

"They're to be betrothed," he said over my pathetic stammering. He put a finger to his lips. "It's a secret. She doesn't know yet."

"Oh," I said again. I looked back to her. "Will she accept, do you think?"

"Without a doubt," he said. "But that doesn't matter. Micah has already done so on her behalf."

That sparked my temper. It didn't matter? Micah had already accepted on her behalf? She shouldn't have to marry Zeke if she didn't want to, and she shouldn't have to marry that stranger, either. I did not think women should be given in marriage, as was the custom. I thought a woman should choose for herself.

"That is absolute nonsense! It is infuriatingly belittling when men presume to—"

Kenai snorted and his sudden chuckle surprised me.

"What's funny?"

"Big words for a little girl like you."

What? I frowned at the ground.

Then I stuck out my foot and tripped him.

He stumbled and looked back. His confusion turned to amusement when he saw I had stopped and drawn my knife, ready for a fight.

I was a little girl, but how dare he call me one!

He chuckled again, low in his chest. "Put that knife away, Isabel, or I'll take it from you," he warned calmly. And I might have, except he added with a deliberate smirk, "That knife is not a play thing like your dolls."

Oh, how I wanted to hurt him in that moment, my adrenaline and fatigue making his words more insulting than they should have been. I would never cut him with the knife—just the memory of what I had done made me shiver—but after what had happened, after being bound and abducted, I felt safer holding it. I wanted to make a point. I was not little, and I was not helpless.

"Come on now," he said. "Put it away."

By now, the others were a distance ahead of us and no one had noticed we were missing. Some rescue mission, I thought as I watched my brothers disappear below a curve in the trail with the others.

Why couldn't my brothers be as protective of me as Keturah's were of her? Not that I would particularly want that. And of course, they thought Kenai was protecting me. Why would they think I needed protection from Kenai?

Suddenly, I was on my back in the dirt, staring up into Kenai's face, and he had taken my knife from me.

"I warned you," he said quietly.

"Give me my knife back!"

He smiled. "You're not old enough to play with this knife."

I squirmed, trying to get up, trying to retrieve my knife from his hand where he held it just out of my reach.

Kenai forced me to stop wiggling by allowing more of the

17

weight from his chest to rest on me. My panic must have shown in my face because he went very still. When I tried to draw in a breath, he slid away from me, hastily withdrawing until he knelt up on his heels at my side.

"Sorry, Isabel," he said uncomfortably and handed back my blade with the hilt extended toward me. He wouldn't look me in the eye. He glanced up ahead, got to his feet, and offered me a hand.

I took it, feeling the dirt on his rough hand and wondering why my cheeks were still hot.

When I was standing, I put my knife into its scabbard. I shot a disgusted look at his turned back, but I said, "It's okay. You're trained to act."

"Yeah," he scoffed under his breath. "Trained to act. Come on."

I walked after him for a few steps and then caught up and walked beside him, still wondering what had happened.

When the group ahead of us entered the village, we heard the relieved cheer go up. Nobody noticed we walked in together minutes behind everyone else.

Kenai put a light hand on my back and led me to where Zeke and Jarom stood together surveying the many reunions. He punched Jarom in the arm and walked away without speaking to me at all, as if walking with me was just a favor he had done for a friend. I tried not to watch him as he met up with his younger brother, Dare, but my eyes followed them as they pushed through the crowd toward home.

Zeke put his hands on his hips, drawing my attention back to him. "I thought I was done with strong-willed women."

It wasn't a compliment.

Jarom smirked, but I disregarded them both, put my chin in the air and set off for home where I could see Mother on her

18

toes trying to spot us. Father stood behind her with his hands on her shoulders looking just as anxious.

I felt Zeke and Jarom fall in on both sides of me as I wove through the groups of tired people, but I didn't look at either one of them. I thought it would be best if I just ignored them, but halfway home I thought *why not?* I slipped my foot out and tripped Zeke. When he stumbled, Jarom chuckled at his expense, but I quickly tripped him too, and then I ran ahead into my Mother's arms. By the time my brothers reached home, tired and annoyed, I was safely ensconced in my Father's protective embrace.

I looked back over my shoulder as I stepped from Father's arms. Darius and Kenai were talking to Leah in their yard across the road. They both glanced at me, and I quickly looked away, embarrassed. Zeke and Jarom's skinny little sister—that's what they saw.

"Isabel, you need to take someone with you when you go to the tannery," Zeke was saying. "It's too far. Even Keturah takes a guard."

"And Keturah's supposed to be my model of behavior?"

He sighed.

"Besides," I said, "I remember a raid that happened right here in this village. Our home is just as vulnerable as the woods. Face it, you wasted six years of your life and it's no safer here than it was before you left."

"Isabel!" exclaimed my mother.

I just gave everyone a scowl and walked into the house.

"As much as I hate to admit it," I heard Jarom say, "She's right. Wickedness abounds, even here in Melek."

"All the more reason she shouldn't resist our protection," Zeke insisted.

A fine time to get protective. I remembered Kenai's chest

pressing down on mine, his eyes searching for something in my face, his sudden movement away when he found it.

"She's not used to it," Father said in my defense.

I gathered up all the things I would need for the work day, filling my satchel with my full set of tools and some food for a midday meal.

Out the side door of our home, I heard Chloe talking to Keturah in the yard. Keturah? Accompanied by a guard? It was ridiculous. Zeke didn't know what he was saying. And did he want to be the one to accompany me everywhere? That was a laugh.

When I stepped into the courtyard ready to go to work, my whole family stopped talking and stared at me. After a moment, Mother offered everyone breakfast, which no one accepted.

Chloe was at work milking the goat. Why shouldn't I go to work?

Well, of course I knew why. I had been kidnapped from the tannery not twelve hours ago. I had been traveling all night. But there was no way I was going to fall asleep. Besides, it was daylight, and I wouldn't be alone. Did they expect me to sit around all day sucking my thumb, looking to be coddled?

"So," I said, looking from Zeke to Jarom. "Which one of you is escorting me everywhere I go now?"

They exchanged a glance.

"I guess I'll go out to the tannery with you," Jarom offered. "But don't you want to get some sleep first?"

He tried to stifle a yawn, but I thought it was a pretend one, so I just stared him down without answering. After a minute I turned and began fidgeting with the tools in my satchel.

"Let me get you all that breakfast," Mother said, and she bustled off to get it together.

By then, Jarom had been home from the war for several

months, and he usually went to the tannery in the morning with Father and me. Zeke had traveled all the way from Judea the day before, and then he had traveled all night to rescue me and the others. Even though I sensed some kind of rift between them, it was kind of Jarom to let Zeke stay home to sleep. Much kinder than I was being.

"I do have an arrangement to meet Ezra at the tannery today," Father admitted grudgingly, a fact I well knew. "I do not want to break my word." He glanced at me, rubbed a hand over his tired eyes, and turned to Jarom. "We could be done early."

Jarom suppressed a sigh but dutifully prepared to leave. When Mother brought out the breakfast and some extra food to take along for the midday meal, a chore that had been Cana's until she married Micah and moved to the far end of the village, we took it and left the courtyard.

We saw Leah and her new husband, Kalem, speaking to a couple at their fire, a woman with a nice smile and a man who looked very much like Jashon and his brothers. Micah was near the gate speaking to Jashon, and he raised a hand in greeting, which my father returned as we passed. Keturah was nowhere to be seen, but the men from the rescue party milled about the yard accepting food from Cana and talking amongst themselves.

"Who are they?"

Jarom glanced over. "Jashon and Lamech, Gid's brothers. Enos, his cousin. I don't know the little one's name."

"Who's Gid? The man who looks like Jashon?" The man Micah had betrothed Keturah to?

"Yes, and from the looks of it, they're to be Keturah's new family."

I thought there was a note of sadness in his voice.

"Is he the reason she won't marry Zeke?" I asked, remembering how she had looked at Gid that morning as the sun rose. I glanced back over my shoulder at the men. I had thought the whole thing was Micah's doing.

"Appears to be," put in my Father. "And I hope she will be very happy." He too had a note of sadness in his voice, but it did sound as though he meant it.

She better be, I thought, *for all the heartbreak she has caused.*

CHAPTER 3

The tannery consisted of a small building with an awning in the front to shield us from rain and an opening in the back for smoke to escape. This was surrounded by the stakes and frames upon which we stretched and cleaned the hides, a few work benches, and a smokehouse. A stream ran along the north perimeter, one of the main reasons Father had chosen this location.

The Lamanites had used our tannery for their meeting ground, but when we arrived, nothing seemed to be out of place. The whole area had been swarming with Lamanite warriors, but they had obviously been more interested in harming innocent lives than in destroying our property.

Already, two men waited near the hut. Several large game bags sat on the ground between them. I had met Ezra before—he was one of my father's friends—but I had never met the younger man, probably Ezra's son.

"Ezra!" Father walked toward them with his arm outstretched in greeting. "So good to see you."

Jarom knew Ezra's son—definitely one of Helaman's warriors—and they started immediately into a conversation. I didn't waste time looking at him, other than to notice he had dark hair like his father and a shortened tunic like many of the soldiers that had recently returned.

I went around to the back of the hut to retrieve the hide I had scraped the previous evening. Had it only been a few hours ago?

It was time to dress it. I had already put it off too long. I would soak it today, then stretch it and smoke it until it was a beautiful shade of honey brown. I had plans for this piece of buckskin, and I wanted it to be perfect.

I removed the lid from the container that held the animal's brain, which Father had reserved when he skinned the elk. It smelled, but I was used to that. I removed it and placed it into a basin large enough to soak the entire hide.

Glancing at the men who were still chatting, probably coming to an agreement on pricing, I reached for an apron to wipe my hands on and tied it around my waist as I went for a bucket. None of the men paid any attention to me, so I went to the stream and filled a bucket with water. I would need several buckets full to soak the whole skin, but I could only carry one at a time.

When I returned, I poured the water into the basin with the elk brain and turned to fetch more.

"Hey, wait up," called an unfamiliar voice behind me.

I stopped to wait.

Ezra's son hurried up behind me with two more buckets.

"Will this be enough?" he asked, indicating the buckets.

"Should be," I replied, giving the buckets a cursory glance. I turned again and started toward the stream.

"I'm Eliam," he said.

I regarded him from the corner of my eye. "I'm Isabel."

He turned and maneuvered a little hop so he could walk backwards in front of me and lay his hand on my shoulder, as was proper. He grinned into my eyes, which disconcerted me. He had a wide, friendly smile that made my cheeks warm.

"My father and I have game to dress."

"Congratulations," I said sarcastically, trying not to show my interest in him, as I knelt to dip my bucket into the stream.

He laughed. "Jarom said you were a snipping little thing."

I looked briefly up into his teasing smile, his handsome face. "Jarom would definitely say something like that." I held out my hand for another bucket.

Eliam traded me an empty one for the one I had filled, and when they were all filled, he carried two full buckets back toward the hut with ease, something I knew I could not do even with a struggle. One was all I could handle, and even then, I never filled them completely.

He noticed me watching him, the same way Kenai had, and I wondered if perhaps I was not as subtle as I believed myself to be.

I could see that he meant to stay by my side for the time being, so I decided to go ahead and make conversation. "Were you in Helaman's army?"

I thought he might have blushed a little when he modestly said, "Yes, I was." He indicated Jarom, who was removing the quartered animal from the game bags. "Jarom and I both served under the same captain."

"Eli?" I asked.

"Do you know Eli?"

"No. I've only heard Jarom speak of him."

I blushed a little because that was a lie. I recalled Cana and her friend giggling once about Eli, how he was the most handsome man on the training ground. And when Jarom and Darius had been placed under his command, they had thought the boys were so lucky. But I didn't think Eliam would care overmuch that my married sister and her married friend had once thought his commander handsome.

"Oh," he said. "Eli was our chief captain, but I meant Kenai."

"Now, I do know Kenai. He lives in my village."

"Ah, of course you would then. Tell me, what do you think of Kenai?"

"I don't," I said too quickly. "I mean, I don't know him very well. I was only eight when he left with the army, and he has not been home for long."

He nodded slowly and sighed. "But you know, at least, that we are all worried about the captain."

It was kind of a question, but I didn't answer it. "You still call him captain," I remarked instead.

He looked down at me. "He will always be my captain," he said simply. "It is not a bond that can be explained to someone like you."

Oh, how quickly my hackles went up. "Someone like me? I could not understand friendship and loyalty?"

He raised both hands in front of him. "Whoa!" Was he amused? "I simply meant someone who has not been in a battle. The bond that forms between people who fight together is strong."

I took a deep breath. "I see. Sorry."

He studied me for a moment. "It's alright."

I thought of the previous night, how Kenai had held me with such care after the fight with the Lamanites, how I had felt strangely connected to him, a man I hardly knew. Was that what that feeling had been then? The bond that forms with someone when you fight beside them for the same cause?

We came to an uncomfortable silence and stood together watching as Jarom began to remove the bones from the animal, probably a buck, from the size of it. Father and Ezra were talking away like the old friends they were.

"Is this your first time at the tannery?" I asked Eliam and added, "I don't remember you."

His eyes came back to meet mine, and he shook his head. "I came with my father when I was young." He took a step back and looked around the tannery. "But this is my first time back since I returned home from the war."

"Your father has been coming here for many years."

"As long as I can remember," he said. "My father and Hemni are friends. That is why he comes. He can dress his own game, you know. I think he just prefers the visit."

I nodded. Father was friendly like this with all of his customers.

"My father said Hemni had acquired a pretty employee and I should come see for myself."

My face flamed. I could feel it, but I raised my chin and looked him in the eye. "Come see what for yourself, Eliam?"

He folded his arms but smiled sweetly at me. "Isabel, surely you must know your father has begun to seek a betrothal for you."

My eyes shot to my father. He was ploying to marry me to a stranger? My kind father, who with thoughtfulness and understanding had brought me to work at the tannery with him because he knew how I struggled at home?

Eliam cleared his throat. "I can see I have spoken out of turn. But maybe it is better that you know, hmm? There will likely be a parade of striplings passing through the tannery now."

Was that why Father had invited me here? To let the young men get a good look at me before agreeing to let me cook and clean for them?

"After you say no, you mean?" Because there would be no more men parading past if he said yes.

He kept the same smile on his face, both playful and

understanding. He reached out like he might touch me, but pulled his hand back, unsure of himself. He really was kind of sweet, and quickly endearing himself to me, even though everything about the situation made me want to scratch his eyes out—but only because he was the one standing in front of me.

"Now, I didn't say that. We've only just met, but I know your brothers well. If you grew up in the same home as them you can be nothing but upright and faithful."

I liked that the qualities he was looking for in a wife were uprightness and faithfulness. Maybe that would overshadow the fact that I couldn't cook. I regarded him for a moment wondering if I should take a chance on him—trust him with more than a haughty look. I lifted one of the buckets from where we had set them next to the basin and poured the water in, slowly so it wouldn't splash.

"I don't desire marriage. I fear I will lose myself, when I have only begun to find myself." I raised an eyebrow in challenge.

"You are honest, too." He reached out again, but only to take the bucket from my hands and return it to the ground. He lifted another and poured it into the basin between us. Then he stepped closer and passed the bucket back to me, but he didn't let go when I took it. We stood for a few moments holding the empty bucket between us.

"I do not desire marriage either, Isabel. At least not the kind you are thinking of. Most people who have arranged marriages fall in love in time, I believe. But for myself, I would like to love my wife before we become betrothed." He gave a sheepish shrug. "But I am not opposed to an introduction. Are you?" He bent a little at the knee to catch my eye.

"I guess not," I said. "It's just, I hadn't even begun to think about marriage."

"Other than not wanting it?" he teased.

"Other than that," I agreed with a small smile.

"Well, you are young yet. Just fifteen next week, your father says? But after some courting and a year of betrothal, you will be old enough." He waited for me to confirm it with a nod. "I am only nineteen," he went on. "Not so very old." He made a little grimace that made me laugh.

No, it wasn't so very old. Exactly the age my father would be considering for me.

He took the bucket from between us and dropped it to the ground. I barely registered its clatter because he took both my hands in his, drawing my full attention to him.

"I will love you before I ask for a betrothal. And you will love me," he said. "Or it will not happen. Can you be at ease with me in that knowledge?" he asked.

"That is really kind of you," I said.

He laughed a little and gave his head a little shake. "It is for me as much as it is for you, I have to admit," he said. "I believe that God is love, and that God can have no part in a relationship that has no love." He looked down into the basin filled with stream water and elk brains. He wrinkled his nose. "Now, tell me what we are doing here."

"Well," I began, much more comfortable talking about my work than about becoming betrothed to strangers, handsome though they were. "This part of the process is called dressing. We mix the brain, though many kinds of animal fat would do just as well, with the water and soak the skin in the solution." I took a long stick and stirred up the solution in the basin. It turned murky, but I knew it would work just right.

"Interesting," he said.

"Have you never done this before?" I asked.

He shook his head. "Not myself, not personally. My father has always brought our skins here."

29

"You have already completed the first part by letting the deer bleed out and then removing its organs." I pointed to where Jarom was working with the skin. "Jarom will remove any remaining meat from the inside of the skin and the hair from the outside. Next, the skin comes here, where I soak it, wring it, stretch it to dry, and then smoke it." I glanced at Ezra. "If you want buckskin, that is."

"We do. What is the most important part of the process?"

"All of them," I replied. "But I think the most important part is the part you are currently working on. You have to do everything with exactness or the finished product will not be of the fine quality for which my father is known."

"The way I hear it, Isabel, you are the one who is known for her fine quality."

I was only fourteen, but I didn't think he was talking about my buckskins. And it was much too high of a compliment for me.

"Eliam, you shouldn't compliment me so outrageously."

His only reply was a chuckle.

When we had soaked and wrung the skin several times over, Eliam helped me stretch it to dry. It was turning out really nice. The whole process had gone easily. It would be a beautiful skin as long as the color came out right, and that would be determined during the smoking process.

When the day was drawing to a close, Eliam said, "You're very good at this."

"I've been working here at it for six years." I glanced to where Jarom was cleaning up for the day. "It's strange to have my brothers back. I'm afraid my father won't want my help anymore, because Zeke and Jarom will be more than enough help for his business." And then I confided, "That's why the talk of betrothing unsettles me. I will not be able to work here once I am married. Being a wife will require other things of my time."

"I think you might be wrong."

He didn't say this unkindly, but I smirked up at him. He couldn't really mean that.

"You would have the freedom to tan all the hides for your household use," he pressed on. "You could do it at home with the little ones around your feet. And until there were little ones, I do not think your father would object to your working here. He seems to be a reasonable man."

I looked back at my father, a lump rising in my throat.

"From the conversation I had with him, I know he cares for you. He hopes to find someone who will love you as much as he does, I think. And if he succeeds, I doubt your husband would mind overmuch if you worked here with your father."

What an oddly intimate conversation to be having with a stranger. But probably not as odd as the one Eliam had had with my father.

"I mean, Hemni let you come here even today," Eliam went on.

"Today? What do you mean?"

"Isabel, Jarom told me all about last night. Your father should have made you stay home to rest. Made sure you were okay."

"But I am okay."

He regarded me for a long moment with deep concern in his brown eyes. "Are you?" he asked.

"Yes," I insisted.

"Still. Can you not see how indulging he is toward you?"

"I'm sure you are right," I said quickly. "I enjoyed meeting you very much, Eliam."

"And would you allow me to come here to work with you again?"

"Well, yes," I said. "Of course. But would you not rather

walk in the woods on moonlit evenings trying to hold my hand or take me to an entertainment in the city?"

He laughed. "Perhaps, but this is what matters to you, Isabel, that's easy to see." He gestured around at the tannery. "This is where you are yourself, so I think this is the place I will learn best about who you are."

"But, where will I learn best about you?"

"That is for you to determine if you ever decide you want to." He glanced over his shoulder.

His father stood with mine, prepared to leave, and they were both keeping an eye on us as they said goodbye. My cheeks heated as I wondered if they had been watching us like that the whole day.

"Until next time, Isabel," Eliam said with a smile and walked toward his father with long, confident strides.

I watched him go, wondering at the extraordinary day we had shared together, two strangers becoming friends.

Soon Jarom was standing beside me.

"Did you know Father arranged for that guy to come?" he asked me.

"Yes, he told me. Do you not like him?"

"Oh, I like him fine. I just never thought, you know, that you would."

"I just met him."

"Well, I can see you don't hate him."

"No," I agreed. "I think he would be very hard to hate." I watched as Eliam followed Ezra from the clearing and Father went to inspect our work.

"And why's that?"

I hesitated, biting my lip. "I told him I don't really desire marriage. He did not take offense or judge me. It was nice."

"You told him that?"

"Sure. He's easy to talk to. It's embarrassing to be a girl, to be given in marriage by a man like he would give away a lamb to the slaughter."

"That's how you see marriage?" Jarom laughed.

I bristled. "Pretty much. I wouldn't expect someone like you to understand."

"Well, it's not easy to ask a man to give you his daughter either, when you know that with you she would definitely be a lamb for the slaughter. It is embarrassing to put a price on someone you love, when you know everything you have, everything you could ever acquire, would never amount to enough."

Turning to my brother, I froze when I saw the longing on his face before he hid it behind dark eyes that didn't look as insolent as he wanted them to.

"You're in love," I said.

He stared at me for a moment and then winced and looked away.

CHAPTER 4

The next morning I added extra food into my satchel for the midday meal. I wasn't sure why. I just did it. A few corn cakes filled with Mother's thick stew, an extra apple, some goat cheese.

Mother watched me from the corner of her eye but said nothing.

I was tired. Though I had slept well, the abduction and then working hard with Eliam the next morning had taken a toll. Maybe the extra food would give me extra energy. That was what I told myself.

Zeke joined us at the tannery that day. My oldest brother was much quieter than I remembered him being. The girl he loved, had loved his whole life, had agreed to become betrothed to another man yesterday. He was understandably sad and melancholy, but it scared me. If things that were as sure as Zeke and Keturah didn't work out, what hope did the rest of us have for anything? It was upsetting. Our whole family felt the loss keenly.

The betrothal would take place in a fortnight and then Keturah would live with Gid's parents near a place called Orihah. Gid had taken a job as a private guard for Captain Helaman, a position that was considered a great honor. He would be stationed in Zarahemla. I had heard the whole terrible story at the evening meal.

It confused me and made me uneasy. Things would be different without Keturah in the village.

I added handfuls of rotten cottonwood chips to my fire and stirred it up. It was ready. The skin Eliam and I had soaked yesterday was ready too. All that remained was to force the smoke through it. This would give the skin its color and its ability to stay soft even after getting wet, a quality neither rawhide nor leather had, and it was a quality nobody in Melek could make come out as soft and pretty as I could.

"You want some help with that?" Zeke asked when he saw me setting up the leather tube through which I would channel the smoke.

"Sure," I said. "You can help hang the hide. I'm not quite tall enough for this one."

So Zeke, who had been cleaning a fresh hide, wiped his hands on his apron and attached the hide to the frames while I attached the tube to the hide.

I coughed the last bit of smoke from my lungs. "Thanks," I told him.

"No problem."

I studied him for a moment.

"Got something on your mind?" he asked.

"How come Keturah is marrying that Gid person?" I hadn't really planned on asking him about it, but I just couldn't get it out of my mind. "Why did you agree to it? I mean, Micah wanted her to marry you. All you had to do was agree and make the deal."

He folded his arms across his chest. "How do you know that?"

"Everyone knows that."

He shrugged. "Ket loves Gid."

"No!" I insisted. "You and Keturah love each other!"

Zeke glanced at Jarom and our father and then took me by the elbow and led me over to the stream.

"Sometimes, Izz, love isn't the only thing that matters. Keturah does love me—a lot—but it is not enough."

"How can it not be enough? How much is enough?" I asked, frowning. "I'm confused."

"What's confusing you?"

"It's just, you and Keturah have been promised since you were little. Everyone expected you to marry. You love each other. So I don't understand why you are not going to do it. Does the expectation of your families mean nothing to the two of you?"

"Izz," he said. "It is much more complicated than that."

"And I'm too little to understand?"

"No, you're not. I didn't say that. In fact, with Father beginning to bring potential husbands for your consideration, I think it is something you should be made to understand."

"So," I said. "Why is it that you do not have to do as your family desires, but I do?"

He smiled. "Don't you think Mother and Father would rather you perfect your skills in the home than work here with the men?"

I looked toward Father.

"He is letting you do contrary to your family's desire, but you take no notice of that, only of what you see happening with me."

"I guess you're right," I said with a little pout.

"Father is good, and he is kind and fair. He will not make you marry a man you don't love, just as he will not make you work in the home when it makes you so unhappy."

I sighed. He had made Cana marry Micah. But Zeke was partially right, and I was being unfair.

"But won't you miss Keturah?" I asked.

37

He didn't say anything for a moment, just regarded me with a very sad expression. I searched his eyes. They were the same shape as Father's and Jarom's and mine. Rich brown like Mother's.

"I know that you love her, Zeke," I said. "So why did you let her go?"

His expression changed. "Will you miss her so much, Izz? Is that what all these questions are about?"

I turned and started pacing. "Well, of course I will miss her. She's nice."

What I didn't say was that when Keturah left the village, everyone would forget that girls could do more than just cook food and wash clothing.

"Yeah, she's nice," Zeke huffed. "Listen now, since it is time for you to consider your betrothal, there is something you should understand. Keturah did choose me. She thought she was making the right choice, but she felt uneasy about it. For a while, I thought it would be enough, what we had. But I knew of her unease, and in the end, I knew that if I let her choose something that would make her unhappy, then my love for her wasn't real. Understand?"

I thought about that for a moment and then nodded, though I didn't really understand how Zeke, who loved Keturah so much, could ever make her unhappy. That must have been the part that was complicated.

He shrugged, but he was far from indifferent. "The Spirit just led her a different way. I can't explain it any better than that."

And couldn't argue with it either, poor guy.

"Come on," he said. "Let's get back to work."

He started toward the tannery, but I called him back. "Zeke, wait."

He stopped and turned to me.

I hesitated, but decided I needed to know. "What...what is wrong with Kenai?" He would say it was none of my business, but I made myself go on. "I overheard Leah tell Mother that he doesn't eat, he prefers to be alone, and he spends a great deal of time sleeping. Why is everyone so careful around him? Why is he acting so strangely?"

He stepped back toward me, placed a hand on my shoulder, and dipped his head to catch my eye. "That is complicated, too."

I just stared at him, trying to look obstinate, but I could feel my face burning.

Zeke studied my face, took in my embarrassment but didn't remark on it. "Kenai saw many ugly things in the war—many more than the rest of us because of his assignments. He was a spy, you know."

"I heard that," I said but wondered why that would make things so much more difficult on Kenai than on the others.

"Well, he was, and a good one. The best. He was always out on his own. When the rest of us came upon enemies, we took them prisoner because we had the numbers to guard them. Sometimes we could even let them go if they made an oath not to fight us anymore. Kenai didn't have that option."

I squinted my eyes as I thought. "So he had to kill them?"

"Yes," he said simply. "He had to kill a great many of them. And he hated it. Now he has the memories he cannot erase and the guilt that torments him."

"Is that how he got that scar on his throat?"

Zeke let out a breath. "I don't know how he got that one. He hasn't said, and nobody has asked him. I think Jarom might know. Maybe Eliam or Mahonri."

"Eliam?" I asked in surprise.

"Yes, he worked under Kenai's command."

39

"Oh! He said Kenai was his captain, but I didn't realize Eliam was a spy too."

"And I didn't realize you knew Eliam," Zeke teased.

I flushed even more red than before. "Father brought him to the tannery."

"Ah," he said. "I see. A good choice."

"I haven't agreed or anything," I said quickly.

"Well you have my hearty approval to aid your decision."

"But I must go with what the Spirit tells me," I reminded him.

He laughed a little. "That is my advice, yes."

I nodded. "Well, thank you for telling me. About Kenai. I don't talk to him much or anything, but I don't want to say something stupid or do the wrong thing."

He smiled. "There is nothing you could do that would be wrong. He will heal in time."

"Could you and Father not give him a blessing?" I suggested as we began to walk toward the hut. "To give him peace."

"Yes, but he has refused it."

"But why?"

"That's personal, Isabel. Only Kenai knows. But you know why someone might shun the Spirit. It is his guilt, I think."

I considered this. I was stubborn myself and hated to accept help of any kind. That wasn't exactly what Zeke was saying, wasn't the same as resisting the Spirit, but I could understand being defensive.

"I'm glad you're back," I said. "At least for a little while."

Zeke did not plan to stay long in the village. Like Gid, he had also taken a job as a guard on Helaman's estate and would leave for Zarahemla in a month.

He slung an arm around my neck and pulled me off

balance into him. "I'll be around, Izz."

I pushed against him to get away and laughed, but we both sobered when I said stupidly, "I'm sorry about Keturah."

He just nodded, swallowed hard, and went back to the skin he had been cleaning.

I stood awkwardly for a moment and then went to check on my smoking skin. I had to watch it carefully to make sure no smoke escaped except through the skin or the final product would not come out as beautiful and soft as I wanted it to.

I had a reputation to uphold after all.

None of the skins were ready to soak by midday and Eliam and his father had not yet shown up, so I decided to take the food I had packed into my satchel and go for a walk out through the forest to give my father and brothers time to finish cleaning the skins.

I told myself I was just going out into the forest, but when I ended up outside the village in the maize fields, I couldn't even lie to myself anymore. I had gone in search of Kenai.

Something in the way he had looked at me when he had taken my knife, when he had given it back, something in the way he had held me so close to him—that was why I was standing there with the weight of an extra large midday meal in my satchel.

I saw him in the field where corn stalks had grown as high as his waist. Months ago, when he had walked into the village with Jarom, his hair had been short, but it was longer now and almost unkempt. He had worn the short tunic of a soldier, but he wore a mid-length tunic now, made from cloth I recognized. The blue and green patterns woven into it were his mother's.

He stopped stabbing half-heartedly at weeds when I walked down the low hill toward him. Leaning slightly on the handle of his spade, he regarded me carefully as he straightened. My presence definitely surprised him, though his troubled eyes tried to hide it. He seemed to be waiting for an explanation and glanced over my shoulder as if he thought perhaps something was wrong at home.

"Hi," I said.

He gave his chin a jerk upward, more to indicate a greeting than to give one.

We stood awkwardly for a moment.

"Have you had your midday meal?" I asked him.

I tried to keep the pity from my face when I saw the intense sadness in his.

"No."

I expected his voice to sound tired or craggy with disuse, but it was clear and made me wonder what I was doing there.

"I've brought you some." I held up my satchel. "But it's cold."

His answer came after a long pause. "The midday meal usually is."

I looked around, tried to offer him a small smile. "Are you ready to eat?"

"I'm not hungry."

He was much too slender. He hadn't been hungry in a while.

I looked at the ground and noticed all the weeds he had dug out. There were so many more, and I thought it was no wonder he felt hopeless. Here in Melek there was so much rain that weeds grew as fast as a person could dig them. I dragged a toe through the dirt and looked back up at this boy—much older than me, much more experience behind his eyes, not a very likely friend.

"Maybe you want to take a rest and watch me eat," I said.

A corner of his mouth turned up. If I accomplished nothing else today, I had accomplished that.

"Maybe," he said.

"Where?" I asked.

Without a word, he stabbed his spade into the ground and led me to a shaded area at the side of the field.

I sat in the grass without a word, took out my food, including the extra I had packed, set it in my lap and began to eat. I didn't say any more, and I didn't offer him any.

He clearly wasn't interested in having a conversation with me, and I chewed miserably, wishing I hadn't come. We sat for a long time in silence listening to the breeze and the birds and the sound of me chewing.

After a while, he reached over and took the extra apple. I heard him bite into it.

I wanted him to eat a corn cake with stew on it, to recognize how it would taste like his mother's, but he didn't touch it.

When I was still chewing the last bite of my meal—I had even eaten the extra I had brought for him—I pushed it to the side of my mouth and said, "I guess I'll go now."

I felt his eyes on my back as I walked away.

Probably, I thought, I had done no good. Probably, I had made things worse for him. What could I do? I was just a little girl.

But that was the thing. I was just a little girl. He would never suspect me of wanting to help him.

And I wanted to so much. I couldn't explain it. I had been so young when he had gone away to war, I hardly remembered him, and I doubted he remembered much about me. I was just a little girl that lived at Zeke's house. I knew that was all he would ever see in me, and I would have thought he didn't even know my name if he hadn't said it two nights ago.

Sorry, Isabel.

It was embarrassing, I would never want anyone to know, but those two words went through my mind over and over and over. I kept hearing my name cross Kenai's lips, huskily and filled with remorse. And not for taking my knife from me.

CHAPTER 5

The next day when I showed up for the midday meal in the maize field, Kenai looked up from his work and stared at me as I walked down from the hill. He didn't say anything, and I didn't say anything either, just walked right past him toward the tree we had sat under the day before.

I was halfway through my meal when he dug his spade into the ground and made his way up to the tree. He stood above me and stared down uncertainly for a moment.

"Did you get a lot done today?" I asked him, and I deliberately moved my apple a little closer to myself. I was counting on Kenai's brotherly instinct to tease me. I had seen him tease Keturah many times, even after he'd come home with so much sadness in his heart. She knew just how to goad him into it, and I had been paying close attention when she did.

He sighed and sat down near me. "Not really," he said. "Not that it matters much."

I nodded and made a little hum like I understood. The truth was I didn't know whether it mattered or not. It seemed to me that the field grew either way. I knew that Father had overseen the fields while Kenai's family was away at the war and he had not had a lot of time to devote to them. They always produced well, and there had been plenty of corn to take to the armies. But Father insisted this had been a blessing from the

Lord, the abundance in the crop yields, that the Lord had made his weakness strong and magnified the time he could spend here.

Personally, I thought the fields just grew well on their own. It rained. The sun shone down. And the crops grew.

Harvesting the crops had been the real miracle.

"Then why do you come if it makes no difference?"

"Why do you?"

I couldn't answer. I didn't know. So I just shrugged and said, "I got a beautiful elk skin bucked today. It turned out really nice."

"From what I hear," he said as he took my apple, "all your skins turn out really nice."

"I just do exactly what my father told me to do and they always turn out. I'm lucky I guess."

"It's not luck."

"How would you know?

"I know," he said and took a big bite of the apple.

"Hey!" I pretended to finally notice the apple. "That's mine!" I made an attempt to get it back, but he simply held it high out of my reach. His half a rusty grin was so endearing I had to work hard to feign annoyance. "Fine," I conceded. "But next time bring your own food."

He swallowed. "Next time?"

"Sure. I like it here," I said, looking around.

"It's a long walk from the tannery."

"How would you know? You don't go there."

He pushed another bite of apple into his cheek. "I've been there. Lots. Before you ever were." He shrugged. "Besides, I have no reason to go there."

Our eyes locked for just a second. "Your best friend is there. You haven't seen him in...how long?"

He looked off into the field and I definitely sensed regret, shame maybe, something sad.

I could hear the breeze blowing lightly through all the plants on the field. I could understand why Kenai preferred being alone here to being with other people.

"He could use a friend right now, you know."

He swallowed and threw the apple core into the bushes. "What do you mean?"

"With Keturah and all."

"Oh." He sighed. "I'd just remind him of Ket."

Like he reminded Kenai of Cana. I wasn't sure, but I had always thought Cana and Kenai had intended to marry.

"Who is that guy, Gid, anyway? I don't like him. He's got a lot of nerve asking for Keturah."

"Actually, Micah sought him out."

"Well, then I guess I don't like Micah anymore either," I said, only half kidding.

He didn't say anything but glanced at me as if he expected an explanation to come spilling forth.

I twisted up my lips, trying to withhold it. "I guess I just don't like to see Zeke hurting," I said finally.

"Yeah," he said quietly, his eyes looking into the distance, looking into the past. "He really loved her."

"He really *loves* her. I don't think he could walk away from her if he didn't."

The frown that crossed his face was different. "What do you mean?"

"Well," I said. "It's like Zeke told me. If he didn't do everything in his power to make her happy, then what he feels for her isn't really love."

He didn't say any more, so finally I got up to leave.

"Hey." He stopped me, reaching out in time to grasp my fingers.

"Yeah?" I turned, my eye catching on our joined hands before I looked up into his face. Though they weren't dark or unsightly, it was hard to miss the scars that ran across his forearms, touched his temple, and the one that cut across the side of his neck. If that cut had been deep, he wouldn't be alive. I knew he probably had many more scars that were hidden.

"What are you going to do with your buckskin?"

I grinned. "Something my mother's going to hate."

While I waited for the skins to soak that afternoon, I got to work on my project. I had gotten the idea a few months ago in the market when I saw several men wearing buckskin legging pants instead of tunics. I didn't think I could get away with wearing them with a short tunic like the men did, but I thought I might be able to fashion a more feminine pair to wear under a long tunic or sarong.

With all the bending and stretching, reaching and lifting I had to do at the tannery, I thought a nice pair of leggings would provide me more modesty than the simple, thin sarong all the women wore.

I didn't have a real pattern to go by, but I had measured myself and thought I had a good idea of how to proceed.

I was bent over the hide at the large table when Zeke came over and asked me what I was doing.

I looked up at him guiltily.

"Uh-oh," he said. "Better tell me."

"I don't want to."

"All the more reason you should."

I stood up straight and regarded him warily. "I'm making buckskin leggings," I said, my eyes daring him to say I couldn't.

"Would you like to take the pattern off of mine?" he asked.

"You have some?"

48

He nodded. "Mostly I use them for dancing. I'll go get them for you if you want to have a look. I made them with some buckskin I got in Judea."

Jarom grunted as he walked past us, and I noticed the scowl he sent in Zeke's direction.

"I...don't think we're the same size," I said.

He laughed. "We'll scale them down. I'm done for the day. I'll go get them for you and you can see what you think."

When Zeke got back, we set the pants over the top of my elk skin, and I inspected them.

"They look okay. Do they look decent when they're on?"

"Of course they do. I'm very handsome in them," he said with feigned offense.

I giggled. "Okay, I'll just take your word on it."

"So, these leggings are for you?" he asked.

I bit my lip and nodded. "Mmm-hmm."

He felt the hide between his fingers and thumb. "This is really well done," he said. "I have some connections from the war who might be interested in this."

"Thanks."

"After we scale down the leggings, you might have enough hide left over for a top to go with them. We'll have to be careful how we cut it, though."

"I was thinking a tunic might be nice."

He looked at me with a considering eye. "No. A sarong I think."

"And you know all about fashion?"

"You weren't going for fashionable were you?"

"No," I admitted. "I thought the leggings might afford me more modesty here while I'm working."

He nodded. "Then maybe a tunic would be better."

"Well, let's do the leggings first and then see if we have

enough left for the top."

"You want my help then?"

"Sure," I said, noting he seemed pleased. "You obviously know more than I do."

So we scaled down the pattern while Father and Jarom worked hides. When Father wandered over and asked what we were doing, Zeke told him. I thought Father might say I couldn't wear the leggings, but he only thought about it for a moment and then nodded.

"It could be a good way to show off the work you can do."

"But, Father," I couldn't help pointing out. "I will be wearing pants."

He shook his head. "No, they will be leggings under your sarong. I don't see any harm in that."

"Well, then I will let you break it to Mother."

"Leave Mother to me," he said with a chuckle, and then he went back to his work.

When Zeke and I had the pattern drawn onto the skin, he stopped and looked down at my legs. He let his eyes climb up my body.

"What are you looking at?"

He clenched his jaw and his neck flushed. "I think..." He cleared his throat and started again. "I think we should make an allowance for your hips." He was staring hard at the buckskin.

I looked down at myself. I didn't really have any hips to speak of, but I shrugged and motioned for him to adjust the design.

"You're a sorry excuse for a grown man if you can't talk about hips," I teased him as he adjusted the lines of the pattern.

"You're my sister," he replied without looking at me.

"Shouldn't that make it easier?"

"Hardly."

"She hasn't got any hips," Jarom said from behind me.

I swirled to see him staring at me there.

"Jarom!" I said and tried to cover myself with my hands, an attempt that wasn't successful.

They both laughed, and after a moment, I joined them.

"Stop it," I giggled. "You remind me of that snake that came courting Cana."

They both stopped laughing and looked at me with the same sudden intensity.

"You know," I said. "That guy, Zareth I think his name was."

"When was this?" asked Zeke.

"Not long after you left with Helaman's army," I said, wondering why they didn't know about it. "But Father saw him in the city one day, and after that he refused to allow Zareth to see Cana at all. In fact, he forbade any of us to speak to Zareth if we ever saw him."

My brothers exchanged a look. "Did you ever see him again?" Zeke asked me.

Both my brothers had sobered considerably.

"What did he do to make you dislike him?" Jarom asked.

I frowned. "It wasn't what he did, just what he was like."

"Why did Father forbid you to speak to him?" Jarom pressed.

"I don't know. I was only eight. Maybe nine. He said not to, and so I wouldn't have. But I never saw him again."

Jarom wandered back to his work, and after Zeke finished drawing the pattern, he told me to cut it out and he went to speak to my Father in low tones that I couldn't hear. Jarom joined them and they all three stood talking with their arms folded over their chests.

Maybe I shouldn't have brought that up.

That kind of dampened the day, but the good news was that the leggings fit perfectly. Zeke had been right about the extra allowance.

After the evening meal, my family went across the road to Kalem and Leah's.

Gid's family was still there. They planned on staying for a fortnight until the official betrothal. The men and boys all slept out in the yard, leaving the inside of the hut as the women's domain.

The younger girls played in the yard, but I sat by myself near the fire. I was too old to play with them anymore.

One of Gid's brothers approached me. It was one of the younger ones, Lamech I thought. He looked about my age, and there was one younger boy named Shad. He was about ten or eleven, Sarai's age I guessed.

I eyed Lamech as warily as he eyed me.

"What're you doing?" he asked.

It was clear I wasn't doing anything so I just shrugged.

"Do you want to get out of here?"

"What do you mean?"

"I mean leave. Let's go somewhere else."

I looked around. "But everyone is here."

He gave a quick glance around too. "Exactly. Do you know where the old training ground is?"

"Of course," I said.

"You can show me." He started out through the gate, and when he didn't stop or look back, I reluctantly followed after him. He would get lost if I didn't.

Zeke and Kenai were talking near the gate. I was glad to see that Kenai was spending more time with his friend, making a concerted effort to reestablish their friendship, though I knew it was for Zeke's sake, not his own.

Zeke was on the outside of the gate. It didn't appear as though he planned to stay either, and I didn't blame him. Keturah was sitting by her Gid and beaming as brightly as the sun at noon day.

Couldn't she see how she was hurting Zeke? Didn't she care at all?

"Tell Mother and Father I'm going for a walk. I'll be back before dark," I told Zeke.

"You're not going alone," he protested.

I tilted my head toward Lamech who had finally stopped near the trees to wait for me.

Zeke looked in Lamech's direction and then nodded, giving his approval. Not that I needed it, I thought.

I turned to go, but I heard Kenai speak in a low voice. "You're letting her walk with him?"

"They're just kids."

"She's old enough," Kenai said roughly.

"Lamech is good enough with his weapons to protect her if need be."

"But will he protect her from himself?"

Zeke laughed. "You were over-protective of Keturah. Now you're going to be over-protective of Izz?"

"*You* were over-protective of Keturah, not me. And perhaps you should take more thought of Isabel's care. You're her elder brother."

"And you're not. They're fine."

I didn't hear any more than that. When I caught up with Lamech he regarded me for a second with his dark eyes. He glanced over my shoulder toward Zeke and Kenai, then turned on his heel and started down the path.

Lamech's eyes weren't just dark colored. The prominent bones of his brow shadowed his eyes leaving him with a deeply brooding look that I suspected would not alter no matter his mood. He wore his thick black hair in two long braids. As I followed along behind him, I wondered what he would look like with his hair loosened and out of the braids. I wondered why he wore it that way, because it definitely accentuated his Lamanite-looking features.

All Ammonites had Lamanite heritage, but most tried to shun as much of it as they could in favor of their new Christian traditions.

"Which way?" he asked after a while.

"Follow the main path," I said. It had been growing over for years now, but it had been traveled enough that it was still visible. Various other trails broke off from the path to the training ground, but it was still the largest and easy to follow.

"Do you like living here?" he asked over his shoulder.

"Sure. What else is there?"

"I live on a farm where all the trees have been cleared."

"Don't you ever go into the woods?"

"Not really. Not if I don't have to."

"Why not?"

He shrugged.

"You're little brother is cute," I said.

His shoulders stiffened but he said, "Yeah, Shad's like one of your dolls. I dressed him and combed his hair myself."

"I don't play with dolls," I said lamely.

"Sure you do. What are you, like ten?"

I didn't think that even deserved an answer, so I didn't give one. When he realized I wasn't going to, he turned and walked backward facing me.

"You're going to trip," I said.

He smiled. "I doubt it."

"Why do you want to see the training ground?"

He turned back around. "I've never seen it, that's all."

"It's a working field planted with squash and beans now. It hardly looks like it did."

"Did you ever see it?"

"I wasn't allowed to go there."

"So how do you know it looks different?"

"I can imagine."

"Ha!" he scoffed. "I see the knife on your belt. I bet you're just like Keturah. You went there without permission, didn't you?"

My knife was tied to my belt underneath my sarong. He'd had to look closely, too closely, to see its outline there at my waist.

I didn't answer that, but asked instead, "Would you have gone there without permission?"

"In a heartbeat."

"Don't you have any respect for rules?"

"Only rules that make sense. It doesn't make sense for me to stay off the training ground. The only place for me in this world is on the battlefield."

"Lamech."

At the sound of his name, he slowed, blocking my way forward.

"What?"

"You don't belong on a battlefield. No one does." I didn't really believe that, though. What I did believe was that it was not the only place for him.

He reached toward me suddenly and lifted my knife out from under my sarong. He let the sarong fall back down immediately, and I did have the leggings on, but I gasped at his familiarity.

He held the knife between us, as if it was evidence of something.

"Just look at me. Do I look like a pure Nephite?"

I wasn't sure how to answer that question. He didn't look Nephite in the slightest. I shook my head slowly.

"I've got a fight going on all the time inside me," he said. He lifted the knife so it caught the fading light. "And so do you."

"I use that at the tannery," I said and tried to take it from him.

He moved it quickly and tucked it into his own belt.

"That's a lie. Trust me, you'll feel better when you stop lying to yourself and just accept what you are. Here."

He pulled a knife from his arm band and handed it to me hilt first. The blade, formed from flint, was stained with blood.

"Go on," he said when I hesitated.

I took it and turned slightly away from him to slip it under my sarong.

When I looked back, he was politely averting his eyes.

"The training ground is just over that rise," I said and pointed to the small hill behind him.

"Good." He gave me one last look and turned.

I watched his shoulders as he walked away—slender, square, straight, proud. His feet were quiet on the earth, his steps carefully placed. He said strange things, but I couldn't help but like him.

A peaceful feeling came over me when we neared the field. I had felt it before, when I had been there, uninvited and without permission just as Lamech had said. I watched him curiously as he wandered out through the rows of plants. He must have felt the Spirit, too, because as I watched, he knelt, bowed his head humbly, and looked to be praying in the twilight.

I had to turn away. It was too personal. As I waited, idly rubbing a leaf between my fingers, I wondered why he had allowed me to see it at all.

When he wandered back to me, we started for the village. This time I led the way. I could feel his eyes on me as I dodged low branches and jutting roots. He had seemed so vulnerable in the field. He was full of contradictions, different at every moment. It was odd, but I felt safe with him, even if I felt uneasy in a very different way. Zeke was wrong—Lamech wasn't too young to be thinking about girls.

"Thanks for having me back before dark," I said because I didn't know what else to say to this boy I didn't know.

"I wouldn't do anything to upset the captain," he replied.

I followed his gaze to where Zeke sat alone at our own fire, far enough away from Keturah and Gid that he didn't have to see them—as long as his back was turned, which it was. But when he heard us arrive at the gate, he stood and placed his hands on his hips, a natural stance I had seen him take hundreds of times. He nodded to Lamech.

Lamech raised a hand to him and then turned and walked away.

"Wait!" I called and hurried after him.

He turned curious eyes to me.

"Why did you let me see you pray?" I felt myself blushing furiously. "You seem so strong."

He hooked a thumb in the strap of his satchel and glanced away, but he said steadily, "Submission to God is not a weakness. It takes a strength of character many do not have."

"And you do." I didn't mean it to, but it sounded like a challenge.

He glanced again at Zeke. "Goodnight, Isabel."

He started to leave, but I stopped him again, stumbling over my words. "Wait. I...wait. You looked like a pure Nephite tonight...to me," I said, and before he could respond, I turned and ran back to my brother.

CHAPTER 6

The next day when I showed up at the maize field, Kenai was already sitting under the tree waiting for me. I hid my smile as I sat next to him and got out my large meal, though I could see that it was unneeded because Kenai had brought his own.

I looked at him as we ate in silence. His brown hair had lightened from spending so much time in the sun, and the ends curled a little. That was something I remembered from our youth, from before the war. His sad eyes were green like a pine forest, made deeper against the green of his tunic, which he wore over a leathern kilt, probably made from my father's leather. It was the kind of kilt carpenters wore when they worked and a style he had taken sometimes to wearing. A rawhide cord hung around his neck, and it looked as though a pendant of some kind hung on it below the neckline of his tunic. I wanted to know what it was, but I would never ask.

And it was obvious he had become much too thin.

He was taking the same catalogue of me as he ate slowly but steadily. I wondered what was obvious about me.

I didn't mention the food or the fact that he was eating, but after I had eaten my own maize-wrapped beans, I reached over and took a piece of his flatbread. I bit into it quickly before he could try to stop me.

But he didn't try.

"I guess I owe you that," he said quietly, his eyes on the green stalks in the field.

I shrugged. Our families shared everything anyway. "What's mine is yours." I took another big bite and spoke around it. "And what's yours is mine."

Kenai finished his own flatbread and brushed the grains from his fingers. He didn't play into my teasing.

"Isabel," he said. "What are you doing here?"

I pushed the bite of bread to the side of my mouth. "I told you, I'm eating."

"You could eat anywhere."

"I know, but nobody bothers me here."

"Nobody...like who?"

"Oh, my family. Yours too. Keturah is driving me nuts with her permanent smile while Zeke is dying inside."

"Yeah, it's hard to watch."

"I just can't believe she's going through with it."

"Zeke and Ket have been through a lot together—a lot of things that you don't know about."

"And you do?"

"Who do you think he came to for advice?"

I couldn't help a small smile. "I guess your advice wasn't very good."

He nearly smiled too, but sighed. "Zeke just wanted things to work out like planned. He wanted to honor your parents and please my mother. He wanted to become my brother. He only wanted to do what he thought was right."

"Yeah, that sounds like Zeke." I paused, not wanting to admit the truth. "I don't think Ket likes when he gets overprotective like he does."

"It irritates her," Kenai agreed. "But when Zeke almost died in Cumeni, she stopped blaming him, started accepting it."

I swallowed and set the remainder of the corn cake down. "Zeke almost died?"

His brows rose. "You didn't know?" When I shook my head, Kenai told me quietly, "He lost so much blood in one of the battles—at Cumeni—while trying to protect Keturah that he fainted and almost didn't make it."

"I had no idea of that."

"I think it embarrasses him a little—to go through all that and it turns out she didn't need his protection. She never did. Never wanted it either. I think that may be why he doesn't protect you as he should."

I knew he was remembering my walk with Lamech. "He's embarrassed?"

He shook his head. "He thinks you don't need it."

"I don't."

"You do."

"From what?"

"Whatever you're hiding from here. And it's not your family."

I looked down at my hands and dusted the crumbs from my fingers. "What do you mean?"

"Don't be naïve, Isabel." He took the small pot of venison stew I had brought and scooped some into his mouth with his fingers.

I felt my face start to heat. I knew what he was talking about. He was talking about Eliam and the possibility of others like him coming to the tannery.

"I'm just a little girl. You said so yourself."

"I was wrong. Isabel, your father is right to begin a search for your husband. It is time."

I laughed, but not convincingly. I was uncomfortable with the subject, and it showed. "Father will have to search a long time for a man who enjoys warm leather clothing and an empty belly. My husband will have to eat his boots."

"This isn't so bad," he said and held up the small pot of stew.

"Mother and Sarai made that. I have no interest in cooking and less skill."

"What do you have interest in, Isabel?"

Why did he keep saying my name like that? I couldn't remember him ever saying it before the war, and now he said it repeatedly as if it were a life line, as if it grounded him. It gave me a heady, powerful feeling.

I bent my knees up and wrapped my bare arms around them. "I like making buckskins."

"Like these?" He fingered the leather at the bottom hem of my leggings.

"Yes."

"But that is hardly worth throwing over a husband and family for."

"Isn't it?"

He slowly shook his head. "No. You could do so much more."

"If I were a slave in my own home you mean?"

His brows rose a little. "Is that how you view it?"

I shrugged.

"That's not an answer. Your mother is not a slave to your father. None of the women in the village are slaves to their men. Where have you gotten this false idea?"

I shrugged again.

"You don't know what you mean," he said with a scoff and went back to the stew.

He meant to brush it off? I shot to my feet. "I hate household work! I hate milking the goat, washing the clothing, weaving, grinding corn flour. Is being made to do things I hate not slavery?"

To my great surprise, Kenai just reached calmly over and tugged on my fingertips. "Sit down," he said.

I stood a moment longer taking quick breaths.

Kenai took my whole hand in a firm, warm clasp and pulled harder. "Sit," he commanded gently.

I made my knees bend and sat again on the log that had become mine during these meals we shared. Kenai had been reclining on one elbow on the ground next to me, but he sat up.

"There is a choice, you know," he said quietly.

I looked at him and shook my head. "No. There isn't, not for me. Father will choose me a husband, but I want to go to the war."

He squeezed my hand. "No, Izz," he said so gently that I couldn't be upset. "It is too ugly."

"Too ugly for a little girl like me?" I asked, still trying to be angry and falling short.

"Too ugly for anyone," Kenai said softly. "Don't wish for it, Izz. Don't."

I closed my eyes, trying to take his words to heart, trying to take them in and trust them, trying to make his counsel part of what I believed. "I want to make them pay for what they have done. I want justice for our people," I said.

I felt him watching me try to control my feelings and check my temper. It usually didn't come out in angry bursts as it had moments ago, but I felt very close to it again.

"You really mean that, don't you?" Kenai said.

I nodded. "I hate that Lamanites have been allowed to go free, even to come here to Melek to live out their lives when so many of the Nephites have died at their hands."

"You have to forgive them," he said.

I opened my eyes to stare straight into his. He sat so close to me. My eyes dropped to his lips, and then closed again.

"You are the one who has not forgiven," I said. As if I knew what I was talking about. I was in way over my head with Kenai. I thought of drawing Lamech's knife and preparing for the fight that would surely come when I said what came out next. "You have not forgiven yourself."

I felt him withdraw. The scowl on his face and the narrowing of his eyes told me I had made a mistake. I thought I had lost any ground I had gained with him. Tomorrow he would not bring a meal, and he would not be waiting under the tree.

"I'll go," I said quickly. This was his place of refuge, and I was intruding. "I'll go," I repeated. "You stay."

I gathered my things without looking at him, discreetly leaving the last roll of maize and beans on his satchel with the remnants of his small meal. Then I left swiftly. He didn't try to stop me.

My work with Father was done for the day, so I went to Cana's.

Cana and I were very different, but I knew she would say something to make me feel better, because that was just the way she was—caring, compassionate, considerate.

It was this last quality that had me puzzled lately. So after I arrived and I was watching her get Micah's evening meal on to cook, I said, "You should stop being affectionate with Micah in front of Kenai. It's not nice."

She cast me a glance from the side of her eye as she cut sweet potatoes into a small pot.

"It's unlike you to be cruel," I pressed. "You let him think you loved him, and then you married his brother."

"We were just children," she said, downplaying it all. "And I had little say in Father's decision."

"I understand that. Still, I think you could show more consideration to Kenai's feelings. You've hurt him, even if you did not intend to."

She spoke in her characteristically gentle voice. "Micah says that we should not coddle Kenai. He is a grown man and would lose respect for himself if he felt we pitied him."

Oh. That made sense.

"It's still hard to watch."

"I'm understanding that more as I watch Keturah and Gid."

I nodded. "It's awful, isn't it?"

"Probably more for us than for Zeke. Oftentimes we hurt more for those we love than we hurt for ourselves."

"No. I've seen Zeke when he thinks no one is watching. He's miserable."

She sighed. "Do you think Kenai is miserable too?"

"Yes," I said slowly. "But I think he is miserable about other things, and your marriage to Micah is just an excuse for him to show it. Because it kills him to keep his feelings all inside. It kills him more every day."

She dropped her hands to her lap and looked curiously at me.

"He hasn't yet dealt with what he did in the war."

"Isabel, how do you know this?"

I shrugged. Anyone could see it. "I've been talking to him, that's all."

She eyed me. "Darius says he hardly talks to anyone."

I avoided her eyes and shrugged again. Then I changed the subject to the tunics she was weaving for her husband, and she was so kind, she allowed it.

After that, I went home and watched my Mother prepare the evening meal.

"Can I help?" I asked half-heartedly.

Somehow, though I had been helping prepare meals my whole life, I still did not know exactly what step would come next. I did not know how to anticipate what ingredient Mother would need next. Cooking was not something that made sense to me.

"No, I've got everything started. Tell me, how is your work at the tannery coming?"

"I love it," I admitted. She knew I preferred it to work in the home, but I had never told anyone I loved working at the tannery, never actually said the words. "Zeke helped me make these leggings. Feel them."

She felt the buckskin between her fingers. "It's very soft. Your best yet." She winked at me.

"You don't hate the leggings?"

"No. They look practical."

"That's what I intended. But I thought you would hate them."

"I don't." She gave me a smile. "Were you trying to make me upset, Isabel?" she teased.

"No. I just wanted them, and I was prepared to wear them even if you hated them."

"Well, I think you look very pretty."

I looked away from her. "Thanks," I mumbled.

I felt her arm around me. "Isabel, you are very pretty. Not even those pants can hide it."

A painful lump formed in my throat.

She squeezed me and kissed my temple.

"I'm not good like Cana," I blurted out. "And I'm not pretty like her, either."

"I don't want you to be like Cana. And you're right. You're not pretty like Cana." She squeezed me again. "You're pretty like Isabel."

"Mother."

She laughed.

Father walked through the mat at the door, ducking his head and standing for a moment to let his eyes get used to the dimness. His eyes went first to Mother, but then he turned them to me.

"Oh, Isabel, there you are. I wanted to tell you the boys and I will be hunting tomorrow, so we will not be at the tannery."

"Okay," I said. I could use a day to myself. "I can finish Ezra's skins alone."

He hesitated. "Both Zeke and Jarom feel it is not safe for you to be alone there. And I agree. I would prefer you stay here in the village while we are away."

"But that's not fair! It's perfectly safe! I'll be fine!" I insisted, though a part of me did feel unease at the thought of being alone there.

He sighed. He didn't want to make me stay at home.

Mother broke in. "Couldn't Darius or Kenai go with her? Perhaps Micah would have some time."

Father gave a nod. "Good idea, Dinah. I will check with them. Will you agree to have one of Leah's boys along?"

"They aren't going with you?" It was not unusual for Father to take all five boys.

"No." Father shook his head. "Zeke just got back. I want some time with my own boys."

I wondered if Mother heard what he did not say. I suspected he wanted to have a long talk with Zeke and Jarom and find out what was wrong between them. He did not want to hunt for meat or even skins so much as he wanted to counsel his sons.

"When will Ezra return for the skins?" I asked and blushed despite my effort not to because we all knew I was not as curious about Ezra as I was about his son.

67

"I'm surprised he and Eliam have not returned already. I'm worried they had to go far to find good hunting. That could mean the boys and I will be gone longer than I want to be."

"Jarom can find game anywhere," Mother said. "Just let him follow his nose and you will all be home soon."

They exchanged a smile, sharing pride in their talented son.

I left them alone, leaving by the side door out into the courtyard, but a little while later I saw Father walk over to Kalem and Leah's and heard him call out for Darius.

Darius was the closest of Leah's boys to my age and the most like a brother to me. Micah was my brother now that he had married Cana, but I had not grown up running through the forest with him. When we had all been little, I had played with Jarom and Darius until they had decided they didn't want a girl along anymore.

I wondered why Father did not try to align a betrothal with Darius. He wasn't quite old enough, but the betrothal could last for a year or more to give us time to prepare. But I was glad Father had made no such arrangements because I wasn't sure I could ever look at Darius as a husband.

Maybe Father knew that.

Kenai and one of Gid's kinsman, the one I had heard them call Enos, came from behind the hut with Darius. They walked to the fence to listen to my father. I hid myself partially behind the corner of our hut and watched as my father explained our problem to them.

"I'll go," I heard Kenai say.

Father seemed a little surprised, but he didn't hesitate to nod his head and accept Kenai's offer. They talked a few more minutes and then Father returned home with the good news. Kenai would stop by in the morning to take me to the tannery.

"What time?" I asked him.

"After the morning meal, I assume," Father said.

Kenai hadn't been awake for the morning meal in a while. I thought everyone knew this, but I didn't mention it. I was probably not supposed to have noticed how long Kenai was sleeping.

The next morning, Kenai showed up at our gate right after breakfast. He hardly looked at me, just waited patiently while I gathered my things. After the way I had left him in the maize field the day before, I wondered why he had agreed to go.

"Thank you, Kenai," my mother called from the doorway as Kenai closed the gate behind me.

He nodded to her and followed me toward the path that would lead us through the thick forest to the tannery.

He yawned. "Your father left before dawn?"

I nodded without looking at him.

"What's so important at the tannery you couldn't take a day off?"

"I have skins to smoke. The buyer is coming for them."

"Your father trusts you to do that?"

"Sure. I do all the smoking."

"It's going to rain today."

I glanced at the sky. He was right. And the air was cool besides. "Maybe."

He grunted. "It's definitely going to rain."

"Would Father have gone hunting if he thought it was going to rain?"

"It wouldn't be the first time he got wet."

I laughed. "I can do my work inside the hut. It's set up to accommodate a rainy day."

"You're okay with me coming? You wouldn't rather have Darius along?"

I stopped walking and turned to look directly at him for the first time that morning. "Father said I couldn't go if you didn't come. I've work to do, and I am grateful to you. Of course I like Darius, but you'll do just as well."

All of a sudden, I understood where the question came from.

"I hate how he teases me," I added quickly, a ploy he would see right through.

Kenai looked into my face. His eyes were dark green like the forest and when I looked into them I thought of the evergreen pine, green even through winter. Jarom had told me of the snow in the mountains near Judea and Cumeni, how it covered everything, cold, pure white, and cleansing.

"You don't like being teased?"

"Not really. It makes me uncomfortable."

"But you enjoy teasing others."

"What do you mean?"

"By tripping them."

I smiled. "I wasn't teasing you. I was angry. There's a big difference. And anyway, I think you were the one teasing me."

"No I wasn't."

"You called me a little girl."

"But that's true."

"You told me to go home and play with my dolls."

He laughed and gestured me on toward the tannery. "I guess it might been teasing if I had said that, but I didn't."

"I think you're teasing me right now."

"And yet you don't seem to hate it."

"Don't I?"

"Isabel."

I glanced behind me. "Hmm?"

"Nevermind."

The tannery stood empty, and I got right to work.

"What do you want me to do?" Kenai asked.

"I don't expect you to work. It's enough that you're here."

"I'm not going to sit around all day and watch you work," he pointed out.

"You can get the fire going."

"That's women's work."

I burst out in laughter, and I noticed a corner of a smile on Kenai's lips.

"Careful how you tease me. I'm likely to take it the wrong way."

He smirked. "Well, we wouldn't want that."

"If you want to help, you can haul those skins into the hut. I think you're right about the rain."

I knew Kenai had worked here before at times with my father and Zeke, but he listened to me and followed all my instructions.

"I've been making fires that barely give off any smoke for so long, it is strange to build one for the purpose of smoke."

"You follow directions like a soldier," I remarked while he attached the top of the ballooned skin to the frame and I attached the base of the smoke tube around the fire.

"And you give them like a commander."

"I would be a good commander," I said, letting a kind of wistfulness sound in my voice.

"I'm sure you would."

"I have heard that you were a good commander."

He finished his task before responding. "I did my job. That's all." After a moment, he added, "And I don't want to talk about it."

I looked up at him, staring so plaintively down at me. I got to my feet and approached him in the small hut. I stood next to him and stared straight ahead into his chest, avoiding his eyes. "I won't ask you to right now. But I will listen should you ever change your mind."

I didn't really mean to, but I reached out and touched his arm. I let my fingers run lightly over a scar that was near his elbow.

The fire crackled and drops of rain began to fall on the roof of the hut, but the roof sheltered us and the rain couldn't put the fire out.

Kenai hooked a finger under my chin and lifted my face to his gaze. "What are you doing, little girl?" he asked quietly, and he wasn't teasing.

I didn't have an answer. I was just a little girl. I didn't know. Something had just happened, something much bigger than what I had done by touching his scar.

"This is just a scar." I slid my fingers over it again. I winced when he narrowed his eyes.

But when I looked again, I saw he hadn't narrowed them, but closed them.

"It doesn't hurt you anymore," I said softly.

He gave a slight shake to his head.

"It is part of who you are now, but it is still just a scar."

He took a deep breath in and let it out.

"Hemni! Jarom!" someone called from outside.

And Kenai took a sudden step back.

CHAPTER 7

I saw Eliam as I ducked out of the little hut. He was coming into the clearing alone.

His eyes lit up when he saw me. I felt Kenai duck out of the hut behind me and saw Eliam's gaze move over my shoulder to him.

"Captain," he said with happy surprise. "I didn't expect to see you here."

"Hemni is hunting with his sons today. They don't want Isabel to be working here alone."

Eliam nodded, looking back at me. "A wise father."

We all stood for a moment, awkwardly looking at one another.

"I'm just smoking the skins now," I said to Eliam. "I'm sorry they are not yet ready."

He waved a hand as if it didn't matter. "That will give me an excuse to come by tomorrow."

"You don't need an excuse." I beckoned him under the awning of the hut where Kenai and I stood out of the rain. "You are welcome anytime."

That was what my father would have said, but Kenai made a soft snort that made me re-think saying it myself.

You wouldn't rather have Darius along?

He hadn't been able to hide the hurt in his voice. I had

heard it. It had little to do with Darius and much more to do with the open affection between Micah and Cana, with the way Kenai managed to disappear whenever they were present for the evening meal. Eliam was as close as a brother to him. Closer. Kenai was probably better friends with Eliam than he was with his own brother.

Father wished for me to get to know Eliam. It was very obvious, even to me, who could overlook things like that. I wanted to do as my father wished, but in that moment I took a step closer to Kenai. If things didn't work out with Eliam, Father would find someone else for me. And in the end I would probably know him about as well as I knew Eliam, which was hardly at all. But I only had this one chance to help Kenai, and despite the fact that he was catching on, I still felt that I was reaching him, if only a tiny bit.

I was about to suggest that perhaps it would be better if Eliam came back the next day, but he drew Kenai into a conversation about the wars.

I went inside the hut to check the wood in the fire and secure the seals on the skins. Everything looked just as it should, so I went outside again. Kenai and Eliam were sitting on their heels under the awning talking about people they knew from the army and what they were doing now, who was married, who was not, who had gone into the regular army under Captain Moroni, who had been promoted to chief captain.

I tried to listen, but my mind began to wander because I didn't know anyone they spoke of. They were just names to me.

"I heard that Teancum is dead," Eliam said.

"It's true," Kenai confirmed. "Gid's brother, Jashon, was with him."

"The same Jashon who was with him when he killed Amalikiah?"

"The same."

"I didn't know they were brothers, but it doesn't surprise me. Have you seen Gid, then? Where is he fighting?"

"Gid is here in the village. He's to be betrothed next week."

"Gid? No! I don't believe it!"

Kenai shrugged as if it didn't matter to him what Eliam believed.

"He's to be betrothed to Keturah," I broke in, because this was something I did understand and about someone I did know.

Eliam's eyes widened as he turned to look at me, but he said, "That doesn't surprise me over much, either." He turned back to Kenai. "Everyone knew he was gone on your sister from that first moment in the training ground."

"What moment?" I asked.

They both looked at me.

Kenai spoke. "You know Helaman told her if she could fight one of the boys and keep all her appendages she could join the militia."

I'd heard the story a thousand times.

I nodded.

"Gid was the only one who would fight her."

"I thought he'd kill her with that first blow." Why did Eliam sound so excited?

"Why?" I asked. I turned to Kenai. "Would he have?"

He laughed and shook his head. "No. He trained her. He knew what she was capable of. In fact, he was probably the only man on the field who could have beaten her that day."

I looked at him skeptically.

"It's true," Eliam put in with real admiration that was starting to annoy me. "Even today, any one of us would have a hard time beating her in a pairing."

"But she's just a girl," I said.

Eliam grinned. "Yeah, an amazing one."

I scowled at them both.

Kenai caught my scowl and said more diplomatically, "Gid and I taught her to fight differently than men fight because she can't depend on her strength. So by the time her opponents figure out what she's doing, it's too late."

I swung around. "You?" I exclaimed.

He backpedaled. "I showed her some defensive moves. That's all."

"You have to show me too."

Their easy speech stopped abruptly, and they exchanged a guilty look.

"It wouldn't be appropriate to do that," said Kenai.

"I agree with Kenai," added Eliam.

"I don't."

Eliam moved so he was closer to me. "But just look what happened to Keturah."

I glared at him. "She got to act with integrity and be true to who she was inside." My voice got louder and more out of control as I lost my temper. "Keturah fought for her own freedom, and she can respect herself for that, but she forgets her duty to her family! Does honor mean nothing? She marries who she will and cares not for who she hurts! She always, *always*, gets everything she wants!"

Fortunately a knot formed in my throat so I couldn't say any more. I couldn't look at either of them, but I heard Kenai's low voice.

"Keturah saw many terrible things. She did many terrible things that she will have to live with. I myself commanded her to do many of them, because it was my duty to command and it was her duty to obey."

That sounded suspiciously like marriage to me.

"Besides," Eliam said gently, trying to placate me. "The war is over. Ammoron has been slain and even now Moroni and his armies are returning to their homes. There is no need for you to learn to fight."

"What about the night I was kidnapped? What if I could have stopped it?"

"You couldn't have stopped fifty men," said Kenai.

"I could have stopped one man," I insisted, feeling the humiliation rise all over again.

They exchanged a glance.

"You both admire Keturah. I can hear it easily enough when you speak of her." I stood and turned, poised to step out into the rain. "And neither of you thinks I could ever be as admirable."

They were both silent. Well, more like tongue-tied. So I took the opportunity to make things worse in every way possible.

"I see you don't deny it." Though I could tell they wanted to and would when they got hold of their tongues.

I turned to Eliam, and even I couldn't believe what I said. "But I am more than a prospective cook and mother for your brood of children."

I turned to Kenai. "And I am more than your best friend's little sister. I can see in your eyes that you know it every time you look at me. I am young, but I know when a man wants me."

That was how my temper came out. Some people raised their voices and yelled until the sun went down. I said the exact truth in words I could not take back.

I looked at them both in absolute regret. I had ruined the possible courtship with Eliam that my father had arranged. I had undermined any positive effect I had made on Kenai. Eliam would leave and never come back, and I would be lucky if he didn't warn other men away from me. Kenai would revert back into his silent state where he slept too long and ate too little.

"I'm sorry," I whispered to them both in the instant before I turned and ran away from them out into the rain.

I heard one of them following me and by the time I reached the trees at the edge of the clearing, I slowed and allowed him to catch up. I thought it would be Kenai, and he would say something about my father not wanting me to be alone and that he would fulfill his promise to my father whether I liked it or not.

It surprised me when Eliam came to my side, his wet hair matted to his head, a huge grin on his face that he was literally trying to wipe away with one large hand.

I glanced back to see Kenai. He watched us for a moment and then went into the hut, ducking his head at the door. I hoped he remembered everything I had told him about the smoke and the system I had perfected. I didn't want those skins ruined.

Then I looked back to Eliam, who had succeeded in diminishing his smile. But he was looking at me with what appeared, strangely, to be admiration.

He looked down at the ground for a moment and then back up at me, water dripping from the tips of his hair. He stepped toward me.

I stood utterly shocked and still when he cupped my wet cheek with his warm, wet hand. "I had a nice time the other day when we worked together. But now, now I know I could really love you, Isabel."

He bent a little toward me, hesitated, and then proceeded to place a wet kiss on my cheek, just at the corner of my lips. Then he moved his lips to my ear and his warm breath sent a chill down me when he whispered, "If you ever choose to let me."

He pulled away and looked into my face. "Think on it?"

I gave a nod and shivered.

"Go on. The captain said he'd stoke the fire so you could get warm. I'll be back tomorrow for the skins."

I bit my lip. I had told Kenai specifically not to stoke the fire. The embers would burn the hide. At my worried look, Eliam said, "You don't have to decide anything before tomorrow. We have lots of time. I told you I want love before marriage, before betrothal. I won't accept less. And I won't be the one to take that option from you, especially now that I know it's of great importance to you."

I nodded again, groaning inside for what I had said under the awning.

He gestured with his head. "Go on," he repeated gently.

I swallowed and blinked rain from my eyes. I reached up and pushed my stringy wet hair from my face. "'Til tomorrow," I said.

I really didn't understand what had just happened. Had he enjoyed my temper? Did he think it was funny? Did my feelings humor him?

The hut was warm, but my face heated from embarrassment when I saw Kenai crouched down beside the fire.

I spoke immediately because I was afraid I wouldn't be able to if I waited. "I'm sorry for what I said to you. It was not polite. It's my temper. I lose it sometimes. I'm just so jealous of Keturah I could spit, you know?"

He eyed me for so long, I was sure he would never speak to me again. But at last he said, "I'm familiar with jealousy. It's nothing to be ashamed of. You just deal with it, repent, and move on."

"But you are ashamed of yours." Why could I not shut my mouth today?

His eyes narrowed.

I went to him and knelt beside him. "You hide behind it.

79

It is a shield meant to keep others away. But admit it, you have long since forgiven both Micah and Cana."

He didn't say anything. I saw his jaw clench tightly, and his fists too.

"Have I spoken falsely?" I asked.

I was sure I looked so small, so innocent, so pathetically wet to him. How could he lie to me? I did not have many chances to ease the truth from him, so I took this one. How much better he would feel when he spoke it. Then he would be able to let it go.

He still didn't say anything.

I pointed to the skin behind him. He glanced stiffly back at it.

"The fire burns," I said. "It makes the smoke. The smoke rises and the skin stops it. Eventually, there is so much smoke that it must pass through the skin to get out. The fire forces it out."

His jaw clenched again. But I took one of his big warm fists in my cold wet hands and began to ease it open one finger at a time as I spoke. I thought again of the snow on the pines, and I looked into his green eyes.

"That is the magical part," I told him. "Once the smoke passes through the skin, the skin becomes soft. It takes on new properties. When rawhide gets wet, you know, it hardens as it dries. When leather gets wet, it hardens as it dries. But buckskin, like this," I indicated the skins behind us. "Buckskin takes the water and stays soft. It can dry other things. It can actually keep you warm when it's wet. It won't chaff your skin. It won't decay. It is pliable and comfortable and lovely."

I got his hand open, and I wove my fingers through his so he couldn't close it again. He tried, but my hand was inside of his. My hand kept it from closing up.

"Say it," I cajoled softly. "Say you're not jealous of your brother. You don't need to be. You know Cana is not right for you, she never was. You have other things to fight. Don't let this get in the way. It is unimportant and untrue besides." I studied his face, dark from the sun, lines starting to form at the corners of his eyes. "Say it," I whispered.

The rain tapped on the roof. The fire crackled. The smoke pushed against the skins. My hand kept his from closing. Kenai breathed deeply. And then he said it.

"I'm not jealous of Micah." His words were halting but sincere.

I let out the breath I had been holding.

"But I am jealous of Eliam."

My eyes dropped to the dirt floor. I couldn't help it. "No you're not."

"Now you speak falsely."

"No, Kenai. What I said, I was just—"

"You were right. You're very pretty, Isabel, and it's impossible for me not to look at you as a man looks at a woman. But, I am much older than Eliam. You can understand, can't you, that I feel wrong looking at you that way?"

"Because I am too young? Because I am Zeke's sister?"

He shook his head slowly. "Because I am old. Because I am Zeke's friend."

"What difference does it make if you look at me that way or Eliam does?" I stared at him for long moments, my heart pounding. "Besides, I am not pretty. I'm too skinny. I don't have Mother's big, beautiful eyes like my sisters do. I look exactly like Zeke and Jarom." I looked him in the eye, daring him to deny it because we both knew he couldn't. "And I smell like animal carcass," I added.

His smile showed in his eyes long before it hit his lips. He studied my face then, my eyes, as if he had never seen them before. "I never realized how pretty Zeke and Jarom were."

I felt my face turn the absolute red of a fiery sunset.

When I couldn't take his scrutiny any longer, I said, "See how the color has changed?"

He searched my flushed face. "I do."

I licked my lips and gave my head a little shake. I indicated the skins and the smoke seeping out in wispy billows. "Just a little longer and the skins will be the perfect shade and soft as can be."

He gave me half a smile. "Are you sure you're only fifteen?" he asked.

"I'm not fifteen. I'm fourteen."

He pretended to fall over backwards as if I had shot him with an arrow to his heart. I giggled.

"You're something else, you know that?"

I looked back down at the dirt floor, blushing fiercely. The heat in my cheeks made me shiver. I was relatively warm under my leggings, but my shoulders were bare, my sarong was thin, and my hair was wet

"You're cold," Kenai said, concern appearing in his eyes.

"Oh, no," I said, folding my arms. "I'm fine." It wasn't the first time I had been wet, either.

"Can we open this so you get more warmth from the fire?" he asked, indicating the tube that covered it.

I scrutinized the skins. "Not just yet."

"Here. Come here."

I scooted toward him.

He picked me up and put me unceremoniously in his lap. He rubbed my arms with his hands, making goose bumps rise on them.

"Why didn't you tell me you were freezing?" His chastisement touched something in my heart.

"I didn't think of it."

"You should take more thought for your health and safety."

"So should you," I pointed out.

He pulled down a warm fur from the table and wrapped it around me, tucking me in closer to his warm chest. "I'll leave that to you and your healthy midday meals," he said, the hint of a smile in his voice.

Once inside the fur, curled against the warmth he shared, tucked within the strength of his arms, I realized I had been very cold.

I didn't care how old Kenai was or if his holding me that way was inappropriate. He had allowed me to help him, and I would allow him to help me in this small thing. I would allow him to be my hero for these moments. I would allow him to show compassion in any way he could. Because the smoke was seeping out just as it was supposed to, just as it had to when the pressure reached its utmost. His heart was softening.

After a long time, long after I was warm, I wriggled away from him and took the knife from my belt to cut the skins free of the frames.

"Where did you get that?" Kenai was staring at the knife.

I turned it over in my hand. "It's Lamech's. He stole mine and gave me this in return."

He quirked an eyebrow. "A trade you are satisfied with?"

"No," I said, feeling exasperated all over again. "But I couldn't very well take my knife back from him."

He nodded slowly.

When we spread the skins between us, they were beautiful. He helped me roll them to set the color and we left them for Eliam to pick up in the morning. Then he walked me home.

That night as I lay in my hammock, I thought about the events of the day. I thought of Eliam, of his camaraderie with Kenai, the easy way they talked. I thought of my outburst, the smile that had followed it which Eliam hadn't been able to wipe away from his face, and his warm kiss.

But when I had thought through all of that, I put it aside and thought of Kenai. Why could he talk so freely with Eliam and not with Zeke? Why could I still feel the heat of his arms around me? I thought of his soft snort when I had invited Eliam to stay. I thought of how he had looked at Eliam and me in the trees for long moments before retreating into the tanning hut. I thought of every word he had said and every touch we had shared. I knew I should not be thinking about any of it, but I could not stop it.

And the next morning when I saw the amount of game my father and my brothers had brought back to the tannery, I had a really great idea.

CHAPTER 8

In my family birthdays were always small but happy celebrations. My fifteenth birthday was happy, but the celebration was larger than usual. Kenai's family had returned to the village after years of traveling with the Nephite army, and they were all in attendance, including his mother's new husband, Kalem, and his daughter, Melia, and her betrothed husband, Muloki.

Also, Father invited Gid's family to come.

It would have been the height of rudeness not to, but I thought it would ruin my celebration. I thought my oldest brother might think of some excuse and leave because Keturah would be at the fire with Gid. The thought made me glum.

But Zeke stayed. He even sat down to a long conversation with Gid. Zeke was right. It was complicated. I didn't understand it at all. Sometimes he was insanely jealous of Gid, and sometimes he seemed to rein it in as if his jealousy and hurt did not exist.

I had to admit I was curious about this man who had ruined everything. As time passed, I began to accept that Keturah was not going to marry my brother. I found it easier to forgive her than I had thought it would be, but I found it much harder to forgive Gid. I guessed it was because I loved her, and I did not love him. Besides, he had known Keturah was promised to Zeke, and he hadn't cared.

My curiosity got the better of me, and even though Kenai sent me a secret scolding look, I eased up behind Zeke and Gid to listen to them talk.

"Helaman wishes you a happy betrothal," Zeke was saying. "He plans to be home in Zarahemla for the winter season and then begin to travel, just as discussed. The church must be reorganized."

"Then I will join him in Zarahemla. He granted your petition?"

"He did."

"Zeke," Gid said, his tone changing. "Thank you."

"I'm not doing it for you," Zeke snapped, but after a long moment he cleared his throat and said more calmly. "Your thanks is not necessary."

"Still," Gid said quietly and then lowered his voice even more. "I know what it feels like to be the one she did not choose."

Zeke took a slow breath, leaned forward, and placed his elbows on his knees. "I will tell you something."

Gid leaned closer to my brother, as what he was about to say was clearly meant to stay between them. I had to inch closer too, and fight my conscience to do it. Mother was looking around for me. I pretended not to see her. Just one more minute. I wanted to understand. I needed to know how a lifetime of Zeke's love was not enough for Keturah.

"A fortnight ago, in the dead of night," Zeke said slowly, as if still deciding whether or not to say it. "I awoke with the uncomfortable feeling that I should come here and end things with Ket. I can't explain it. I didn't want to, but knew I must. I knew her heart was still divided, but I had decided to proceed with the marriage contracts when I returned home. I thought I had given her adequate time, more than adequate, to consider fully and change her mind if she was going to."

There was a smile in Gid's voice when he said, "Keturah does things her own way."

"She always did," Zeke said, trailing off as if he was remembering something from the past.

"I will tell you something," said Gid when Zeke did not offer any more confidences. "I too woke in the night to an irrational feeling. It was the same as for you. I could not deny it." He paused while Zeke took this in. "I felt so foolish. I thought she was already betrothed to you."

Zeke glanced at Keturah as she laughed with Kalem's daughter and Cana. "She wasn't. She never was."

"That night, I think it was the night before she went to Micah, the night she finally came to a decision she felt at peace with."

"Micah told me every painful detail of that conversation. She is kind and brave, but it would have been a mistake." Zeke took a deep breath and let it out. "I knew that if you were willing, it must be you."

I moved away from them as subtly as I could. I did not understand all that had happened, but I wasn't so upset with the three of them anymore.

That alone eased my mind enough to be a great birthday gift. But it was not my favorite one.

As I moved away from Zeke and Gid, Kenai kicked himself off the fence where he'd been sitting alone and followed me toward the fire. The scolding in his eyes had turned to disinterest, as if it made no difference to him if he were here with his family and friends or alone somewhere else.

He had talked to Jashon for a while but had spent most of the evening avoiding contact with everyone. Everyone but me. I had been watching him all night, catching his eye, and I knew he was not disinterested.

As Mother, Cana, Leah, and even Keturah began to serve the food, Kenai took a seat on the ground next to me.

Cana came to serve him his food. I understood why, but I glared at her anyway. Kenai wouldn't look at her, and she walked away with her shoulders sagging.

And he didn't eat the food. Any of it. But every so often he reached over and took something from my dish and popped it into his mouth.

At first I pretended not to notice. After a few times, though, after I judged he had eaten enough, I started to giggle when he did it. Finally I reached down and took a large piece of fruit from his untouched dish and put it into my mouth. He glanced at me and our eyes caught and held. I grinned slowly. The juice dripped over my lips and down my chin. Reaching up, he wiped the juice from my chin with a bent finger, and though it didn't touch his lips, there was a smile dancing in his eyes.

When I looked away and glanced around at the party, I saw that more than one person had noticed.

Zeke's eyes darted away without meeting mine. Mother gave a small knowing smile, probably thinking of all the extra food I had been taking. And Leah. His mother. She stared at us and let huge tears slip down her cheeks.

And still, this was not my favorite gift.

Lamech got up to take his empty dish to my mother, and when he returned to the fire, he sat on my other side, offering a brief wave of his hand in greeting to Kenai. He began asking me question after question, and soon I was talking more than eating.

I thought his constant talking odd until I noticed him glance at my sister, Sarai, who was sitting with Chloe a short distance away. And when she thought he wasn't looking, she edged a little closer to us. I shared a private smile with Kenai, though he didn't seem to know what it was for.

Lamech's questions had nothing to do with me. He probably had little interest in my answers. His interest was in my sister, and it occurred to me that Sarai might have developed an interest in this handsome warrior, too.

Lamech was very handsome. But it was more than that. He was handsome in such a unique way—not like Father or Zeke or Kenai or anyone I knew. He was mysterious, so dark, almost mesmerizing. When he spoke to me, I had to respond, even after I knew he didn't care what I said. I had gotten the impression before that he didn't say much to other people. It was like a strange gift he bestowed on someone when he spoke to them, though everything he said was completely normal. I was very much at ease with him, and he got me to say many things about myself that I had never given much thought to.

Kenai sat silently on my other side and listened, pretending not to, but with every word I said, I felt the weight of his attention.

"Have you given any thought to what I said?" Lamech asked me.

"Of course I have," I said. "You are right. But I don't see how I can act on it."

"Don't you?"

"No. My choices are limited."

When Lamech got up to go back to camp at Kalem and Leah's with his family, Kenai got up too.

"Give me the knife he gave you," he whispered.

I didn't know what he could want it for, but I passed it over to him.

"Be right back," he said. "Meet me behind your hut."

I watched him slip into the twilight behind Gid's family. Somehow, between my hut and his, he disappeared.

I took my dish to Keturah and Melia who were taking

stacks of dishes toward the stream, and then I went to wait behind the hut.

Presently, as the light began to fade, Kenai reappeared out of the dimness.

"Oh!" I said. "You startled me." I put my hand to my chest.

He took it by the wrist and pulled it to him. I felt the familiar hilt of my own knife as he placed it into my hand. I had to look twice.

"How did you get this?"

He chuckled. "Lamech doesn't even know yet."

"He doesn't...know?"

He shook his head. "Happy birthday, Isabel."

I licked my lips and looked at him in a way that probably showed too many of my feelings. I didn't care.

"Wait here," I said. "I have something for you too."

Before he could say anything, I darted around the hut and slipped inside. I went to my hammock and got a bundle from underneath it. I had tried to plan a way to give it to him that night, but nothing I had dreamed up was as perfect as this.

I slipped back outside and around the hut, where Kenai still waited. I had half thought he would be gone.

"Here," I said and thrust the package into his hands.

"What's this?" he said, taking it and turning it over in his hands. He glanced up at me. "Isn't it unusual to give gifts away on the anniversary of your own birth?"

It was unusual, and this had become an exchange of gifts, a custom of my people that could mean little more than a handshake in farewell, or it could mean a great deal and often did in the courtship years, which was one of the reasons exchanging knives with Lamech had made me so uneasy—I didn't know what it meant.

I watched as Kenai opened the bundle I had carefully wrapped with a length of Mother's patterned cloth and when he felt the buckskin beneath it, his hands stilled.

"They're leggings, like Zeke's—and mine," I said. "Remember that day we smoked buckskin together?" When he didn't respond, I started to worry for the first time that my gift had been too impetuous, too presumptuous, too much.

"I am unlikely to forget," he said gruffly after a moment.

"Don't you like them, Kenai?" I asked when he didn't make a move to take the buckskins from their wrapping.

He closed his eyes, and when he opened them, they were shining in the moonlight with tears like melted snow. "I like them very much, Isabel." His voice was husky with emotion.

This was my favorite gift, the one I gave to Kenai.

Relieved, I grinned stupidly and then I foolishly, recklessly put my arms around his middle and hugged him.

I didn't feel his arms close around me, didn't feel his hands tenderly caressing my shoulders as they had the night he had rescued me, but when I broke away and hastily said, "Goodnight, and thank you for getting my knife back," he grabbed my arm to stop me from leaving.

He stared at me for a long time without speaking. I held his gaze in the dim glow from the distant fire for as long as I could but finally looked down in embarrassment.

"Did I do something wrong?" I asked uncertainly.

He huffed. "Something wrong? No."

"Then why are you grasping my arm so tightly?"

He loosened his grip by degrees, apparently unaware that he was hurting me.

"Sorry," he mumbled.

"It's alright," I said, rubbing my arm and thinking about the long scar on his.

Then he was looking past me, his expression blank, his eyes pools of dark intensity.

"Go on back to your party," he said. Then he looked down at me and let himself smile—that rusty, unused one that had quickly become so endearing to me.

"Alright," I said, unsure why he had suddenly become so guarded, but when I turned to leave, I saw the reason.

Zeke leaned against the corner of the house with his arms folded over his chest, staring intently at us.

I couldn't read his expression in the shadows, not with the fire behind him as it was. I had no idea how much he had seen and heard, what he was thinking, or what mood he was in, but I knew I deserved to have him listen to my private conversation.

When I finally got my feet moving and passed him, he tugged on my hair and said, "Goodnight, Izz." But he kept his attention on Kenai.

I chanced a look back at Kenai, who stood rigidly facing his best friend, holding my gift tightly under one arm.

"Come on," I heard Zeke say behind me, and there was kindness, compassion, and utter authority in his voice. "I'll walk with you. You can tell me what happened the day you smoked buckskin together."

The next day when I left the tannery at lunch, Zeke watched me closely. I thought he intended to let me go, but in the end he jogged after me. "Wait up," he called out.

I turned and waited.

"Where are you headed?" he asked. As if he didn't know perfectly well. But before I could reply, he said, "You're going to see Kenai, aren't you?"

"I'm taking him his midday meal." I tried to keep my voice from sounding defensive. I was doing nothing wrong and had nothing to hide.

Except that my reasons for doing it had so foolishly, so imprudently, so unwisely changed.

"Does he eat it?" Curiosity flooded his tone.

"Yes."

"Does he...mind?"

"Does he mind that I go there? Did he say he minded?"

He shook his head almost as if he couldn't believe it. "No, he said nothing of the sort."

"Oh. Well, he doesn't seem to mind."

"Does he talk while you're there?"

"Yes."

"What does he talk about?" Zeke was curious and a little confused.

"Not the war, if that's what you're worried about."

"I am a little. I don't want you to hear about it, and I don't want him to lose it when you're, you know, alone with him."

"He's never come close to losing it."

"Yeah, well I heard what happened with Muloki."

"I think that was an isolated incident, Zeke. And who could blame him? Muloki was an enemy soldier."

"None of the other men tried to punch Muloki in the face," he pointed out.

"No," I agreed. "You heard about his reaction to Muloki, but did you hear that he stopped immediately when Kalem commanded him to? Did you hear that he cried by himself for the rest of the night?"

"How do you know that?"

I looked away from him.

"Izz," Zeke pressed.

"I heard him."

He gave me a puzzled look. "From our home?"

"No," I admitted. "I couldn't sleep. I went outside for

some air during the second watch and I saw him in the glow of his fire. It was just coals, but I saw him."

He had seen me too.

Zeke heaved out a burdened sigh and rubbed a hand over the back of his neck, hooking it there and leaning his head back.

"Is he expecting you?" he asked after a moment of thinking.

"Probably."

"Okay. You better go. But tell me if he does anything unusual."

"He's depressed, everything he does is unusual."

He smiled a little and waved me off. But after I had turned to go he said, "Izz, wait. Are you, you know, taken with Kenai?"

I thought that was kind of obvious.

"Honestly, Zeke?"

"Yes, Izz, honestly."

"Are you going to tell Father?"

"Depends on your answer."

I glanced over his shoulder at Father and Jarom. Would he walk straight over there and tell them?

I licked my lips. "Zeke, I like Kenai very much."

He settled back and folded his arms, watching me curiously as I continued.

"If there were not the obstacles of my age and his illness, I think I could love him more than any person on this earth."

Besides the slight widening of his eyes, he didn't reply.

I sighed. I might dream of other things, but I would always do what was right, what was expected of me, and what was required of me.

"I will marry who Father deems best. You needn't worry on that score," I assured him. "I trust Father."

Zeke nodded, and it seemed a bit of color drained from

his face. He waved me away again, and I left.

My heart was pounding. I shouldn't have told him. But when I walked into the maize field and saw Kenai working there, wearing his new buckskin pants, my heart lifted and I laughed.

CHAPTER 9

The day of Keturah's betrothal ceremony arrived quickly. Sarai wasn't feeling well, so Chloe was busy with Sarai's chores, and Mother asked me if I would milk Sachemai.

"I think it would be nice if you milked Mui, too. I'm sure Keturah has many other things on her mind this morning." She paused. "But it is up to you. I know you hate it."

"No, you're right. I should do it today." It was better than fixing the morning meal, which I would almost surely burn.

I thought of Zeke and what a hard day it would be for him. Losing Keturah was hard for our whole family, as we had long considered her our sister already. I was sad, but my heart ached for Zeke.

I milked Sachemai without incident and then went across the road and let myself in to Leah's crowded yard. Mother was right. No one had yet thought to milk the goat.

"Hello, Mui." I knelt next her. "I'll behave if you do."

After a moment, a pair of sandaled feet stepped into view. I would have known them anywhere, especially there in his own yard.

"You'd think with all these people here, someone could have troubled himself to milk Mui," I said to the sandals.

"But Kenai becomes jealous when other men get near his special girl."

I frowned. "Kenai has a girl?" And she milked their goat for them?

I did not want to think about why the thought of Kenai having a girl made my heart pound and my face get hot.

"Mui," Darius laughed. "They've been quite the couple for a long time."

I took a moment to stretch my back, leaning around Mui to look at him. I nearly asked him what he meant—it must have been some kind of family joke—but it was too silly and I giggled. I noticed Kenai standing near the door of their home, and I gestured him over but he didn't seem to see me. He was directing a dark scowl at his brother.

A funny, sick feeling formed in my stomach as I watched him stalk off through the gate and head toward the woods.

Darius followed my gaze.

"Did he hear that about Mui, do you think?" I asked him.

"Maybe, but that joke never makes him mad. He started it himself. Must be something else."

"All he saw was..." *Me laughing up into your eyes.*

"Us laughing together," Darius finished. "Wonder why that set him off."

"He thinks..." I bit back the words. It would sound silly, maybe even prideful.

"He thinks what?"

I worried my lip, looking to the place Kenai had disappeared. "He thinks I prefer you to him."

"Why would that—?" His eyes followed Kenai too. "Oh."

"You see why that would bother him?"

"Not unless he cares for you, Isabel."

I looked down at the ground, fidgeted with the meagerly filled bowl of milk, twisting it this way and that.

"Izz?"

"He doesn't," I said. "That would be ridiculous."

He was silent for a long time. I glanced up to see him looking at me thoughtfully, but I looked away and started again to milk the goat. People moved around the yard—it was crowded with people. But Darius just stood over me silently thinking about what I had said.

Finally, he knelt next to me. "I'll finish that," he said gently. "You'd better go find my brother and straighten things out. Make sure he knows that, you know, there's nothing between you and me."

"Do you even know how to milk a goat?" I asked, avoiding the whole idea that there could ever be anything between me and Darius.

He tilted the bowl to look inside. "At least as well as you," he teased. "Go. Please? He won't hear it from me, I'm sure of that." He bent closer and lowered his voice. "Izz, if you can reach him, in whatever way, you have to. Understand?"

I nodded and then stood up. I brushed the dirt off my leggings and started to leave.

"Isabel," he said, stopping me before I got two steps away. "We have to be careful about what Kenai sees between us from now on."

"There isn't anything to see," I pointed out.

"I think he's going to see what he wants to see. Don't you?"

"Okay."

"And Izz? There never can be anything. I mean, unless things drastically change for Kenai."

"Darius, I didn't think...did you think..."

A telling flush crept up his neck.

"Well, the thought crossed my mind, Izz. Your father's too."

"My father has talked to you?" This shouldn't have surprised me as it did. Darius was the most obvious choice for my father. He would likely only pursue other candidates if Darius had said no. "Did you refuse?" I demanded suddenly.

"No," he said defensively. "But Mother did. And now I think I know why."

I remembered the tears running down her face as she had watched Kenai eating from my dish, teasing me. And I knew why too. Leah had known something long before I had ever walked out to the maize field with my satchel loaded with food.

"It doesn't matter. We can talk about it later if you want. Right now, just go find him. And don't ever look at me and giggle like that again," he added with a wink.

"Just so long as you don't wink and say something funny," I promised unnecessarily, because any feeling Darius may have had for me was clearly overshadowed by his love and concern for his brother.

He didn't laugh. He stood and took the few steps toward me, cast a glance at Leah who was watching us from the corner of her eye. Darius drew me toward the gate away from the people in the yard for a little more privacy.

He didn't look at me when he spoke and his voice was very low. "I can't let it matter either way—I just want to know, Isabel. And I'm only going to ask it once." He ran his hand though his dark hair. "Is Kenai right? Do you...prefer me over him?"

I didn't give it the thought I should have. I just said, "No."

He let out a breath. "Good," he said, but it didn't sound like he thought it was. "One more thing."

I glanced toward the woods. "I've got to go, Darius."

He grasped my arm gently so I wouldn't.

I looked down to his fingers on my arm.

"Do you prefer Kenai over me?"

I didn't think about that either. "No!" I looked away, uncomfortable under his assessing gaze. "Not before. Not until that night. With the Lamanites. I didn't. Something happened that night. I don't know what."

He nodded slowly. "Okay." Darius was good-natured and easy-going. I was not used to seeing a frown on his face. "He seems to be listening to you. Will you help us get him back?"

"Well that's a silly question. Of course I will. Now, let me go do it." I looked pointedly at my arm where he still held it.

He let go and stepped back. "He probably went to the maize field. If he's not there, you might check at the falls. The grazing land is a possibility, but I'd check there last."

"I'll find him."

And I did. But he wasn't at the maize field.

I had followed Keturah to a meadow near a beautiful small waterfall once before the war. While she had been away, I had gone there sometimes when I wanted to be alone, but I hadn't been back since she had come home. I knew it was her place, the place she went to be alone, and I wouldn't encroach upon it.

I wondered why Darius had thought Kenai might be there, but it must have been a special place for him too because that was exactly where I found him. He was sitting on the bank of the river with his knees pulled up to his chest.

I made plenty of noise so he would know I was there, but he had probably known I was there long before he could see me.

I didn't pause when I entered the meadow, just took a direct path toward him. As I sat down next to him, I wondered what on earth I was going to say.

He was staring into the water and didn't take his eyes off of it. His locked arms held his knees up and he rested his chin behind them, so his voice was muffled when he said, "Isabel, go away."

101

"Okay," I said, but I didn't move to leave.

"Keturah spouts off some nonsense about water being like the love of God," he said as if he had forgotten he had just told me to leave, as if he had forgotten I was there at all. "I don't buy it, though," he went on.

"Is that why you're here?"

He snorted.

"But don't you remember Lehi's vision?" I asked. It was one of our oldest tales and explained many of our religious beliefs. Our ancestor, Lehi, had experienced a vision in which he had seen a river that flowed toward the tree of life. Our elders taught that the water was a representation of God's love.

"That was only figurative. It was used to help people understand."

"But to help us understand what, if not something literal?"

His eyes flicked to me for a second and encouraged by that small flicker of interest, I went on. "Just look all around you, Kenai! There is water everywhere. It makes the things flourish and grow. It seeps into all the small places. We must have it to live, but you don't have to stay by a source. You can collect some in your water skin and take it with you. Compare that to the love of God."

"You don't know what you're talking about. What about the fabled flood. Was that the love of God wiping out all of mankind?"

"It isn't a fable, and He was wiping out all the wicked so the good could go on," I corrected. "And I don't know, but I think that was love."

He didn't say anything.

"Well, anyway," I said, looking around. "What are you doing here when you could be back in the village with me?"

"You and Darius, you mean?"

"Sure," I said easily, feeling anything but easy about it. But I had the strangest feeling I should let him think I liked Darius. "Why not? You don't need me all to yourself, do you?"

"Of course not." His words were listless, and I could tell he didn't mean them.

"Good, that's what Darius said."

"What did Darius say?"

"That you already had a girl. I would hate to make her jealous. I'm no threat to her relationship with you. You can assure her of that."

Kenai's chin finally came off his knee. "He said what?"

"That you had spoken for some beautiful girl, and that I should just forget about you and marry him instead."

He looked confused, probably trying to decide what to laugh at first—that I thought Darius would marry me, or that I thought he would.

"What girl?" he finally asked, genuinely perplexed.

"Some girl named Mui," I said, forcing a straight face.

His lips cracked into a smile, a genuine one.

Relieved, I offered him a smile of my own.

"That's what we were laughing about. That's all. Mother suggested I milk Mui for Keturah today. That's the reason I was there, nothing else."

He shrugged as if he didn't care, but I knew he did, or he wouldn't have been here sulking in the first place.

"Tell me something," I said. He didn't refuse, so I went on. "Tell me one thing about the war that you didn't hate."

His expression changed to surprise at my sudden change of subject, but I could see that he was thinking about it.

"I liked that my family was there."

He hadn't refused to answer.

"A blessing not many of the boys had, I'll bet."

"No, I guess not."

"And I know I said I wouldn't ask," I pried a little more. "But tell me one thing you hated about it."

He went back into his thoughts. I was sure nobody had asked him to talk about it since he had been home. Everyone gave him a very wide berth. No one asked him about his experiences. No one asked much of him at all.

While he continued to think on it, I slipped my sandals off and rolled up my leggings, and then I put my feet over the edge of the river and let them dangle into the water.

"Here," I said, reaching over to pull Kenai's sandals off too. "Put your feet in with me." Once I accomplished the task of coaxing him into it—which wasn't difficult since he did not seem to care overmuch about anything—and his feet were in the water next to mine, I asked again. "What did you hate about the war, Kenai?"

"I hated being a commander," he said flatly. "It's one thing to kill a man because it is your duty, or because if you do not kill him, he will kill you." He swallowed hard, the only sign that the memories disturbed him. I reached over and took his big, scarred hand in mine. "It is quite another thing to command others to kill unsuspecting men—to decide who will die and when. And how."

I squeezed his hand tighter.

"That is what I hated, Isabel."

I ached for him. But I looked at our feet together in the water. He hadn't protested much really, not to me. We stayed there for a long time, letting the water run over our feet and legs and listening to the quiet sounds of the meadow.

"Now you tell me one thing," he said at last.

"Okay." I was leaning back on my hands by then, my feet

still in the water, watching the white clouds roll through the opening of trees in the meadow.

"Just tell me now if you..." He couldn't even finish.

"If I like Darius?" I ventured.

I saw the muscles in his jaw tighten.

"Of course I do," I said. It was true, but not exactly what he was asking. And again, I wasn't quite sure why I felt I should say it that way, why I should let him believe that I loved his brother.

When he didn't respond, just took his feet out of the water and shoved them, still wet, into his sandals, I said, "Was that not what you wanted to know?"

"No, that was it."

"I have heard my father thinks to arrange a betrothal between us." I had also heard it would never happen.

"Would you agree to that?"

"I trust my father," I said with a shrug.

He threw me a smirk. "I thought you didn't believe women should be given in marriage."

He remembered that?

"I don't. But I do believe in honoring my father and mother. I will not go against their wishes."

He regarded me in silence.

"You think that's foolish—to put so much trust in my father."

"No. I think it is good. But with Keturah..." He shook his head. "I'd forgotten there were still girls who were obedient."

I didn't care for the way he worded that, but he was right. What I wanted was to be an obedient person. "Zeke says Keturah tried to go along with Micah's wishes, but in the end she had to follow what the Spirit spoke in her heart."

"And what would you do, Isabel, if your heart led you

down a different path than your father wanted for you?"

"What would you do?" I turned back on him.

His eyes were bleak when he said, "I would do exactly as I was commanded."

"And yet you take on the guilt for things you were commanded to do. You needn't take responsibility for someone else's decisions, nor the blame."

I heard a margay in the trees, the small wildcat with big eyes and spotted fur that roamed the forest. I ignored it as I always did, but Kenai casually turned and repeated the call, replicating the sound with ease before I realized it had not been an actual margay.

Before I could ask if there was danger nearby, the only reason I knew for the secret call, Keturah came through the trees.

We watched in silence as she approached.

"Hi guys." She looked between us with a small, secret smile playing at her lips. It was different from the smile she had been wearing for her Gid these past weeks.

"Hi," I said, and Kenai nodded his greeting.

She sat on the other side of Kenai and took a moment to look around at the falls and the beautiful meadow, the rich blue of the sky. "I just had to come here one last time. We leave in the morning."

"You're really going to live with that man's family?" I blurted out. "Gid's, I mean."

She peered around Kenai and smiled at me. "Yes. If our families lived closer, I would stay in my mother's home for the duration of the betrothal. But, Gideon and his brothers will be leaving again and there will be no protection for their parents on the farm if I do not go. It is intended to be an opportunity for us to get to know one another."

"Oh," I said. "But we will miss you."

A tender look fell over her face. "Ah, Isabel, I will miss you all too. Very much."

"Even Zeke?" I couldn't help the pointed question.

"Especially Zeke," she said softly and cast a quick glance at Kenai.

He read it and said, "I'll leave you girls to talk."

"Where will I find you later?" I asked him.

He got to his feet and stood over us. He cast his own glance at his sister. "I'll be at home for the betrothal festivities." He stayed for a moment and then said, "You don't have to follow me around, Izz. I'm not going to harm myself or anything." He sounded irritable, but I knew it was for Keturah's sake. If I were him, I wouldn't admit that I liked me hanging around, either.

I smiled up at him. "If harming yourself even crossed your mind, then I do have to follow you around."

"If I wanted to harm myself, you couldn't stop me," he said with a snort.

"And you can't stop me from following you around,"

He made an irritated noise—fake—and threw a hand in the air, then left.

"He needs you," Keturah said as we watched him go. "I feel more comfortable leaving, knowing you are here to help him."

"I don't know what you mean," I said.

"I'm not blind, Isabel. For some reason, he is listening to you. And you know it very well."

I sighed. "Every day I pray I won't do or say the wrong thing."

"He just glowers at everyone else and walks away from them. The fact that he's letting you do and say anything is significant. What you are doing for him is amazing."

"Not so amazing as going to war to save your people."

She looked around the meadow, at the trees that surrounded it. She seemed to find what she was looking for, and I followed her gaze to a tree that looked as if it had been hacked at with an axe.

"I helped save my people, yes, but did it never occur to you that you could save one man?" She let that sink in for a moment. "Is the worth of one soul not great in the eyes of God?" Another pause. "Do you love him?"

I blushed from my toes to my ears.

She giggled. "I don't blame you. And I think," she touched my chin, "I think he might love you, too."

I shook my head vigorously. "No. I am just a baby. He only thinks of me as Zeke's annoying little sister."

She was quiet for another moment, considering me— probably wondering how I could be so naïve.

"He's too old for me," I added hastily and wanted to bite my tongue off.

"No he's not. And in a couple years, the difference won't even be noticeable. I bet you didn't even know there is a great age difference between Melia and Muloki. She is twenty-one, and he is twenty-nine."

That was eight years difference, just like Kenai and me, and she was right—I had not known. She looked at me until I shook my head in answer.

"And I doubt Kenai sees you as annoying," she continued. "Is it perhaps the way you see yourself?"

I looked down into my lap, ignoring her question. "Keturah, why did you hurt Zeke? Why did you go against Micah's wishes and agree to marry that other man?"

"It's complicated," she said gently.

"That's what Zeke said."

I wasn't looking at her, but I heard the smile in her voice

when she said, "Zeke's heart will heal. Once, on the battlefield, he was given a blessing, the most beautiful of blessings that his heart would heal and he would love again. I thought it was me he would love." She sighed, remembering. "But now I know it will be someone else."

"But why did you choose Gid?"

"I didn't. I chose Zeke. When I came home from the war, I was determined to marry him, but every day I felt uneasy about it. I was so confused, for I thought marrying Zeke was what my family wanted, what God wanted me to do. One morning your mother told me something I will never forget. How I will always love her for it."

Her eyes were bright, but of course she did not let any tears fall.

"Dinah said there is the kind of obedience that is strict observance of the commandments, or in my case, doing exactly what my brother asked of me. This strict obedience takes faith and courage. Then she spoke of the Holy Spirit, of listening to what it tells us inside our own souls. That is obedience too. Following the guidance of the Spirit, taking that step into the darkness, also takes faith and courage. There is a time for both."

"I understand," I said. "I guess I never thought of going against my Father's wishes."

She laughed. "I thought of it every day! But I truly wanted to be in harmony with what Micah thought was right. I think once he fell in love with Cana, his perspective changed."

"You think he is in love with Cana?" I asked in surprise. I knew it was an arrangement my father and Micah had made with little consideration to either of their feelings.

"I know they are in love. I see it every time they look at each other."

"I didn't think Father cared much about their feelings."

She laughed again. "You should ask Cana about how it all occurred. And you should talk to your father. Hemni does not disregard feelings."

He did not regard Kenai's.

I slipped my sandals on and stood. "I will let you have your last moments here alone," I said. "See you at home."

She stood too and wrapped me in her arms. "Good luck, Isabel, in all you have ahead of you."

I drew back and looked at her. "And to you, Keturah. I hope you will be very happy."

"I will," she replied and then walked away toward the waterfall.

Chapter 10

Zeke stayed through all of the celebrations, ceremonies, and festive meals for Keturah's betrothal, but by late evening, I saw him set his travel pack near the entrance of our home.

He walked with deliberate strides toward Keturah and Gid, and his shoulders squared when he neared them. I watched curiously—and I wasn't the only one watching—as he clasped arms with Gid. I wished I could hear what they were saying. Then, only after he had spoken to Gid, did he turn and place a hand on Keturah's shoulder. He smiled into her eyes, but he did not linger.

He had to feel everyone's eyes on him as he left the brightly lit center of the village and turned into the dim twilight. He walked alone to our home and picked up his travel pack, hefted it over his shoulder, and walked out of the village toward the West Road.

Lamech appeared at my elbow and asked, "What are you crying for?"

"Oh!" I touched my wet cheek. "I didn't realize I was."

"That's dumb."

"You're dumb."

He snorted.

"So dumb you have no idea how I got my knife back."

He shifted his weight to his other foot and looked at me.

His face was half in shadow and his dark eyes stared into mine—maybe angry, maybe amused, maybe puzzled. I didn't know him well enough to guess.

I couldn't stop the smug smile that stole my lips, and I couldn't get it to go away once it was there.

"Are you going to dance?" he asked, completely avoiding the subject of the knife, and I would have bet anything his dark eyes hid embarrassment.

I looked nervously toward the fires that burned brightly in the center of the village. "Oh. I'm not very good at it," I said, backing away.

Those dark eyes just stared at me with an indiscernible expression.

"Really," I emphasized.

I looked again toward the dancers, so beautiful in their best dance costumes and ceremonial clothes. The bright colors swirled and flounced in rhythm with the drums.

"But you want to," Lamech said.

"The girls dance," I said and folded my arms over my chest. "I can never get the steps right." I saw Keturah had begun to dance, spinning and stepping perfectly, and laughing through the firelight. Laughing. So happy. So sure of herself.

She knew who she was.

"Come on," Lamech said. He took my arm and pulled me into the firelight. "Stay here," he commanded. Then he walked to the drum circle and spoke to his cousin, Enos, who drummed and sang there. Enos gave him a strange look, but nodded.

I glanced around. I hadn't lied to Lamech. I was about as good at dancing as I was at fixing meals and milking goats. Which was to say I was not a good dancer at all.

"Alright," Lamech said when he returned, hopping a little on his way like he was so excited he couldn't contain it, or so

112

athletic he just moved that way. "When Enos starts the music, you just follow me." And then he crouched a little and started to show me the steps of a dance I had only seen once.

Everything about that night was seared into my mind. The burning fires on the field. The movements of the dancers—hardly resembling dancing at all—that depicted battles as they moved slowly in and around each other. And that drum beat—slow, incessant, filling the air, reaching up into the night with the embers of the fires.

The new song started, and it all came back so vividly as Lamech towed me out into the clearing. Most of the other dancers had shuffled away, confused when they heard the beat. A war dance at a betrothal?

I looked at Lamech, panic making knots in my stomach. There was no way I could dance a dance meant for war. Not in front of all these people. Not ever.

"Come on," he coaxed gently. "It's okay. Everyone else needs a rest anyway." When he saw the look on my face at the thought of dancing alone, he smiled but didn't laugh at me. "Sorry. It's easy. Just like this." And he continued to show me the steps.

A few of the other striplings joined us. There were plenty of them there, as many of them lived within a day's walking distance. Some had come from even farther away. Gid had been their captain, and the men loved him. Most of them seemed to be friends with Keturah too. More and more of the men joined us on the clearing and whoops and cries went up through the night.

Gid and Keturah joined the dancers, and suddenly the war dance did seem fitting at this particular betrothal. Keturah and Gid had met and fallen in love during the war.

I took a deep breath, turned my eyes back to Lamech and began to study the movements of his feet. It didn't look so hard.

So I began to move my feet. I wasn't good at it, but I tried.

Lamech caught my eye, and I laughed as he exaggerated his steps. He really wasn't so bad. He was much nicer than he looked.

Over his shoulder, I saw Leah coming through the dancers on a path set for me. I sobered and straightened, watching her warily. I thought she would tell me this dance was not a dance for young ladies, but to my surprise, she smiled, took my hand, and danced with me.

And she knew the steps perfectly.

After that, I looked at Leah differently. I had seen her many different ways through the years as I had grown up. I had seen her as a neighbor, a healer, my Mother's absent friend, a survivor, a woman at my church, a bride as happy as Keturah was tonight.

Most recently, I had seen her as the mother of a soldier, worried sick, and crying just to see him eat.

But tonight I saw her as a woman, my own friend, a fellow daughter of God. Tonight, the gap in our ages did not matter. We were sisters—that was all.

When the song ended and the dancing was over, Leah hugged me. It was a familiar embrace, just like my own mother's a few mornings before, the morning she told me I was pretty in my buckskins.

I didn't know what to say to her. I eased my arms around her, and she responded by holding me more tightly. I felt her body jerk with a sob, but she released me after one more moment. I caught the hope in her eyes before Lamech appeared at my elbow.

"You were right about..." He glanced at Leah as she dabbed her tears away. "Your dancing," he finished, opting to be polite in front of her.

I shrugged. "I tried to tell you. But Leah showed me how."

He nodded.

Leah placed her arm around Lamech's shoulders.

"Come with me, Lamech. There are many friends I want to introduce you to, and after that, there is more, much more, food you must eat."

He nodded politely and only glanced back at me as Leah led him away.

Something about Leah's embrace made me feel like Zeke. I wanted to leave the party too. I wondered if she had hugged him like that, so tight, as I wandered back toward home.

I saw Kenai sitting in his own yard working with some wood, making a stool or a chair maybe. I couldn't tell which.

I went to the gate to say hello, but I didn't plan to stay with him. Leah was counting on me. She was desperate for it. But as I watched Kenai work, it all felt out of my control. He needed so much from me and had been taking increasingly more. It was good—he was giving me his trust, offering his wounds to be examined and cleaned—but I needed some time to think things over because every time I was with him, I became confused.

"What are you working on?" I asked him.

He looked at it and a small corner of his mouth turned up. "Just a chair," he said. But I could tell that to him it was more than a chair.

"I'm sure it will be sturdy and beautiful," I said, and covered a yawn. "I'll see you tomorrow." I thought of the food Mother had in the house. "Would you rather have squash or sweet potatoes for tomorrow's midday meal?"

He put the chair down and stood. "I'll leave that to you."

"Alright. Goodnight then, Kenai."

I was halfway home, which was to say I had taken about ten steps, when he appeared at my side and said, "I'll walk you."

115

I slowed and turned to stare at him. Fires glowed all through the village, but here at our far end only moonlight fell on Kenai's face as he walked slowly beside me down the road.

"It's only ten more steps."

He shrugged.

We took a few more steps in silence.

"I danced the war dance," I said. "Did you hear it?"

"Yes, I heard it." His words were soft and even warm.

The steady thrum of the drumbeat made the village seem small, but the sounds of the night were there too—the owl, the crickets, the breeze in the trees—and they made me feel miles away from the revelry.

"Your mother danced with me."

"She likes to dance."

"She's worried about you."

"She'll get over it."

We came to my home. Kenai opened the little gate and followed me through it.

I turned to him. "Only when you do."

"I think it drives her crazy that she can't just give me some herbs and make me well."

That hadn't occurred to me. "I imagine it would be difficult for a healer to be unable to heal her own son."

"I can't just snap out of it to make her feel better."

"Nobody expects you to."

He raised an eyebrow. "Not even you?"

"Especially not me. I just want you to eat."

He looked at me skeptically.

"Really, Kenai. I'm not angling to get anything."

"Because I don't have anything you want." It was kind of a question.

"Right," I agreed in answer. "What have I to gain? Now,

why are you not over there dancing at your sister's celebration?"

He rolled his eyes. "How come you aren't? You're the one whose father must show her off to the eligible young men."

I looked away. "You should be showing off yourself. It's time for you to marry. Much more so than it is for me. You're old."

He shook his head. "No. I'm...messed up if you hadn't noticed. No. It wouldn't be fair to some poor girl to be yoked to someone like me."

He made it sound like a joke, but I had witnessed his silent tears, his apathy, his mood swings, his anger at God, and his confusion.

"Would your wife be just some poor girl to you?"

"I never really thought about her—what she would be like."

He had obviously thought of Cana at least once, but I didn't mention that.

"I told Eliam I had never really thought about marriage. I told him I didn't want to be married," I admitted.

"What did he say to that?" he asked, surprise touching his voice, though I didn't know which part surprised him.

"He was nice about it. He said he would not pursue a betrothal until we were both in love."

"Do you want to be in love then?"

"What kind of question is that? Of course I do."

But I knew I put off the appearance that I didn't. I could be testy and impatient, and I ignored a lot of things, including the village boys, to work at the tannery.

Kenai didn't make a reply to that, just waited for the rest of mine.

I sighed, wishing I had just said goodnight and ducked into the house. I looked off toward the place in the trees where

Zeke had disappeared. "I do. I want love," I said with a note of wistfulness that I couldn't disguise.

"And marriage? You lied to him, didn't you?" The warmth was still there in his voice. He took a step closer to me. Then another.

"Yes," I whispered back.

"And children?"

I looked up into his eyes, swallowed hard.

"I'll be so bad at it," I said. "I can't even cook."

He was quiet. What could he say? I couldn't cook.

"Well, goodnight," I said after a few moments.

"Couldn't you learn to cook?" he blurted as I turned to go.

I shook my head at the preposterous idea. "You and I would make a ridiculous pair," I said. "I can't cook, and you won't eat."

With that and a nervous laugh, I swept back the mat over the threshold and went inside my family's home.

I heard Kenai's voice behind me, soft in the darkness.

"Goodnight, little girl."

I had barely stoked the fire to build the light a little when I heard Jarom talking to Kenai in the yard. He sounded agitated.

"Father says he's taken off for Judea!"

I went to the mat and pulled back the edge so I could see Jarom and Kenai, shadows near the gate.

"But he is no longer stationed there. He's expected in Zarahemla in just over a fortnight," Kenai said, seeming unperturbed while Jarom paced anxiously.

"He's gone there to bring back a girl!"

"So soon? That seems uncharacteristically rash for Zeke."

Jarom stopped pacing and looked pleadingly at Kenai, his whole manner filled with apprehension.

"Father has sent Zeke with betrothal contracts and authorized him to negotiate on our behalf."

"For whom?"

"For me!"

Kenai leaned back on his heels and let a smile touch his lips. "I meant for what girl. Are you angry because Hemni did not send you to do your own negotiating, or angry because you do not like the girl?"

Jarom threw up his hands and started pacing again.

I was completely shocked—the idea that a man could be betrothed without his consent to a girl he didn't like had never, ever, occurred to me.

But who did my brothers know in Judea that would consent to come here and marry Jarom? And what about Zeke? He was the eldest son. He was expected to take a wife first. But then again, since Zeke hadn't married Keturah, I no longer expected that he would do anything he was supposed to do.

"I thought you liked her," Kenai was saying. "You told me you did."

"She drives me crazy!"

That ghost of a smile touched Kenai's lips again. "I know the feeling."

Jarom stopped pacing and turned to Kenai. "Captain, if my little sister makes you feel like this, I'll skin you myself."

Kenai laughed—actually laughed—a hearty and genuine laugh.

"You could try," he said, still chuckling.

"In seriousness, Kenai, idle threats aside." His agitation turned to concern. "What's going on with you and Izz? She's disappearing for hours at midday, Mother says she's taking an extra portion of food each day, and Zeke says you exchanged gifts on her birthday."

119

I hadn't realized so many people were taking note of our friendship because we usually kind of avoided each other in the village.

Jarom stepped closer to Kenai and lowered his voice. "Darius won't go near her. He says he won't run the risk of you misinterpreting anything between them."

Kenai had been staring at his sandal, but he looked up suddenly. "He said that? I thought they were considering a betrothal."

Jarom shrugged. "Of course Father presented the idea to Darius before he approached anyone else with it. But your mother and Kalem refused the offer. You didn't know that?"

Kenai turned slowly toward the door, easily making eye contact with me through the slit in the mat as if he had known I was standing there. Was he figuring out that I had lied to him? First to Eliam and now to him. He would surely think I was nothing but a little liar.

Kenai put his hands on his hips and turned his attention down to the ground in front of him again. He chewed on his cheek for a moment, hesitating, considering. Then he shook his head and took a step back. "Nothing's going on."

"Be straight with me," Jarom said, his demeanor completely different than it had been moments ago when he had been falling apart. It was brotherly. It was authoritative. It was protective. It no longer sounded like he was talking to his commander. "I saw you myself, standing with her here in the moonlight. Standing too close, Kenai. What were you doing here like that if there is nothing going on?"

Kenai met Jarom's eyes. The drums thrummed on and the crickets were slow. Everyone said Kenai had this crazy way of talking with his eyes—silent communication they said—and I thought maybe he was using it just then.

But when Jarom glanced behind him at the house, and said, "Oh, I forgot," I figured Kenai had just glanced pointedly toward the door.

After a few uncomfortable seconds while Jarom realized I was inside the house and had likely heard their entire conversation, Kenai changed the subject, returning it to Jarom's predicament. "So, Zeke is bringing your bride to you."

Jarom's mood instantly changed at the reminder, though I wasn't sure if it was a production for my sake or if he really couldn't help it. He gripped both his hands in his hair and looked to the star-lit sky. "What am I going to do?"

"Die a happy man?"

Jarom groaned.

"This is what you wanted, is it not?" Kenai asked.

Jarom made another sound of frustration. "Once, maybe," he admitted.

"You're not still stinging from what she said, are you?"

Jarom treated Kenai to a glare.

"It's been so long. Could you not forgive her?"

Jarom made a disgusted sound. "I'm just a poor replica of the original, elder, better brother?" He snorted. "Not likely."

I had known Jarom was in love with a girl.

I hadn't known he also hated her.

CHAPTER 11

Nearly a fortnight had passed when Zeke strode back into the village with two other soldiers and a family of four.

The man, the soldiers, and Zeke each hauled a pack full of leathers and furs. The woman, a girl, and a younger boy each carried their own gear. Travel worn and dusty, they gazed anxiously about the small village.

Father, Jarom and I were just returning home from the tannery for the evening meal. Jarom and I glanced at each other, and I knew we were both heartily wishing we had stopped at the stream with a chunk of soap on our way home.

Zeke led the people right up to the gate.

So this girl, whoever she was, I thought as I watched her eyes dart around nervously, had accepted Jarom.

It seemed there were nerves on both sides of this betrothal. Jarom had been very worked up on the night of Keturah's betrothal, but since then, he had become unusually withdrawn. Father had tried to bring it up one day at the tannery, but Jarom only listened sullenly. When Father had given up, Jarom went off alone into the woods and didn't return for two days.

"Father," Zeke began the formal introductions. "This is Paachus of Judea. Paachus, my father, Hemni."

The two men clasped arms.

"Welcome!" my father said warmly.

Zeke continued to introduce our family to theirs. Paachus's wife was Ophelia. The boy was Lucius, and his sister's name was Eve.

Eve was a small girl with pale skin, dark hair which she wore in a knot at her nape, and light eyes. She was short and curvaceous. She was pretty, but I didn't think she was outstandingly beautiful—just normal like me, I guessed. And she was not at all the type of girl I pictured Jarom going crazy over.

When she made eye contact with Jarom, her pale complexion turned a very pretty shade of pink that reminded me of the first rays of dawn. But she put her chin in the air and looked away from him.

That could have meant anything. Her pink cheeks seemed to contradict her stubborn chin, and I liked her right away.

When the introductions were done and the travelers had come through the gate, I took Eve by the hand and pulled her further into the courtyard where she could sit and take off her pack. I sent a sharp look to Jarom, hoping he would be gentlemanly and come over to help Eve remove her gear, but he just stared at her for a moment and then went to talk with Zeke and our fathers.

I touched Eve's shoulder. "He's nervous," I said quietly.

She watched him. "No. He dislikes me."

I laughed, drawing her attention to me, and I shook my head.

"You will find that you are wrong. Now, let me help you with this pack."

"Thank you," she said. "It was a long journey."

"Willingly traveled?" I asked.

She looked back to Jarom. "Nervously traveled. A long time ago, I said something that hurt him. I was so young, only

124

twelve. I never got a chance to make it right, you know, before the army marched out." She looked back to me. "I was beyond surprised when Zeke called at our door."

"How do you know my brothers?"

"Zeke has long been a customer at our shop in Judea." She gestured to the racks the men had hauled into the yard. "My father sells pelts."

"Probably reminded him of home," I said.

"I think it did." She bit her lip and blushed again. "Papa and Zeke have made a trade agreement."

"Is it...part of the betrothal?"

She shook her head. "No, thank goodness."

"I can take you to the stream to wash if you want. A quick bath will make you feel better after your long journey."

She hesitated, but only for a second. "Okay," she agreed. "That would be nice."

"I could use a scrub, too. I've been at the tannery all day."

She nodded her understanding, and her eyes lit. "Zeke brought us some of your lovely buckskin. That is what convinced my father to trade at such a distance."

My eyes found Zeke across the yard. He could hardly make this agreement if Father didn't plan to let me continue working at the tannery. Perhaps Eliam had been right and I was underestimating my father.

I turned back to Eve's bright eyes. Not very many girls would describe buckskin as lovely.

I told Mother and Ophelia where we were going and invited Ophelia to come along too. She declined politely and said she would freshen up in the basin inside the house.

I gathered my things and hurried Eve out of the yard before my brothers could insist we needed a guard to walk to the stream.

"It's beautiful here in your village," she said.

"What's your home like?"

"Much the same as yours. We are higher in the mountains. We live inside the city so I do not see much of the forest, not up close. Until the war ended, I'd never even been out of the city."

"Eve, what was it like with the army there?"

"Well," she said. "Before the stripling reinforcements came, Antipus and his men were barely able to maintain the city. The embattlements were in disrepair, their weapons were barely serviceable, and the food stores were running low. The striplings changed all that."

"How?"

"They went right to work rebuilding the embankments and walls of timbers. They went hunting when we could not. They harvested the crops and tended the flocks outside the gates. And after they had provided for us, they lured the Lamanites out of Antiparah so Antipus and his men could slay them."

"That is more than my brothers have told me about their whole six years in the army," I told her.

"I'm sure it's difficult for them to talk about. There were many pleasant, even happy, times for them. At least, Zeke was always happy when I saw him." She smiled at that, but then her expression clouded. "But though the striplings were all kept safe and alive, many of their Nephite brothers were not. I think that would have been a hard blessing to bear."

I bit my lip. I had never thought of that.

"How old are you, Eve?" I asked as we drew close to the stream hidden far behind my home.

"Eighteen," she said.

"Jarom's age then."

"Yes."

"Can I ask you something personal?"

We put our satchels down on the grassy bank of the stream.

"Of course, Isabel. We are to be sisters." She gave a little smile. "I've never had a sister."

I returned her smile. "Eve, why did you agree to marry Jarom if you believe he dislikes you? Wouldn't you prefer to marry a man in whose love you could trust?"

We knelt by the stream and each wet and lathered a small cloth.

"Well, several boys have asked Papa if they could court me, but none that we could both agree on. See, he always kind of favored Zeke—and I must confess that I did too—and no man that came to the door was enough like him to suit either of us."

I frowned, and anger churned in my stomach on Jarom's behalf and rose through my throat, burning it. But I did not let it escape through my words. Much.

"And Jarom is enough like Zeke to suit you?"

Despite the terse question, she actually smiled. "I favored Zeke only until he brought his brother along with him and introduced us."

"But why did you—?"

"Say what I said? You heard about that." She sighed. "I was twelve. So was he." She gave me a sheepish look full of pink cheeks, embarrassment, hope. "I thought...when Zeke explained the arrangement he had come to offer, I said yes immediately. I had thought of Jarom every day for six years, and I had seldom thought of Zeke. Father had never met Jarom, and he took more persuading. But I knew I was unlikely," she scoffed at the word, "to get the offer again."

Mollified, I washed up in silence, the only sounds between us the sounds of splashing water and the wind high in the trees.

"Are you angry?" Eve asked after a while.

"No. I should have said that. Sorry. I was just thinking." I wrung the water from my rag. "So, you've loved Jarom since you were twelve? Without ever seeing him again?"

She shrugged. "I don't know if you can call what I felt at twelve love, but..."

I looked over at her when she didn't go on. She was biting her lip and blinking back the bright moisture in her eyes.

"What is it? Go on," I coaxed gently.

She leaned forward. "I knew Zeke was coming. The whole week before he walked into our shop, I just had this feeling. I didn't know it would be Zeke. I didn't know he would bring betrothal contracts. But I knew...something. When I saw him, I knew that whatever he had come there for was what God wanted for me. The Spirit confirmed it before he even arrived in Judea."

"Well," I said. "You're lucky. Jarom is an amazing person. You will make each other happy." I giggled. "And you must believe me when I say he does not dislike you."

Skeptically, with a slight reprimand in her tone she asked, "Did he say that?"

"No. He said you drive him crazy."

She looked at me for a moment, then laughed too and splashed me.

"Here," I said. "Lay back on the bank and I will wash your hair for you."

Someone cleared his throat behind us.

Eve and I both turned to see Jarom had followed us. He was standing across the small clearing with his arms at his sides. His thumb tapped his leg in agitation, but his gaze had settled on Eve and didn't waver. His clean tunic was damp from his wet hair and his face was freshly scrubbed, though I could see he had not taken the time to shave, something I was sure he would have done if he had felt there were minutes to spare.

"I will wash her hair," he said, walking toward us with slow strides. He didn't take his intense gaze off of Eve.

But Eve's eyes shot to me in alarm.

"Jarom," I said. "I really don't think that's appro—"

"I don't care what you think."

He still hadn't looked at me at all. I didn't know what to do. I looked to Eve, but she had no answers, only looked back at me with luminous eyes.

I stood. "I won't stand by and let you drown her! We've only just met!" I stomped my foot petulantly for effect.

Jarom broke his gaze on Eve to look at me at last. He rolled his eyes, and I felt assured then that he wasn't as angry as he looked. No matter how she had hurt his pride.

"Okay," I said to him. I picked up my things, gave Eve an encouraging smile, and left the two of them to work out their future and their feelings.

Good luck, I thought with a bit of silent sarcasm.

I wasn't surprised when Jarom and Eve missed the evening meal, but Ophelia was alarmed.

"Jarom met us at the stream. They had much to talk about," I told her.

But it was only Zeke's assurance that eased her concern. "Jarom is the most honorable of men, and he can protect your daughter from anything out there." He jerked his head toward the forest as he accepted a plate of food.

He was sincere, as always, but there was a note of resignation in his voice too. Was it Eve he and Jarom had been at odds over?

But I couldn't worry over their concerns. I had enough of my own.

When I passed Kenai on the road that evening, he

glowered at me. Just a glower, nothing more, and this had been going on for a fortnight, since Jarom had told him I was not to be betrothed to Darius.

"Zeke, will you find Darius and ask him to meet me?"

"No," Zeke said without even looking up from the scroll he was reading in the firelight.

"I need to talk to him and he doesn't want Kenai to see us together."

"I know. That's why I'm not going."

"I'll just get Sarai to do it," I said, but I was stunned that Zeke, like Jarom, knew Darius was avoiding me and why. How many other people knew?

"She won't go either."

"Of course she will."

"I won't let her."

"Zeke!"

He finally sighed and looked up.

"What do you want with Darius?"

"I want to know why Kenai is glowering at me as if I were one of the rest of you."

"Want my advice?"

"No."

"Go straight to the source. Just ask Kenai."

"But—"

"I mean it, Izz. Be honest with him, and make him be honest with you."

"I doubt I could make Kenai do anything."

Zeke scoffed. "You are the only one who can make Kenai do anything."

"I hardly think I should take relationship advice from you." I instantly wanted to slap my hand over my mouth. "Sorry," I said. "I didn't mean that."

He gave me a wry smile. "We learn by our mistakes, so you should definitely take relationship advice from me for I have made many and am very wise."

His attempt at humor fell flat for me. I sat next to him. "What went wrong with Keturah?" I asked.

His eyes flicked away. "She fell in love with someone else."

"No, I mean, what did you do wrong?"

"For one thing, I didn't listen to her. I heard the things she said, even thought I understood them. But I always thought I knew what was best for her. I thought I knew that she was wrong, and more importantly, that I was right. I didn't listen to what she was really saying. Didn't pick up on what she needed from me, which was friendship and understanding, not protection and jealousy."

I skimmed my foot through the dirt.

"Just work it out with Kenai and skip Darius," he said. "Because even if I went for him, he wouldn't come."

I nodded, got up, and walked away, and I went all the way to the tannery.

It was eerily similar to that night I had been abducted. The evening had been just like this—the sun was still above the treetops but sinking quickly into a purple sky.

I didn't care how quickly it was sinking. I felt troubled and I wanted to be alone.

The quiet at the tannery eased my heart immediately. I hadn't planned on working, but I absently got out an unfinished hide, stretched it over the log Jarom used outside, soaked it with water, and began the long, slow, scraping strokes that would make it clean and smooth.

I didn't know how long he had been in the clearing when I finally sensed him behind me. I stiffened. I didn't look at him, but he must have noticed the change in my posture because that was when he spoke.

"You lied to me about Darius," he growled. "You knew you weren't getting betrothed to him. Did you want it to be true? Is that why you said it?"

"You lied to Jarom about us," I shot back, leaving the scraper on the hide and turning to face him.

"No, I didn't."

"You said there is nothing going on between us."

"There isn't."

"There is, and you know it."

"No, there isn't." He shook his head forcefully as if that would make it true. "And the way I look at you sometimes, like you said, doesn't count. It doesn't mean anything."

I glared at him.

His hand flew up, as if to wave it off. "I've never acted on it. I've never kissed you, never touched you. That makes it nothing."

No, he hadn't kissed me. Not with his lips. But his eyes had kissed me many times. And never touched me? That was debatable, I thought, as I remembered being cradled against him in the tanning hut, remembered his chest on mine while the others walked away through the darkness, remembered how he held me after the Lamanites had all been killed as if I were his to comfort.

"I don't need this," he went on. "I've got enough to deal with without everyone expecting me to marry you."

"Nobody expects that."

Did they?

Shocked, hurt, I retaliated. "But maybe a wife would give you something other than your own self-pity to focus on."

"You don't understand." He took a step back.

"Neither do you," I broke in. "You're the best one of them, of all the striplings! Do you know that? The best one! And all you can see are the things you did that would have been wrong only in times of peace. But it wasn't a time of peace! You were called of God to fight that war. Your position as captain, that was a calling, specifically designed for you. Try thanking God for once!"

"Thanking Him?"

"Yes, Kenai, thanking Him. For preserving your life hundreds of times! Ask yourself why He did that for you. Thank Him for giving you the means—the skills and talents—to preserve your own life."

My words met silence. Kenai's nostrils flared slightly as he breathed deeply. His eyes glittered with passion, anger, confusion. He swallowed hard.

I stood still, but my chest rose and fell as if I had been running. I was shaking inside. Everyone was so careful with Kenai, and I had just yelled at him, talked about the war, about things I knew nothing of. About things he knew too much of.

"I am not the only one who thinks poorly of myself," he said after a moment, his voice coming from deep in his chest. "You underestimate your own worth."

He had kept his distance from me, like a wild animal circling, but he stepped toward me. The intensity in his eyes scared me, and I stepped back. Zeke was right. Kenai was going to lose it, and I was alone in the woods with him.

I realized with sudden wonder that his eyes were speaking to me. But I couldn't understand what they said, because what his eyes said conflicted utterly with what his mouth had said.

When I tried to retreat from Kenai's advancing steps, my hips hit the log behind me. He placed both of his large hands at my waist trapping me against it.

"I thought...I thought you said you wouldn't touch me."

"I said I hadn't touched you."

I swallowed.

He moved his hands around to my back, pulling me away from the log, and now I understood that his hands, too, were saying the same thing his eyes were saying.

"*Come here, little girl.*"

I took the small step toward him and had to raise my face higher to see into his.

"You were right," he said softly. "We do make a ridiculous pair."

He kissed me then, and not with his eyes.

I had never been kissed before. I had nothing to compare Kenai's kiss to. But of one thing I was sure—no other man's kiss could compare to his.

CHAPTER 12

Weeks passed. We held the betrothal ceremony for Jarom and Eve who had, it seemed, worked out their misunderstanding. Eve left with her family to await the marriage at her family's home in Judea. I missed her. But she would be back to stay in one short year.

Zeke had received leave to stay in the village for Jarom's betrothal, but he left the next morning for Zarahemla and his new duties as a captain's guard for Helaman and his brethren.

Finally, when the weather began to warm, the men in the village began building a home for Jarom which was situated near Micah and Cana's. I didn't have much occasion to pass near the site as it was not on the way to anywhere, but sometimes I went there with the excuse of visiting Cana just to see the progress, to see if Kenai was there.

Since he had kissed me, he had been acting differently. I told myself it was the cooler weather that kept us indoors more. We still ate midday meals together, still sat by each other at family functions in the village, but he stopped talking to me about the things that mattered. He never mentioned wanting to kiss me again, for instance.

He was in a full-fledged retreat on that front.

I was no longer the only person he talked to. I saw him in the village talking to other men, even laughing with them. The food I brought for him was no longer the only food he ate. And once, Sarai said she had seen him walking with another girl.

I couldn't imagine him with another girl. I couldn't imagine Jarom married, someone's husband, someone's father. I couldn't imagine Zeke as a guard in the city, either. Everything was strange.

One morning, when Father and I were walking together to the tannery, just the two of us like it had been before Jarom had come home, I asked, "Father, where does Eliam live?"

He turned to me. "Do you have a need to know that?"

It wasn't that I hadn't seen Eliam. He came by the tannery often enough, sometimes to my home for the evening meal. But I had spent too much time worrying about Kenai and not enough worrying about my own future.

"I want to talk with him. I would like to go there."

Looking pleased, Father said, "He lives in Ezra, on the north side of Melek."

"You have no objection to me going then?"

"I'd rather you didn't travel alone, but no, no objection otherwise."

"But the boys are busy with Jarom's house," I said.

Zeke had come home every other fortnight, but he was gone just then traveling with Helaman. Darius still wouldn't come near me. And I wouldn't dream of asking Kenai, not to take me to Eliam. Jonas? Mahonri? Another of the striplings? Micah maybe?

"Perhaps Muloki would take me. I'll ask Eliam to bring me back."

"I like the way you think," Father said with a smile.

I took a deep breath. I needed to know. "Do you intend for me to marry Eliam?"

"If you like him," Father said easily.

"You weren't even going to discuss it with me?"

He looked at me with surprise. "I just thought you'd like to meet and come to know Eliam before we made any plans."

"Oh." That was thoughtful. "Then thank you. What do you like about Eliam? I mean, why did you choose him?"

Father frowned a little as he thought, but not from anger or displeasure. "He is honest, brave, has faith in God."

"But surely there are many men here in Melek that are honest and brave."

He chuckled. "You're right. I like Eliam's family. They will take care of you, love you."

"Still," I said. "There are many good families in Melek." I paused for a moment, actually nervous to say the next part. "Including Leah's. Would you not consider Leah's boys?"

"Of course I would. I already have."

"Just Darius?"

"Kenai is not looking for a wife just now."

"Neither is Darius," I pointed out.

"Hence, I have sought Eliam," he said with a teasing glint in his eye as if he were very smart indeed for thinking of it.

When I did not respond to this, he sighed heavily and said, "I love Kenai like my own son. You know that."

"I know."

"But he could not do well by a wife at present."

"And I will not do well by a husband. I can't even cook."

"But you can sew."

"I can't take care of the goat or tend the garden."

"But you can tend children, and before long you could assign those other tasks to your own children. And besides, this is one of the things I like about Eliam. He is not interested in a traditional arranged marriage to a meek wife."

"He's not?"

"No. But Kenai is more inclined that way, and I think he will need a wife with more interest in the domestic arts."

"More skill you mean."

"No. I did not say that, neither did I mean it. You must trust me in this. I know things you do not. I see things you cannot see from your viewpoint. I am thinking of your ability to be happy in the future, not how you feel in just this moment."

"I understand," I said. And I did. Father knew more than I did and that was a fact.

We completed what work we had at the tannery and were approaching the site of Jarom's new hut well before the midday meal.

Many of the men from the village were there and Kalem was happily supervising the clearing of the land on which they would build the hut. The ground was muddy, but covered with new green grasses and still soft enough to pull the large roots from the ground.

I hung back at the edge of the little clearing while Father approached Muloki and spoke to him. Micah, Kenai, and Darius were all lending their strength to this project.

Muloki dusted his hands off by brushing them together and returned to me with my father.

"Do you wish to go right now, Isabel?" he asked me.

I glanced at the position of the sun. "We should."

He gave a quick, decisive nod. "I'll just get my things."

Father gave me a kiss on the top of my head and went to take Muloki's place.

"So, will you tell me why we're headed to Ezra today?" Muloki asked as he retrieved his water skin and satchel from the base of a tree where he had tossed them.

"I want to visit a friend is all," I said. "Someone Father wishes for me to get to know," I added a little awkwardly.

"Ah," he said knowingly. "Come on then."

I wanted to resist, but I was not strong-willed enough to keep from glancing back at Kenai, who had straightened from his work to stretch his back. He wasn't staring broodingly at me like he would have been a few months before—not like I selfishly wanted him to. I missed the Kenai who would only talk to me and nobody else.

When I met his eyes, Kenai smiled. He nearly raised a hand in greeting, but Kalem said something and his hand stopped halfway, like he had already forgotten me, as he turned to laugh with the others.

It was irritating. Irritating that I hardly merited a greeting to him. Irritating that I had to share him with everyone else. I didn't want to share him—not with his family, not with his friends, not with other girls. And it was silly, because even before I had spoken to Father that morning, I had begun to suspect he was right and Eliam was the better choice for me.

That was why I was going to the place where I could best learn who Eliam truly was.

Muloki and I traveled on a small, narrow road that would circumvent the city Melek and come out of the trees in Ezra. Father had given both of us directions from there, though he had spoken more to Muloki than to me.

I didn't know Muloki well enough to converse easily with him. I saw him a lot, but he was almost fifteen years older than me—we didn't have many conversations.

But I did know that Muloki's own betrothal ceremony had happened not long after Jarom's. He was to marry Kalem's daughter, Melia, who had come all the way from the Land of Nephi to find her father after her mother had died. Muloki was also from the Land of Nephi, and he had been an actual enemy soldier to the striplings during the war. But he had met Keturah, followed her to Melek, and ended up finding the Gospel, the church of Christ, and Melia.

"Are you excited for your wedding?" I asked him.

"You could say that." He gave me his grin, the one all the girls, no matter their age, giggled about. Muloki was dark-skinned, wickedly handsome, and what I had heard some of the older women refer to as eager. When I had asked her, Mother said she thought this meant he had an enthusiasm for life. He was genuinely happy, and it showed.

"It's a few months away still?"

"Yes."

"But you haven't built a house in the village."

"Melia and I will live in Kalem's old home in town, where I stay now."

"Oh. So why are you waiting the full year of betrothal if you don't need to build a house?"

"Melia and I both arrived here in Melek with nothing. We had no material possessions, no livelihoods, no friends, no family besides Kalem, and we didn't have the Gospel. I have accepted the Gospel now, as you know, but Melia is more reluctant to do so. I would like to be baptized together before our marriage if she will accept the Gospel and agree. She needs the time." He glanced at the sky. "We have many ways in which we must prepare a home, not just a house."

"I see," I said. "Muloki, what was the war like?"

"The war?" he asked as if he hadn't heard me right.

"Yes. Was it very terrible?"

"The war is over," he said, clearly trying to put an end to the subject.

Muloki had fought on the enemy's side, the Lamanite side of the war, and I thought he would have a very different perspective of it than the men in Melek did.

"I should think that, of anyone in Melek, you would know the wars are not over."

"What do you...?" he began, but he sighed in resignation. "You're right," he admitted too quickly. "The Lamanites will continue to fight."

Everyone I knew insisted the war was over. The striplings were home as proof, and that was that. But it wasn't true, and it felt strange to have Muloki confirm it.

When we arrived at the home my father had described, a striking and large stone structure, Muloki called out for Eliam.

A woman appeared in the doorway with a curious but pleasant smile, looking first to Muloki and then to me.

Muloki greeted her with a hand on her shoulder. She said her name was Rebekah and blushed as all the women did when he spoke to them. I tried not to roll my eyes. He couldn't help it.

"This is Isabel, daughter of Hemni. She wishes to speak with Eliam. Is he here today?"

"Eliam is working at the quarry with his father. It is such a pleasure to meet you both," she said. "I have heard much about you, Isabel."

My turn to blush.

She smiled and gave us directions to find Eliam. "Wait here just a moment," she said, "and I will pack you a meal to eat together."

My stomach dropped, and I recognized it as a pang of guilt. I ate my midday meals with Kenai.

Muloki elbowed me in the ribs while we waited, making my face heat even more. I elbowed him back.

I thanked Rebekah and avoided Muloki's eyes as we set off again toward the quarry. The path was hilly and we had to climb for quite a while before we saw the men working in a vast hole in the rock of the mountain.

"Thank you for bringing me," I said to Muloki. "Eliam will take me home."

"Let's just go make sure," he said.

I vigorously shook my head. "That's not necessary," I insisted, but Muloki just laughed happily. Was he enjoying my embarrassment?

As we approached the work area, I saw Ezra point us out discreetly to his son. Eliam looked back over his shoulder and broke into a grin that lit his face when he recognized me.

He put his tools down, hopped off the large boulder he was standing on, and jogged down the hill toward us.

"He doesn't hide his feelings, now does he?" Muloki said under his breath.

I didn't have time to respond before Eliam was standing before us. We just stared at each other smiling until Muloki put out his arm.

"I am Muloki. Hemni asked me to escort his daughter safely to you—if you are Eliam."

Eliam clasped arms with Muloki. "I am."

"Hemni would like you to escort her home."

"Of course."

Muloki embarrassed me with a wink. "Have a pleasant day, Isabel."

"I've brought your midday meal," I said to Eliam when Muloki had mercifully gone. "From your mother," I added stupidly. Why hadn't I thought to bring him food?

He glanced at the sun. "Alright. There's a stream and a shaded grove down this way."

He took my hand and led me away. But the shaded area was not close by and we held hands for a long time as we walked there. I could feel that his hand was dusty and calloused from work, but it felt nice clasped around mine.

142

"Does your father have a meal?" I asked him.

"He'll return home before too long. Mother will feed him more than she should."

I nodded. She had certainly packed plenty for Eliam and me.

"What are you doing here?" he asked.

"I thought I should find out where you are most yourself," I said.

He tried to hide a grin, but he was only able to play it down to a smile, so he turned his face away from me.

"And anyway, you've made the journey to see me at the tannery so many times, I thought my turn was long overdue."

"What did your father say to this whim?"

"He was pleased," I admitted.

"And you?"

"Nervous."

"There's no need for that, Isabel. You're safe with me."

"I'm not nervous about my safety."

He squeezed my hand. "I love how honest you are."

"And you are honest too."

"I try to be."

He pulled me into the grove of trees, and a small stream ran through it just as he had said it would.

I set my things down and went to the stream to fill my water skin. I held out my hand for his. "May I fill yours also?" I asked.

He slowly removed his water skin from his belt and passed it to me. He didn't take his eyes from mine.

Generally, filling another person's water skin—a tedious chore, a necessary chore—was considered an action that showed love. It wasn't a declaration of love, exactly, but still, I could see that he thought it was meaningful.

After that talk about honesty, I wondered if I did the right thing. I still didn't know if I loved Eliam. I was still only fifteen— I knew I didn't know what love would feel like.

Eliam stood over me for a moment and watched me fill the water skin. "Thank you," he said in a voice that had turned slightly gruff when I passed it back to him.

"It's nothing," I said.

I thought of what Kenai considered nothing between two people, and wondered again if I spoke the truth.

We sat together in the shade, which was almost too cool with the spring breeze, and ate the food his mother had packed.

"I have to tell you something," I said and gave a little shiver.

"Alright. Are you cold, Isabel?"

"A little," I admitted.

"Do you want to go sit in the sunshine?"

"No. It's so pretty here."

"Alright," he said again. "What is it you want to tell me?"

"I don't want to tell you, but I feel you should know."

Worry filled his eyes. "What is it, Isabel?"

I fought another shiver and folded my arms for warmth. *I really should make a tunic with long sleeves*, I thought.

Eliam moved close to me and put his arm around my back pulling me into his warm side. I leaned into him and it seemed as natural as could be. I closed my eyes in relief. That was one of the things I needed to know, one of the things I had come there to find out.

"Eliam," I said, "I am a lousy cook."

He was silent for a moment. "That's what you wanted to tell me? You came all this way to tell me that you're a lousy cook?"

"Well, yes."

He began to laugh.

144

"And to see you," I added, frowning at his amusement.

He was shaking with laughter. It seemed he could not stop.

"What are you laughing at?"

"You are adorable," he said, still chuckling.

"What do you mean?"

"Isabel, your father already told me you can't cook."

"He did?"

Eliam nodded, his eyes shining.

"You've known all this time? Then why are you still courting me?"

"Oh, Isabel." He slipped his other arm around me as easily as if he had done it every day. "I can cook. I doubt we would starve."

"You? But you're a man."

He laughed again. "Who do you think cooked in the army? You can skin an elk and soak its skin in its brains," he pointed out. "And you are a woman."

"Well, not exactly," I said, embarrassed.

"You can't skin an elk or you can't soak its skin?"

"I'm just a girl, not really a woman."

"Izz," he said and he stopped laughing. He looked into my eyes and brushed my hair back from my face. "For the time being, maybe. But that's not what I see when I look at you. I see the woman you are becoming."

I frowned. "But...I can't cook."

"That's not what makes you a good woman, and it's not what will determine if you're a good wife. You are honest and hardworking. Loving. Those things make up for any lack you may have. I know you don't wish to marry, but really, Izz." His tone had taken on a reprimand, the first time I had heard him sound that way. "We'll hire a cook if you're that worried about it."

"But that would cost so much!" I shook my head. It wasn't even an option.

"Not so very much, and I'm not poor, Isabel."

"But..."

"I make a good living mining ore from the hills. We could provide work for a woman who needed it—there are widows in Ezra who would do it gladly—and you would be free to tan your hides." I felt one of his large hands slip around my waist. "And when the children came," he said more softly, "I'm sure it wouldn't even slow you down."

Something stirred inside of me. I studied his face. Kind, intelligent, light brown eyes, crinkled at the corners from smiling so much. Smooth dark hair that was growing out from a very short cut. Lips that made me wonder what it would be like to kiss him. Strong. Tall. Dependable. Honest. Open with all his feelings. Would this indulgent and understanding man who saw so much in me that I couldn't see, would this man be my children's father?

My own father had been right. Eliam really was the best choice for me. But I was starting to understand Keturah, because even as Eliam so sweetly wove his fingers into my loose hair and so tenderly kissed my lips, dispelling my curiosity, I couldn't stop thinking about Kenai.

CHAPTER 13

The walk with Eliam back to my village was pleasant and much slower than the walk with Muloki had been. He walked me into the village and all the way to my courtyard where Mother welcomed us and invited Eliam to stay for the evening meal.

"I would like that," he told her, "but only because I know Isabel did not prepare it."

My mouth fell open and I smacked him in the chest, comfortable in the familiarity we had developed over the past months. The pleasant day we had shared together had only increased our ease together.

Mother and Father kept stealing glances at me, and Sarai and Chloe kept stealing glances at Eliam. Jarom and Eliam fell easily into conversations that covered many topics, topics that I didn't pay very much attention to until they began to speak of their captain.

"You should see him," Jarom said. "He's doing so much better—talking to people, helping out, teasing the girls." His eyes flicked apologetically to me. "Often, he seems to be his old self."

Eliam didn't say anything, and I realized it was because he couldn't. He had actually choked up at the good news.

"And it's all because of Izz," Sarai put in, trying to be helpful.

Eliam swallowed hard and turned to Sarai.

"All because of Izz, you say?"

Nervous at the sudden attention, Sarai just nodded.

Jarom cleared his throat. "Isabel took the time and care to befriend him when he was at his worst. He regards her friendship very highly."

I flushed to hear it described that way. "It's not as big as all that," I said as I noticed Father deliberately keep his eyes from meeting Mother's.

Later, when we were alone outside, Eliam questioned me further. "I didn't know you were friends with Kenai. In fact, I remember you telling me you weren't."

I fibbed a little. "It was after that day, after you said all his men were worried about him, that I decided to see what I could do to help."

"For my benefit? Because he was my captain?"

"No," I admitted. "I don't know why. He seemed to allow it, so I did." I looked at my hands, twisting in my skirts. "And when his family saw what was happening, they begged me to keep doing what I was doing. But they needn't have begged. I was glad to do it."

I thought of Darius, how he avoided me, so easily, like it didn't bother him. I thought of how tightly Leah had hugged me at Keturah's betrothal.

"What did you do exactly?" Eliam asked, shifting his weight to his other foot, not even glancing at the sun, though it was getting late. He would need to start for home soon.

I bit my lip under his curious scrutiny. Then I sighed and let my posture sag. Lowering my voice, I said, "I got him to eat."

"Eat? How?"

"I don't know how. By not expecting it of him."

But nobody else expected anything of him, a small voice inside me said, and that hadn't worked for them.

All Eliam's scrutiny seemed to be bearing down on me as he searched my face. I bristled. Did he know? Had he guessed how I felt about Kenai? Had he guessed it was not what it should have been?

But in his expression, I only saw concern. My defenses dropped. It was my own guilty conscience making me nervous, and I knew it. Of course he was concerned about his military captain, a man he clearly loved better than a brother, with whom he shared a bond that he could not explain to someone like me.

The crickets were chirping again. The owls called. The breeze rustled in the tops of the trees. Children ran through the village road. Chloe pointed Eliam and me out to her friend, who observed us with wide eyes.

Eliam went to his heels on the ground near me, and I dropped into the grass too and waited while he decided what to say. I could see he was debating with himself.

"Once when we were to take the city Cumeni, we had to disable a guard of three hundred men. Kenai was second in command. And see, the guard blocked the only passage into the city, and we could not lay siege until we had traversed it. It was Cumeni's greatest defense, only having one way in, but also its greatest weakness, because there was only one way out."

Lay siege? I knew nothing of that. "You don't have to tell me." Tentatively, I put my hand on his arm. His muscles flexed—flinched?—and he covered my hand with his.

"They had to be taken out." He glanced at me. "Killed, without alerting the army inside the city to our presence. Kenai and I and a few others had already tracked their scouts and killed them. The Lamanite army had no idea we were coming for them."

"Eliam."

He just continued on. "We moved in while they slept. Only three sentries sat awake." He shook his head, giving a small

149

humorless laugh. "Only three sentries to keep watch for the entire city."

"Not enough?" I asked.

"Not against us." His eyes were unseeing, looking only back into the past, and he was quiet for a moment.

"What happened?" I prodded gently.

"Kenai and Mahonri and me, it was our job to take out the men who were awake." He swallowed, remembering. "And we did. It was easy. We'd been training for a couple years. Practicing actually. We killed them in the same methodical way we killed the scouts we found. Methodical, but so fast you couldn't think, you know? And it was better anyway that you couldn't think about it."

I looked down at his hand on mine. Tanned, calloused with work, strong. But I had felt his hands be gentle. I couldn't help wondering what exactly it had done to those men.

"The three men were eating at the time, sharing a contraband midnight snack."

When he stopped talking, we fell into silence, each staring down at the ground in front of us. I knew what he was implying, that for some reason this was why Kenai had been unable to stomach food.

"I've never told anyone that," Eliam said quietly into the twilight.

"It was a long time ago," I said.

"Yes, and yet sometimes it seems as if it were yesterday." He took a deep breath. "Isabel, I'm going to stay in your village tonight. It's getting too late to start for home." He winked at me, and I knew somehow that he could make it home safely no matter the time of day or night. "I'll stay with the captain. He'll have an extra bedroll."

No. He couldn't.

"Isabel, what is it?"

He had to know, so I had to tell him. "A few months ago, it would have bothered Kenai if you stayed at his home—I mean, in order to court me."

Eliam's brows knit, but a look of understanding fell over his face too. "Is the captain courting you too, then?"

I looked away from him. "No."

I felt his eyes on me. "But you want him to?" He didn't wait for an answer. "He's become attached to you. You've both become attached."

I gave a little shrug. "I thought you should know. He probably wouldn't care now." I heard the bitterness in my own voice and knew he heard it too.

"I think you're too wonderful not to have more than one suitor," he said and brushed a finger along my cheek.

"I'm not wonderful," I said.

"Izz."

"I take him his meals in the fields. Sometimes I help dig the weeds."

"I'm sure he is appreciative of a beautiful girl in his fields."

I couldn't help a little smile, but I shook my head. "There is a portion we have decided to leave overgrown with weeds."

"Won't they choke out the good plants?"

I shook my head again. "I think they will shade the small plants until they've strength enough to survive. Kenai agreed to experiment."

"Your idea then?"

"Yes." I bit my lip. "Darius thinks Kenai favors me. He won't be seen with me because of it."

"This saddens you."

He was reading my face well. "We used to be friends."

Eliam leaned forward and kissed me on the temple,

brushing my hair aside. "I'll borrow a pallet from Jonas."

We stood and walked together to the edge of the yard.

"Do you have a lot of work to do at the tannery tomorrow?" Eliam asked me as he went through the gate.

"Not so very much," I said.

"Would you rather go fishing?"

"Fishing!" I giggled. Fishing was a boy's job like milking the goat was a girl's. "I would love to go fishing."

He nodded. "I'll come by after the morning meal."

He started to walk away.

"Won't your parents be worried?" I called after him.

Turning back, he shook his head, a small smile playing over his lips. "I survived four years in the army fighting Lamanite soldiers." He took the steps back to me and bent closer. "They know I'm gone courting the girl I want to marry. They will not be overly concerned about my absence. And," he added, "I'm a grown man, in case you hadn't noticed."

I bit the side of my cheek and looked him over. "I noticed," I said boldly.

He laughed. "See you tomorrow, Izz."

When morning came, Father was inordinately pleased that I would be going fishing with Eliam.

"Fishing?" my mother said. "That seems so..."

My father cleared his throat.

"That seems so nice," my mother finished, slipping another corn cake onto the grill to cook.

I watched how she did it. I would surely have burned my fingers, and I had burned them more than once—more times than I could count actually.

"When Eliam becomes her betrothed," Father began.

I cleared my throat.

"*If* Eliam becomes her betrothed," he started again with a

152

chuckle. "What is appropriate behavior for her will be up to him."

But when Eliam showed up at the gate with not only spears for fishing but with bows and arrows, knives, axes, and slings, even Father wasn't so sure anymore about letting me go.

I looked up at Father and grinned.

He just said, "Have fun." But he gave Eliam a stern look. "Back by sundown."

Eliam nodded and opened the gate for me. He placed a hand on the small of my back and escorted me through it.

We walked for about an hour before Eliam stopped near the river and set down all the gear he had hauled.

"Are the fish so fearsome?" I asked.

"Hmm?"

I indicated all the weapons at our feet.

Eliam grinned. "I thought if the fishing was good we might get time to hunt a little, too."

"Hunt?"

He raised his brows.

"You would teach me to hunt?"

"Wouldn't you like to bring home your own game to skin?"

That thought was appealing.

"That's what I thought," he said when he saw the look on my face.

We took off our sandals, and I rolled up my leggings. Standing in the river a spear's distance away from each other—I guessed he didn't want me to stab his foot—Eliam taught me the fine arts of fishing.

It only took Eliam a few minutes to spear a fish. I secretly thought he could have done it faster, taken any fish he wanted, but he waited until I became comfortable holding the spear before he fished in earnest.

When he had tossed his fish to the bank, he waded toward me and positioned himself behind me.

"Like this," he instructed and he put a hand at my waist and used the other to correct the movements I made with the spear. He lingered for a moment, making my heart thunder within my chest, but then he stepped back and allowed me to snare the fish myself.

And I did!

I pulled the spear from the water and turned to him with a huge grin. I surprised him when I jumped into his arms, but he caught me, and we both laughed.

"Thank you!" I said, and I gave him a quick kiss.

He stared into my eyes for a moment and then set me back down into the water with a splash. "Alright now," he laughed. "You've scared them all away."

We waited, talking quietly until they came back. I speared another while Eliam easily speared three more.

"My feet are frozen," I said as we slogged to the bank.

"I'll make you a fire," he said, and he set about doing it. "Can you clean those fish?" he asked as he got his flint out.

"Yes."

"There's a knife over there." He nodded his head toward the pile of weapons.

"I'll use mine," I said and brushed my sarong aside to retrieve it.

"You carry a knife?"

"Sure. Don't you?"

"Well, yes."

"Does it bother you?" I tried not to sound defensive.

"No. I like it. You know how to use it?"

"Not really." I couldn't defend myself with it. "But I can gut a fish."

154

When I was done with two of the fish, I rinsed them in the river and took them to Eliam.

He didn't take them.

"You get them started. I'll go find some seasonings."

And he turned and walked out of our little camp.

I stared at the fish, the fire, and the sharpened sticks he had set around as a kind of grill.

I frowned, wondering why he had walked off so hastily. Had I done something wrong? I looked at the fish again, sighed, and set them over the fire to cook.

"Will you rub the fish with these?" Eliam asked as he returned through the trees. "I'm going to wash my hands off."

I took the herbs he brought me, smelled them and, satisfied they were the right ones—all but one of them which I tossed aside—I applied them to the fish.

Eliam took a long time at the stream. He actually got soap out of his satchel to wash his hands. Then he decided to wash his face. He got a cloth out and dried thoroughly. Then, with a surreptitious glance toward me, which I didn't miss because I was watching him closely, he went to the stack of weapons and began inspecting them. He tried the sling, measured its length against his arm. He pulled back the strings on both bows, testing their tautness.

"The fish are almost done," I called after a while.

He reached into his satchel again and brought out two plums and a wrapped bundle of corn cakes.

"From Jonas's mother. Can you heat them? I prefer them warm."

I took them, and he wandered away again, filling the water skins, staring at the sky, testing the strength of tree limbs.

When I had everything ready, I called to him.

Smiling, he returned and sat next to me.

"It smells great. Will you pray over it with me?"

I nodded, and he said a blessing of thanks over the food.

I had cut up the fish and plums and we ate them inside the warmed corn cakes. Everything was done just right.

"It's been a long time since I had a warm lunch," I said. "We usually eat them cold."

"We?"

I had just taken a bite, but I stopped chewing. "Me and Kenai," I admitted through a mouthful of fish.

He just nodded. "He looks like he's been eating better."

"Thanks to my mother," I said. "But then, she cooks exactly like his mother does."

"So, what is it exactly that you can't cook?" Eliam asked when he finished his fish and cake.

"Everything," I replied.

He stared at me for a moment and then let his eyes drop pointedly to the cake I still held in my hand.

"Oh, I didn't make this!" I protested. "Jonas's mother did."

"Isabel," he said. "Who told you that you couldn't cook?"

"Nobody. I just can't."

"Then you're lying to yourself. Do you realize you just cooked our meal and it was delicious? You even knew not to put the achiotl on it." He glanced to where I had tossed it.

I sat up straighter. "Were you putting me on a trial?"

"In a way, but not the way you're thinking. Tell me something," he said as he leaned back on his elbows, an action that reminded me of Kenai. "Tell me, what would you do if you heard of a new tanning process that was purported to be better than the way you do it?"

Hurt, and not understanding why he had changed the subject, only glad that he had, I said, "I'd find out how to do it,

156

learn it as quickly as I could." I put my corn cake down and folded my arms across my chest.

"What if it was difficult to learn?"

I shrugged. "I'd practice until I got it right—if it turned out to be worth knowing, that is."

"And because you do well at tanning with your current process, you feel that you could adapt to a new process?"

"Sure."

"And because you can cook fish to perfection, do you not think you could learn to mix up a corn cake? If it was worth knowing how, that is?"

"Eliam."

"Well?"

I pursed my lips.

He reached over and took what was left of my fish and corn. "If you knew that your husband liked corn cakes very much, would that not make it worth knowing?" Then he stuffed what was left of my food into his mouth in one big bite.

He watched me blatantly as he chewed and swallowed, clearly enjoying the color I knew had crept into my cheeks. But after a moment he jumped to his feet and held out a hand to me.

"Come on. I'll teach you to hunt."

Eliam slung a bow over my shoulder and showed me how to tuck a sling into my belt so it wouldn't slip and fall off, how to release it so I could use it at a moment's notice, something that would obviously take a lot of practice since my fingers kept getting caught in it.

"Move your belt to the outside of your sarong," he said. "At least for today. You will be able to reach things better."

"Okay," I agreed.

He turned his back as I did it, and he asked over his shoulder, "Why do you keep your knife hidden?"

"I carry it for protection. Anyone who tried to harm me would be surprised, I think, to find a knife in his gut."

"But how would you get to it?"

"Look."

When he turned, I showed him how it was not difficult to move the overlapping flaps of the sarong to retrieve the knife.

"But your clothing comes nearly undone," he said, and I could see that there were light stains of red on his own cheeks.

I laughed. "No it doesn't. And besides, I am wearing the leggings."

"Do you find a lot of people want to harm you?" he asked, trying to change the subject and still adorably uncomfortable.

"I don't think my Lamanite abductors wanted to take me fishing," I said dryly.

We had talked only briefly about the kidnapping, and that had been several months ago right after it had happened. He didn't know that I had used my knife to cut my bonds, he didn't know I had fought with the others, and he didn't know I had stabbed the man who had taken me.

"Is that when you started carrying the knife?" he asked quietly. "Did that incident scare you?"

"I've always carried it," I said. "And no, I wasn't scared."

He looked at me like he didn't believe me.

"You said you wanted to get to know me. This is me." I slipped my knife into its scabbard which was now obvious on the outside of my clothing, left my hand on the hilt, and hitched a hip. "I fought tooth and nail to get free, to run home to get Zeke and the others. But I heard a child cry out. I couldn't just run away, so I settled down and let them tie me, but I don't think they wanted to take me."

"Why not?"

I smiled a little, remembering. "They had scratches,

bruises on their faces and hands—wherever I could reach."

"Nobody told me that," he said, frowning. "You've never told me of that night."

"You've never asked."

"I thought you wouldn't want to talk about it, to re-live it." He sounded defensive and maybe a little hurt.

"Your thoughtfulness does not offend me, Eliam," I assured him.

"I wish I had been there. Instead, I was at home sleeping off our long hunting trip."

I shook my head. "You couldn't have known. Jarom only warned our village and then ran to the next for Jonas and Mahonri. Gid and his kinsmen happened to be in the village, so they felt they had enough men."

He blew out a puff of air. "It was a successful mission. They saved you."

"No. I saved myself," I said with my chin high. "They didn't know I had a knife—it was hidden—and I stabbed the man in his stomach."

His eyes narrowed. "What man?"

"The man who took me, bound me, carried me away. The man who..." I choked on the word a little because this part I hadn't told anybody—not Father, not Mother, not Zeke, not even Kenai in all our talks. I started again. "The man who touched me."

Eliam went very still except for the sudden hard clench of his jaw and the fury in his eyes, which rolled in waves.

When he spoke, his voice was low, gravelly, and filled with restrained anger. "Touched you where, Isabel?"

I had thought many times of telling this to Eliam. I had thought telling him about what that awful man had done might embarrass him. He flushed alright, but not with embarrassment.

I just stared at him, unable to say the words.

His voice gentled. "Somewhere he shouldn't have?" I could see he wanted to step toward me, but he held himself back for some reason.

I was the one who was embarrassed, something I had not considered in all the times I had thought of this moment. I hadn't intended to tell him, not really, and certainly not that day. But I had wondered many times what it would be like to tell someone the whole truth.

Now I knew. My chin trembled and I dipped my head slightly. "You're looking at me differently," I whispered.

Then he did move toward me, and to my relief he took me into his arms—but he was hesitant, too gentle.

"No." He shook his head. "No, I'm not. You're as beautiful to me as when you caught your first fish. More." His arms tightened, but then he pulled back. "Is this...is this okay?"

"Of course it is. I know that your touch is loving and appropriate. I...I like your...I like when you..."

He pulled me close again and I felt his large hands caress my head and smooth my hair away from my face and neck.

"Oh, Izz. Now I really wish I'd been there. You truly killed the man?"

I shook my head. "I stabbed him, but he didn't die quickly enough, so Jarom finished him off."

He nodded. "An excellent brother."

"He didn't know. And don't tell him. Don't tell anyone. It wasn't anything."

He pulled back and looked down at me doubtfully.

"I'm fine," I insisted. I laid my forehead against his chest. "The man is dead, and it's over."

I felt Eliam go still again. But when he leaned down and whispered into my ear, I heard leashed delight in his voice instead of anger.

"Look right over there."

I turned to look in the direction he indicated with the slight tilt of his head.

"Can you find a use for the meat?" he asked quietly.

"Father and Jarom keep us supplied with plenty of venison," I admitted a little reluctantly.

Eliam nodded but drew my bow from my shoulder and helped me position it. I didn't agree with hunting for sport and thought perhaps I had found the first thing about Eliam that it would be hard for me to love.

He positioned an arrow and helped me pull the string when he saw I couldn't pull it back far enough on my own. He tilted it up a little and whispered, "Let it go."

Despite my reservations about shooting the deer, I put my trust in Eliam, in what I knew of him, and let the arrow fly.

Eliam was not far behind it, off and running the moment the arrow hit the deer. I took a few breaths and then followed.

He was sitting on his heels next to the dying buck when I drew up. He looked up at me with a grin.

"Great shot!' he exclaimed quietly. "But stay back until it's safe."

"Do you have need of the meat?" I asked. I couldn't take my eyes off the beautiful animal.

"No," he said, and remorse churned in my stomach.

He rose smoothly and came to stand behind me, and we both stared down at the animal whose breathing sounded labored and hoarse. There was fear and panic in his eye.

I wanted to turn into Eliam's chest for comfort. And I wanted to push him away in disgust. But I just stared down at the dying animal.

"Can't you make it faster," I said. My own hand went to my knife.

He stayed it with his. "It will only be another moment. It was an excellent shot."

"But for what?" I demanded. "We don't need the meat."

His chest was hard and warm behind my back. His words were gentle and understanding. "My father and I keep three widows of the war supplied with meat." I could hear the smile in his voice. "And I am glad you become angry when you think of killing for sport."

He had unsettled me. And maybe that had been his aim.

His fingers found the nape of my neck. I felt him bend to speak into my ear. His voice was low and smooth and calm. "Are you in love yet, Isabel?"

I swallowed. And I panicked a little.

"Eliam, I don't know. I don't know. What is love supposed to feel like?"

He considered for a silent moment, then wove his fingers up through my hair. "Do you like when I do this?"

"Yes," I whispered.

He gently turned my face toward him. "And this?"

I nodded, afraid my panic was showing in my eyes.

"And this?"

He bent and kissed me, and in the quiet of the forest there was no sound but our breath and his lips against mine. Even the labored breathing of the buck stopped.

"Yes," I said against his lips when he stopped moving them.

He took a deep breath and let it slowly out.

"That's a good start," he said. Then he turned his attention to the lifeless buck. "Would you like to carry him home, or shall I?"

Chapter 14

The air was hot and muggy as I roamed through the market. I waved to Kalem and Leah at their little shop. I hadn't planned to stop by, but Leah motioned me over.

"Look, we've got some of your buckskin," she said happily, motioning to a corner of the table that displayed my buckskin along with the pelts and skins Father had received from Paachus.

Father thought the market was a spectacle. He had never sold his leathers there, and as he made enough doing business out at the tannery, he never had to. But Zeke's trade agreement with Paachus stipulated that his goods be sold at the market on market days.

So Father and Zeke made an arrangement with Kalem to sell the pelts in his shop. Father didn't have to attend the market, Paachus's pelts got sold, and Kalem got a share of the profits. Everyone was happy with the arrangement, and Father figured since he was selling Paachus's product, he may as well sell mine too.

"I hope it's not too much trouble," I said.

Leah laughed, and Kalem, who had just finished a transaction with a customer, joined her in it.

"No trouble at all," he assured me.

"Here," offered Leah as she passed me a bright pink

pitaya fruit. "These are in season in the southern lands. Take one." Then she added, "Maybe you'll find someone to share it with."

Of course I knew she meant Kenai. And she was right. If I saw him that day, I would feed him the fruit. Even though I knew apples were his favorite, I would find a way to get him to eat the pitaya, and so I slipped it into my satchel.

Leah must have known her son was there at the market, because I saw him right away. He stood at Pontus's tables looking over the merchandise. Was he looking at jewelry? Was he purchasing something for some other girl, perhaps the one Sarai had seen him with?

The jealous thought hit me so fast and hard I had to stop for a moment and take a deep breath. It wasn't fair of me to think this way. I had Eliam, and I was even falling in love with him. Kenai could—Kenai *should*—have other friends, even girls. I had told myself that a hundred times, and I repeated it in my mind while I stood still in the busy market until I almost believed it. When I thought I had my feelings under control, I made my way toward him.

"See anything pretty?" I asked as I sidled up next to his elbow, and I saw immediately that he was looking at a tray full of small, ornate knives, not jewelry at all.

He turned to look at me. "I do now," he said with the hint of a smile.

I couldn't think how to reply. "What are you looking at?" I asked instead.

He picked up a knife. "Knives."

I glanced at the one in his hand. "See any you like?"

He shrugged and put the knife down, aligning it perfectly next to the others.

"Those are pretty," I said, and I pointed to some steal

arrowheads that lay next to the knives on the tray.

He snorted. "They're not pretty. Perhaps you should direct your attention to the jewelry if you're looking for pretty." He made a shooing motion with his hand toward the other end of the table where Pontus stood with his hands clasped in front of his large belly just waiting to be of service. "Pick something if you like. I'll get it for you."

I didn't own much jewelry—and nothing I hadn't made myself sitting around the fire with my family. I wouldn't even know what to choose or how to explain it to Mother and Father. Or Eliam.

I was panicked inside but just said, "That's sweet, Kenai, but no thank you."

He pushed me over to the jewelry side of the table, knocking me off balance and then righting me with his strong hands. "You can skin, tan, and sew me pants, but I can't buy you a necklace?"

"It's not the same. You got my knife back. It was an exchange." I floundered for more reasons.

He picked up a turquoise beaded necklace. Bright, long, impossible to hide. "Then you'll have to think of something to give me in return."

"There's nothing of you in that," I said hurriedly, indicating the gaudy necklace.

"Sure there is. I picked it out."

"No, you picked it *up.*"

Our eyes caught, and we both laughed.

"Select something else then, Isabel."

Maybe it was the sound of my name on his lips that made me acquiesce.

"Alright." I cast an embarrassed glance at Pontus, a man I knew by name only.

He was grinning and not even pretending that he hadn't noticed our argument. He probably witnessed a lot of couples arguing over his jewelry.

"How about this?" I mumbled and reached for a plain but pretty braided leather cord.

When Kenai didn't say anything, I looked up at him

He was scrutinizing a tray of beads.

"Put these on it, will you, Pontus?" he said and picked out two red beads from the tray.

"But those are agates," I said in a loud whisper.

Agates had mystical properties in many of our old legends and stories. Agates were said to help their wearer discern truth and encourage honesty. They were said to help him accept his circumstances and to heal emotionally. And though they weren't particularly rare, the two together did cost more than any jewelry I owned.

Kenai stared at me for a second. "And this," he said. He reached up and slipped the simple rawhide cord from around his own neck. I had noticed it there before, but I had never seen what hung on the end of the cord under his tunic, couldn't guess what lay there against his chest. He pulled it free and handed it over so quickly that I didn't see what it was until later.

Pontus took a few moments with his back to us to assemble the necklace. When he turned, he handed me a small, tied package that contained the gift.

"Thank you," I told him.

"Don't thank me. Thank your young man," he said with a wink.

"Are you ready to go home?" Kenai asked as he handed some coins over to Pontus. "I'll walk you."

I glanced around. There was nothing in the market I needed.

"Sure."

We started across the market square. Kenai pushed through the people where the crowds were heavy, and I followed in his wake.

I looked at all the faces, thinking it strange how few people I knew in Melek anymore. There were many strangers, many refugees, widows, orphans, displaced people of all kinds.

And I thought I saw someone who was none of those things. But it couldn't be. I hadn't seen one glimpse of him in six years.

I tugged on Kenai's tunic and he turned immediately to me as if he could sense it was I who had touched his clothing and not one of the many other people we pushed past.

"Do you know that man?" I asked him and discreetly pointed out the man across the square who I knew only from a past memory as Zareth.

We stood together and watched the man approach Pontus's tables.

I saw the serious consideration of the man in Kenai's eyes but no recognition.

"No. Who is he?" he asked.

"He looks like a man I met once, that's all."

We left the crowded square and walked through the city together. We passed the large buildings, and farther out, we passed homes with small yards full of children playing and women preparing their midday meals.

"Aren't you going to open your package?" Kenai asked.

"Oh!" My mind had been preoccupied with thoughts of Zareth. The man had looked older, meaner than I remembered, but I was almost sure it had been him.

I untied the strings and pulled back the fabric from the necklace inside.

I fingered the strange pendant.

"Kenai," I said. "Did you know this is an arrowhead?"

"Yeah," he laughed. "You said you wanted a gift that had something of me in it."

Actually, I hadn't really wanted a gift at all. Well, that wasn't exactly true either. I was coveting the necklace even as I held it in my hand. Accepting it was going to be difficult, but not more difficult than refusing it.

"This is what you've been wearing around your neck? Does it have significance to you?"

"It does."

"Well?" I prodded when he didn't go on.

"That is a barbed arrowhead," he said.

"I can see that. It looks dangerous."

"Nah. I filed it so it's not even sharp. I bought it when I got back from Nephihah. It reminded me of the war—of who I'd become because of it. See, the barb makes it difficult to remove from its victim once it's found a place there."

"I think I see," I said. "You're letting it go?"

"Well, lately," he said and he rubbed a hand over the back of his neck. "Lately it's been taking on a kind of new meaning."

We walked a few steps, and he didn't continue. I turned my eyes up to see his profile. His green eyes flicked to me, but then returned to what he had been looking at in the distance.

"It's like you," he said. "The barb."

I frowned. "Painful? Unnecessary? Cruel? Kenai, are you insulting me?"

"No, Isabel."

I studied him. He wasn't. And he wasn't joking.

He kept his eyes ahead. "It's just, you've kind of gotten inside me—in my mind, in my heart, Isabel—and I can't get you out." Then he looked down at me. "And I don't want to anymore."

His manner was halting, his words awkward, but they were the sweetest words I had ever heard.

"Will you tie it on?" I asked him.

He lifted it from the cloth wrapping in my hand. We halted on the path, and I faced him as he tied it at the back of my neck. I stared at his chest, at the place he had worn the barbed arrowhead so close to his heart.

"Thanks, Izz, for bringing me food and making me eat it. For picking up a spade and helping in the field. For not giving up on me when everyone else did. Thanks for everything, little girl," he said.

I rolled my eyes. "Do you have to call me that?"

His eyes shone. "Yeah, I do."

"Have to remind yourself I'm too young for you?"

"Something like that. More like too innocent."

"I'm not so very innocent," I said, thinking of the Lamanite man I had stabbed and why I had done it. And I was thinking of how much I was enjoying this walk and how I was accepting this gift with even more meaning than Kenai intended.

"Oh, Izz, you are."

I looked away from the raw honesty in his green eyes, but remembering the pitaya Leah had given me, I reached into my satchel for it. "Here." I held it out to him.

He stared at it for a moment, a strange look on his face, and I wondered immediately if he had some bad memory connected to this kind of fruit. But he reached for it and took it into his big hand. The fruit had felt large in my hand, but it looked small in his.

"You know, these are only good if you share—" Stopping abruptly, he cocked his head to the side as if he were listening. Taking his cue of silence, I didn't say anything, just waited.

Only a few seconds had passed before he leaned toward

me and put his lips in my hair. His arms went around me.

"Kenai—" I protested, but only on principle.

His whispered words were low and quick. "Someone is following us, and not openly." He brushed his lips over my hair, my brow, and then he was back to my ear. "I'm going to see who it is. You walk on alone as if everything is normal. Don't try to be quiet."

Okay, now Kenai was losing it. He was mentally back in the war. But I humored him.

"Alright," I said.

And with no other words or instructions to me, he disappeared into the trees, slipping the pitaya into his satchel as he went.

True to my own word, I walked on as if everything was normal. Because it was. Everything except for Kenai going crazy and imagining he was still stalking Lamanite spies. This was the unusual behavior Zeke had warned me about. It was finally showing up, and I dreaded telling Zeke about it.

I was passing a turnoff that led to the maize fields when Kenai appeared by my side.

I jumped, startled, but before I could say anything he took a firm, almost painful, grip on my elbow and led me down the path toward the fields.

After we turned a bend in the path he said, "Run."

I didn't question him. I just ran, Kenai right on my heels. He pulled me to a stop when we reached our tree, the place we ate our meals together.

He let me catch my breath before he said, "That man you asked me about in the market—who is he?"

"His name is Zareth. He courted Cana not long after the striplings left with Helaman."

"He did what?"

"He courted Cana for a time," I said carefully. "But Father sent him away."

Zeke and Jarom had honed right in on all the reasons Father might have sent a man away. Kenai took a step back and anger flashed across his eyes.

"She allowed him to court her?"

His reaction confused me. He had said he was over Cana, and I believed him. Mostly. "Well, she couldn't really ask him to leave. That would have been inconsiderate."

He barked with laughter. "No, she wouldn't dream of being inconsiderate."

I cringed. I didn't know what to say to that, so I asked, "Why are we here?"

Kenai sobered, reined in his temper. "Is there any reason that Zareth would be following you, Izz?"

"No."

"Have you seen him before?"

"Not since Father said we were not to talk to him. That was about six years ago."

"And you're sure it was the same man?"

"Sure enough to get a prickle on the back of my neck when I saw him."

He ran a hand through his hair and paced for a moment. He was clearly thinking this all over.

"Alright. I'll teach you to defend yourself."

"You said that wasn't a good idea."

"Well, now it's a better idea."

The crop in the field was high, to the top of my ears and nearly to Kenai's shoulder. I gazed out over it, wishing I could see through it.

"Why? Zareth was following us?"

"He was following *you*."

The very idea put the prickles on the back of my neck again.

"Okay." I took a breath. "I would appreciate anything you will teach me. Show me what you taught Keturah."

"That's the plan. Come here."

I did, and with grave patience, Kenai began to instruct me.

"One thing you can do pretty easily to an attacker is break his nose. If it doesn't break, it will probably bleed, which will give you a few seconds to hit him somewhere else. You can always hit the nose again, but it's best to just break it the first time."

Kenai said this so matter-of-factly that I could only stare at him. I had always wanted to learn to fight, at least to protect myself or others, but the stone cold way he talked of hurting another human being made me wish I had never asked it of him.

"Now, since you are much shorter than me, throwing a punch like this isn't a good option." He balled a fist and pretended to throw it at my face—the way he had thrown it at Muloki when he had first come home. Then he knelt in front of me. "So you will want to hit with the heel of your hand like this. That's how Keturah does it. It will be a more forceful hit, an edge you'll need." He pushed the heel of his hand up through the air toward my face again.

He stood. "Now, you try it."

I hesitated a moment, but pushed my hand up through the air toward his face as he had shown me, stopping short of his nose as he had done with me.

"No. Go ahead and hit it."

I laughed nervously. "I'm not going to hit your nose, Kenai."

"It's no big deal. I've been hit hundreds of times."

"No." I shook my head.

"It's the only way to get the feel of it, to gauge how hard you must hit."

"Uh-uh. No way."

"Hit it. Keturah would."

I glared at him.

"I was right," he sighed. "You are too young for this."

I shoved the heel of my hand up and hit him.

He stepped back, and his hand went to his nose. He blinked a couple times and shook his head as if to clear it. He stretched his mouth down from his nose as if it itched.

"Okay. Good. I saw stars, but it's not even going to swell. Harder this time."

I didn't want to, and I winced as I did it, but I did thrust the heel of my hand at his face again.

His recovery took a little longer.

"That was better. This time, don't close your eyes."

I shook my head. There was no way I was hitting him in the nose again.

He placed his hands on his hips and looked at me. Then he gave a sharp nod.

"Got the feel of it?"

"Yes."

"If you ever have to do it, hit harder than you did that last time. Okay?"

I nodded.

"Good girl. Next."

He drew his knife from the band on his arm, and taking his cue, I drew my own knife.

Kenai closed his eyes for a moment as if he were praying for patience. When he opened them, he said, "Isabel, you have got to find a better place for that knife."

I laughed at him. "That's what Eliam said."

A shadow passed through his eyes, but he said, "I see you didn't listen."

I ignored that. "Okay, so what next?"

He took a breath. "When you stabbed that Lamanite, you stabbed him in the belly."

"Yes. But he didn't die. Why?"

"If you need your attacker to die immediately, you have to hit a vital organ—brain, heart, lung." He pointed to his head and chest with the tip of his knife.

I nodded. "Like with deer."

"Yes. If you happen to have a club or an axe or even a rock, you could try for the brain. But again, you've got the problem of a height difference, at least with Zareth, probably with most men. Keturah cuts off the air at the throat." He drew an imaginary line over his scar with his knife. "The only strength that takes is strength of will. But if I were you, I'd go for the heart. A man's heart is in easy reach for you." He beckoned me forward with a small motion of his hand.

I took the few steps toward him.

"A man's heart would be very vulnerable to you."

I looked down, not missing his double meaning.

Abruptly, he sheathed his knife and grasped my hand in his. He separated out two of my fingers and placed them on his side at his ribs. Then, hand over hand, he trailed my fingers up over the ridges of his ribs, counting softly as we passed each one.

"There," he said. "If you slip your knife between these two, your opponent will be dead. With practice, you can get very good and very quick at finding the right place, even without the man knowing."

"I'm not going to practice on you," I said.

He laughed. "Just practice finding the spot. You'll probably never have to use that knowledge because, Izz, we don't

174

kill unless our own life is in danger." He paused. "Our life or our virtue, and I know you know that." He reached out to tilt my face up to meet his gaze. "So you want to tell me why you stabbed that man?"

I actually felt the color drain from my face. I had told Eliam. I could tell Kenai. But I hesitated.

He noticed the change in my expression. From the hard and worried look that came into his eyes, I could tell it confirmed his suspicion.

"Did he hurt you, Isabel?" he asked quietly. "Before I got to you?"

"No."

"Did he try to?"

"Yes."

He didn't say anything for a long time, only let his eyes roam over my face. And I let mine roam over his.

"You did the right thing," he said at last. "And I think the gut wound was a good choice. He'd have bled out for a long time. Death would have been too kind. It *was* too kind."

Then he looked down. He released my chin and scrubbed his hand through his hair. He took a step back and cleared his throat. "There is another fast way to incapacitate a man so you can run away."

A slow smile spread across my face because I already knew what it was.

"But before I let you practice that on me, I will let you hit me in the face a thousand more times."

Chapter 15

Kenai also taught me the move he had used to take me to the ground the night of the kidnapping. He said it didn't have a name, but that Keturah called it his four-count drop. It really did take only four movements which did not require strength or even much skill, and I was able to drop Kenai to the ground several times before we decided to head for home.

"There's something I've been wondering," Kenai said as we walked through the trees.

"What's that?"

"Remember the celebration for the day of your birth?"

"Kenai, that was almost a year ago. You've been wondering about it for this long?"

"Well, kind of."

"Okay. What did you want to know?"

"Remember when Lamech asked if you'd given any thought to what he had said?"

"Vaguely. Why?"

"I've just been wondering what it was he said."

"It was such a long time ago." We walked on in silence for a few moments as the memory came back. "Okay," I said finally. "Do you remember when he and I left and went walking in the woods?"

"Vividly."

"On that walk, that's when he took my knife—pulled it right out from under my sarong. He said any girl who carried a knife like that had a fight going on inside of her. Something like that."

"He reached under your sarong?"

"Maybe."

"No maybe about it. I know where you keep your knife, Isabel."

"Well, that's beside the point."

"That is absolutely not beside the point."

I just gave a one-shouldered shrug. "It's in the past, Kenai. Anyway, he said I would be happier if I just admitted what I was and lived it with integrity."

"That goes for anyone," Kenai agreed.

I shrugged. "I told him I agreed with him, but the truth is, I don't know how you choose between obedience and integrity. He's just a dumb kid. He doesn't know anything."

"Actually," Kenai said, "I think Lamech knows a lot more than the rest of us—he had to accept things at a young age."

"What things? What do you mean?"

He didn't answer.

"Kenai?"

He hesitated again but said, "Lamech's birth was the result of a...brutality. Lamanite raiders sacked his parents' farm and one of them forced himself on his mother. If he didn't look so different from his brothers, even he might be able to overlook it more easily."

"That makes so much more sense now."

I thought of Lamech asking me if he looked like a pure Nephite. I thought of him praying alone on the training ground.

"What makes more sense?"

"Oh, just something he said." I waved it off. "That's

horrible. How horrible for their family."

"His family loves him—that was easy to see when they were here." He paused. "I remember also being kind of jealous of him that night."

"Jealous enough to steal my knife back?"

"No, that was for you."

I rolled my eyes.

"It was. Mostly."

"But jealous, why?"

"Because you talked so easily with him. You barely knew him, yet he got you to say so much about yourself and your feelings. Half of what I know about you I learned in that night, listening to another man talk to you. I can't say I wanted that for myself at the time, exactly, but I wanted to know how to do it."

"You've figured it out okay."

He grunted. Maybe agreeing. Maybe not.

When we approached the turn-off to get to the grazing lands, Kenai slowed and said, "Isabel, stop."

I did and turned to face him.

"I'm going to walk out to talk to Micah. I owe him an apology that's a long time coming. Will you..." He took a deep breath. "Will you keep me company while I walk there?"

Sudden tears stung my eyes, but I blinked them back and nodded. "Sure. But just now, when I told you of Cana and Zareth, you seemed so angry still."

He shrugged. "I'm working on it. Entertaining a proposal from Micah is one thing. Entertaining one from a stranger, entirely different."

We saw both Micah and Darius when we arrived. Micah sat on an outcropping of rock writing in a scroll. Darius played ball by himself.

"Uh-oh," I said.

"What? I'm the one with the apology to make."

"Darius," was all I said.

He couldn't have missed the fact that Darius hadn't so much as glanced my way in months.

"Go talk to him," Kenai urged.

"He'll run the other way."

"He won't. All you have to do is smile at him and he'll be spellbound. Go."

Kenai waited until I started toward Darius. Behind me I heard him take another deep breath and start in the other direction toward Micah.

Darius saw me approaching, but he didn't run the other way, just kept playing ball, a game the boys played by trying to keep a small, soft leather ball off the ground with any part of their body but their hands. Darius hadn't dropped it once since I had spotted him from across the field.

"Hey," I said.

He glanced at me. "Hey."

He bounced the ball toward me, and I hit it back with my foot. I had never actually played this game—I thought it was a big waste of time—but I had seen it played a lot.

Darius bounced the ball around for a minute and then hit it my way again. This time I caught it with my elbow, dropped it to my foot, and hit it back over to him.

"Not bad," he said.

The compliment pleased me.

"Don't start that," he said.

"Don't start what?"

"Blushing like a pretty pink flower."

"I'm not blushing."

He smiled and bounced the ball back. He had the same smile as Micah where one side of his upper lip rose slightly higher

180

than the other. Leah said, always with a softness in her eyes, that it was their father's smile. Kenai didn't have it. He had a smile all his own. I hit the ball a couple times and returned it again.

"You are blushing."

"Then don't praise me."

"Then don't be praiseworthy."

I laughed. "I know," I said. "Don't start that either."

We played for a few minutes more without another comment.

"What are you two doing here?" he asked after a while.

"Kenai wanted to talk to Micah. Something about an apology."

His surprise showed. "Kenai doesn't owe anyone an apology, especially not Micah. I think it's the other way around."

"I think so too, but Kenai was intent on it."

"I wish he would take it easy on himself for once."

"He's working on it."

Darius cast a look at his older brothers sitting side by side on the outcropping a distance away.

"You know, Dare, you're driving me crazy with this silent treatment. It makes me feel like I did something wrong."

He shook his head. "The only thing you did wrong was grow up so pretty while we were gone."

"Dare."

"You know why it has to be this way, Izz."

"I know. I admire you for it. I can tell you really love him." I watched his reaction. "Now don't you go blushing," I teased.

"Shut up," he said and passed me the ball.

"Do you really think it's helping? Ignoring me?"

"I don't ever want to see that look on his face again."

I knew the look he was talking about.

"That's how I felt too. I had to help him if I could." I

lobbed the ball back over to Darius and said quietly, "He's coming over."

Kenai walked toward us with long strides and a straight back. I saw Micah watching him from his place on the rock.

Kenai was still a distance away when Darius kicked him the ball, which I was amazed to see Kenai catch on his knee. He tossed it about from knee to arm to ankle as he walked toward us.

Darius grinned at him when he tossed it back.

"Darius, stop for a minute," Kenai said. "I want to talk with you, too."

"Should I go?" I asked, already starting to back away.

"No. This involves you."

Darius and I exchanged a glance.

Kenai took a deep breath and ran a hand over his jaw. He looked from me to Darius.

"I want you to start talking to Izz again." He stepped closer to Darius and lowered his voice. As they stood next to each other, I could see that Darius had grown taller than his older brother. "It hurts her feelings. I know what you're trying to do, but think of Izz, not me. Okay?"

Darius didn't even glance at me. He just looked his brother in the eye. "If that's what you want."

"It is."

I admired Darius for his determination not to hurt his brother, even though he knew he was hurting me. And I thought it was sweet that Kenai was more worried about my feelings than his own. But I didn't like that they thought they could choose who would be my friend and who would not. That choice was mine, and in just that moment, I didn't want to be friends with either of them.

I glowered at them both, though neither one noticed, and I turned and left. Micah noticed me, though, and waved.

182

I sighed when I became aware of Kenai at my side before I even made it to the trees.

I felt him looking at me. "Something wrong?" he asked.

"You boys," I said, trying to control my temper. "You cannot choose my friends for me."

"But we may choose our own friends."

I sighed deliberately.

He chuckled. "I didn't mean to hurt your feelings, Izz."

I sighed again, more naturally. "I know," I admitted. "It's just, I will marry whomever my father deems best for me, but until then, I will choose my own friends."

"Has your father introduced any other suitors?" He cleared his throat. "Besides Eliam?"

"No. That's unusual isn't it? After Darius turned him down, he got pretty set on Eliam."

"And Eliam?"

"Are you asking if Eliam has agreed to it?"

"I guess."

"Not yet. He said he won't until he knows I love him."

"And do you?"

"I don't know."

"Your father is right. Eliam will be perfect for you. I know him well."

That hung in the air between us for several moments.

"He told me about Cumeni, about the guard there," I said.

"What did he tell you?" Kenai asked cautiously.

"That the two of you and Mahonri killed the sentries after hunting down and killing the spies."

He let out a quick breath. "He shouldn't have told you."

"I am no worse for wear because of it," I pointed out gently.

He didn't reply.

183

"Kenai," I broached. "How did you get the scar on your neck?"

I didn't think he would tell me how it happened, only thought to let him know that I cared about it.

"A young Lamanite. Just a kid."

I stopped walking, and when Kenai noticed, he turned to face me. He glanced up and down the path and continued to speak, quietly and tonelessly.

"We were eating the midday meal. Eliam, Mahonri, Jonas, and me. We were laughing."

"Where were you stationed?" This was the first question the boys always asked each other when they talked about the war.

"Manti."

I nodded, staring at the ground.

"It was noon-day, bright as could be, and some kid gets his knife to my throat. Mine!" He let out a harsh kind of sound intended to be a laugh that fell far, far short of it. "Jonas was down at the stream filling the water skins. That's why they struck when they did—there were only three of them. Eliam and Mahonri both sensed their men. But not me. I got the cut," he said as he lifted his chin so I could get a good look at it, long but thin, "when I swallowed what was in my mouth."

"Oh, Kenai." I swallowed hard past the lump that had formed in my throat.

"The kid couldn't do it, though. Truly, he was younger than we were. Mahonri was still battling his man, but Eliam had killed his quickly. And then he killed the kid."

I reached up to touch the scar at his neck, as if my fingers could sooth all his obvious pain. He let me, but then he encircled my wrist with his long fingers and gently pulled my hand away.

"I owe Eliam my life."

"In other words, if you knew Eliam loved me, you'd turn

184

around and walk the other way." Like Darius, I thought.

He shook his head slowly, keeping his eyes on mine. "No, Isabel. I'd run."

But the way he looked at me, the things his eyes said, the way he still held my wrist—somehow I doubted he would even turn around, let alone run.

And the guilt of that would kill him.

We walked home with confused and heavy hearts.

We passed Father on the way into the village. He was talking to a neighbor, and he watched Kenai walk me to the gate of our courtyard.

I didn't want Father to see Kenai upset, so I changed my own mood and said with a shy smile I didn't have to force, "Thank you for the necklace, Kenai." I shifted my weight and dragged a toe of my sandal through the dirt, watching as it drew a line. "And for the piece of yourself you gave me with it."

Kenai slid a finger under the braided cord and slipped the pendant out from under my sarong. The sensation sent chills along my skin.

"If you will be friends with whoever you want, why do you feel you have to hide this?" he said.

Because it means more than friendship to me.

There was no way to answer him, so I just stared up at him without words.

But maybe I could talk with my eyes, too, because he gave his head a slight nod as if he understood, and a small smile touched lips that had once kissed mine.

"The agate stands for honesty," he said. "It is unnatural to hide it."

He pulled me by the hand to a stool by the fire. I watched as he took the pitaya fruit from his satchel and sliced it in two with his knife. The outside of the pitaya was bright pink, but the

185

inside was pure, translucent white. He handed me one of the halves.

"This is the first food you've ever offered me," I said as I took it.

"You offered it to me first," he said.

We looked into each other's eyes over the fruit as we brought it to our lips and ate it. And I forgot that my father was watching us.

I love you, his eyes said silently.

"That will make things complicated," I said out loud.

"I know," he replied. Then he raised an eyebrow, silently asking if I was up to the challenge.

"Hello!" Father called from the gate.

"Father!"

"Hi, Izz," he said to me. Then he turned to Kenai. "Kenai, I wonder if you will help me cut some firewood."

"Gladly, Hemni," Kenai agreed readily, but we all knew Father did not want firewood.

I watched as they got the big axes and left through the back of the yard for the dense forest. And oh how I wished I knew what Father would say to Kenai.

The next day, Zeke arrived home from Zarahemla, and he showed up at the tannery in the afternoon to talk to Father.

Zeke had been able to make business contacts during all his travels and had been able to get Paachus's pelts even farther north where they were greatly needed and in short supply.

Father considered this Zeke's share of the work, so even when he was in the village, he no longer went to the tannery with the rest of us to skin animals and smoke their hides.

The rift between Zeke and Jarom was something I had observed but not understood. When Zeke went for Eve and arranged for Jarom to marry her, things had changed, though I couldn't describe how. Father had noticed the tension between my brothers, but I thought Mother was still unaware it had ever existed. That's how good they were at sparing her from it.

When Zeke had finished talking to Father and was preparing to leave, Jarom wiped his hands on his apron and approached Zeke.

"Can I speak with you, brother?" he asked with an unmistakable note of humility in his voice.

Zeke regarded him for a moment, nodded, and set off toward the trees. Jarom followed him.

Father came to stand by me. He put his arm around me as we both unabashedly watched Jarom ask his brother's forgiveness, and we both had tears in our eyes when he was finished, when they were hugging each other so tightly there was no room for pride or embarrassment between them.

That night at the evening meal Zeke regaled us with stories about Zarahemla and the people there. He spoke twice of a girl named Eliza, a girl he claimed was more trouble than Keturah, and he probably thought no one noticed the light in his eyes when he said her name. The best parts were his tales about Helaman and the way he gently brought people to repentance as he restored the organization of the church.

"It comes so naturally to him. There is no question he has the mantle of the priesthood," Zeke told us.

As Zeke talked on, I studied him. I was beginning to see him differently. He had been nearly a stranger to me when he had come home from the war, but he wasn't a stranger any longer, and I was starting to trust him.

I thought of the reason he traveled to Zarahemla alone each month. I had figured it out. That was the arrangement he had with Gid. Zeke did Gid's job in Zarahemla so Gid could spend the time courting Keturah properly.

187

I thought of Zeke traveling all the way back to Judea to arrange the betrothal for Jarom to the girl he secretly loved. He had known the feelings of his brother's heart. I thought of Zeke granting forgiveness immediately when Jarom had asked for it that afternoon. Not even Micah had been able to grant that so easily to his brother.

And in my mind, I saw Zeke holding his younger brother with fierce protectiveness while he cried in remorse.

It was an image I would never forget.

I thought, too, of what Kenai had told me of Cumeni. Zeke had been bloody and weak and willing to fight to the death for Keturah, even after she had chosen another man in her heart. I thought of him staring into our fire while Keturah smiled at her Gid in the light of her own fire. I thought of him clasping Gid's arm at the betrothal.

I remembered Zeke helping me scale down the pattern for my leggings. I remembered him in the darkness behind the hut watching me with Kenai. And I remembered his refusal to fetch Darius for me.

I felt such admiration for him when I approached him after nearly everyone had left the fire. "Zeke, I need to talk to you." When he turned to me, I said, "I saw Zareth in the market yesterday."

"Cana's Zareth?"

I nodded. "I was with Kenai, and he followed us home."

He thought for a moment, then he really looked at me. "For now, even though I know you hate it, Izz, don't go anywhere alone."

I nodded. "I won't. I don't like that man, Zeke."

"Good. I'm going to go talk to Kenai."

"Okay." I paused. "And...thank you, Zeke."

CHAPTER 16

I didn't see any more of Zareth before we left the village to travel to Gid's for his marriage to Keturah.

The weather was cooling down. It would be time to harvest the maize soon and, like I had done the year before, I would help Kenai harvest his field.

Zeke was back in Zarahemla. Mother and Father had been busy preparing for Jarom's marriage, which was to take place in a fortnight. Everyone was busy. I thought they might have forgotten my birthday if Leah hadn't reminded them.

The celebration was much smaller than it had been the year before, but I was surrounded by everyone I loved, including Eliam and his parents. Eliam had five sisters and a brother, but he was the youngest and the only child remaining at his parents' home. I had met both Ezra and Rebekah on several occasions and had come to like them both very much. I could see why Father had thought their family would be a good one for me to join.

It made me nervous having both Eliam and Kenai sitting near me at the same time, but they got along well and truly were good friends. Eliam was the man my father had chosen for me. Kenai was his captain. And they both spent the meal distancing themselves from me for the other's sake. It was all very polite. I had known it would be polite, but I had imagined that it would be forced, and it wasn't. They both respected each other so much, liked each other, had that bond they couldn't describe. It was easy and natural between them.

It was my own politeness that was forced. I didn't know how to act. I felt very naive and very inadequate.

I knew Father wanted to weigh my feelings into his decision. He was watching me with an eagle eye, probably trying to determine which man I preferred. But there was no way he could determine it.

Because I just didn't know.

With Eliam, things were easy. Every look and touch was honest. His intentions were clear—he was just waiting on me to say I could love him. Eliam never made me feel I had to give more than I was ready to give. He only made me feel wanted and valued and cherished. I had come to love him, and I knew it.

But I knew I hadn't come to love him until Kenai told me how he got his scar.

I stole a glance at Kenai as I lifted my cup to drink. Though Eliam was perhaps the more handsome of the two, just looking at Kenai made my heart skip. I loved catching glimpses of him in the village, and to be honest about it, I always had. I felt something more for him that I didn't feel with Eliam—couldn't feel with Eliam. I didn't know if it was because we had fought the Lamanites together, because he was the unattainable friend of my older brother, or because a measure of my concern for him had turned to love when he no longer needed the concern. Everything about Kenai, every word spoken, every touch, every look between us, everything was tangled with our history together and the way our families were entwined.

Eliam was not the only one I had grown to love.

But I knew that even if my heart did not get over Kenai right away, I would not be unhappy with Eliam.

When the evening came to an end, Father and I walked

190

Eliam and his parents to the end of the village road.

"So what do you say, Isabel? Should we get the betrothal contracts in order?" Ezra asked me with a big smile.

My heart dropped. Had Father started the arrangements then? Had Eliam? He had said he would wait. But the question was no longer whether or not I could love Eliam—the question was whether or not I could stop loving Kenai.

"I would like to think on it just a little longer, Ezra."

He chuckled. "Come now. You get along so well. What is there to think over?"

I glanced at Eliam, so handsome, so funny and kind, so honest and dependable, so perfect for me. And I glanced at Father who was frowning slightly, but not at me—at Ezra.

Eliam put his arm around me and drew me close to him. "Father, Isabel is deciding between two men, and the other is the better one." He smiled down at me, no hint of jealousy in his eyes. "If she chooses me, it will be out of pity."

"Oh. I see," Ezra mumbled, seemingly as embarrassed as I was.

Eliam squeezed me and turned me to face him. Then, in front of his parents and my father, he kissed me gently on my lips. It might have seemed bold, but Eliam made everything so natural and easy.

"You remember what we talked about that first day?" he asked me.

I nodded, unable to look away from the tenderness in his face.

"Good." He turned then to his parents. "A love like Isabel's is not something that can be won overnight. If it was, I wouldn't want it, because it would hardly be worth having." He turned to Father. "Hemni, think of Izz, not me. Let her be sure. She is still young, and I am in no hurry."

Finally, he turned back to me and pulled me into his arms. He held me against his chest for a moment and whispered into my hair, "Take your time, sweetheart."

A rush of emotion went through me. Relief, gratitude, appreciation, love.

He released me and turned to go. "But not too long, huh?" he said with a teasing smile.

I shook my head. "Thank you, Eliam."

He nodded to my father and turned to leave with Ezra and Rebekah.

"Eliam! Wait!"

He turned back, surprised when I flew the few steps right into his arms again.

"I do love you," I said into his shoulder, muffled but irrevocable.

He stilled, and I thought I had perhaps been too impulsive. But after a moment, I felt a rumbling sound of approval in his chest. "And I love you, Isabel."

As Father and I walked back toward home, he placed his arm across my shoulders and teased me. "So what do you say, Izz? Should we get those betrothal contracts in order?"

I giggled nervously.

Father laughed and gave me a squeeze. "After Keturah's and Jarom's weddings, we'll work it out, one way or another."

"Okay," I said, but I felt very uneasy.

It must have looked to our parents as though I had decided, as though I did have a preference for Eliam—what with that last impulsive, ardent embrace. It must have looked that way to Eliam, too. But when I walked into the yard and caught the sight of Kenai talking to Jarom by the fire, I knew I hadn't decided.

And what was worse—I knew I never could.

This was the reason, I thought, why fathers made these decisions. How much easier it would be to trust Father's judgment and do as he thought was best.

Eliam then.

But I knew Father had spoken to Kenai, and hadn't Kenai been courting me in his own way since that time? He had gone from walking me everywhere I went to walking me to nowhere in particular. He had overcome Father's main objection which was that Kenai was not emotionally ready to take on a wife. He was better—getting better anyway, and clearly working on it each day. He had improved his skill in woodworking and could make a living from it if he chose. He had asked Micah's forgiveness. He had accepted a blessing from Kalem and my father. He had even formally asked Father if he could court me, I thought.

And it appeared Father had given him permission.

But why, if he had already decided on Eliam? That raised a terrible thought. I looked closely at Father as he went to Mother, kissed her on the cheek, and exchanged a troubled look with her.

Father was as unsure as I was.

I looked across the courtyard and caught Jarom's eye. He gave me a commiserating look, and it embarrassed me that he seemed to know all that was going on in my heart. But it made me sad, too, that he was soon to move away to live with his wife, and I had only just come to know him and find a friend in him.

The morning arrived when we were to travel to the southern-most part of Melek for Keturah's wedding ceremony. My family waited in the courtyard for Kalem and Leah and their boys, a silly term for the two grown men who came through the little gate carrying the extra parcels filled with Leah's gifts for their sister. Darius, grown very tall by then, taller than both his brothers, skipped the gate entirely and just stepped over the fence, clearing it easily.

I giggled. He sent me a reprimanding look, but then allowed himself a grin. I sighed. He still could not get used to the idea that Kenai wanted us to renew our friendship.

When Micah and Cana arrived ready to leave, we walked together in a large group out of the village. It was safest to travel this way.

I observed Micah and Cana as I walked with Mother and Leah. Micah appeared to be his usual pleasant and agreeable self, but he had a guarded look whenever he focused on Kenai—which seemed to be frequently. Cana looked, in a word, miserable. Her pale face was drawn, and when she thought no one was watching, she slipped into the bushes off the side of the road.

I didn't stop to stare, but I didn't have to wonder what was wrong for long because Mother said, "I think she is with child," in a quiet, hopeful, and oddly conspiratorial tone to Leah. "She looks exactly as I felt when Zeke was coming. You remember how ill I was."

Leah took Mother's hand and squeezed it. How wonderful for them, I thought, that they had been blessed to raise their children side by side as mothers, and now they would be grandmothers together. It was rare to find a friend so true.

I threw a glance over my shoulder and saw Micah waiting patiently for his wife while everyone else walked on.

I quickened my pace until I caught up with Jarom.

"How long will it take to get there?" I asked him.

Jarom squinted at the sky and said, "It will take half a day to get to Gid's. The striplings made it by the midday meal, but women always slow things down."

I reached over and jabbed him hard in the ribs that protected his heart—I had gotten good at finding them, as Kenai had said I would if I practiced.

I expected a tussle, retaliation of some kind, but he just

placed a hand over the spot and gave me a questioning look. He was wondering if I knew the significance of that spot, or if it was just a coincidence that I had poked him there.

I shrugged, loath to reveal why I knew it. "Are you nervous for your wedding?" I asked him. It would take place in just weeks. His home was ready and the last time he had come back from visiting Eve, he had said that she was ready as well.

"No, but I am a little nervous for the marriage," he admitted.

"Jarom," I said. "You will be a great husband."

He snorted.

"Yes. I heard Leah tell Mother of your first battle, when you lured the Lamanites from Antiparah."

He glanced down at me.

"You were on the front lines."

"Yes," he affirmed quietly.

"You were just thirteen."

"Yes."

"That was right around the time you met Eve, wasn't it?"

He nodded, eyes ahead, staring into the past.

"That is the boy she fell in love with—the one Helaman put on the front line who came away completely unscathed as a testament of God's power, so that all would know that only He could save your army of boys. If Helaman had placed stronger, more experienced, older boys there, couldn't we all have denied it? Take that knowledge into your marriage, Jarom, and you will do fine, for it is God who supports us and makes us what we are. And just as He made you an unstoppable warrior, He will make you a caring and noble husband."

I was watching the road ahead, but turned to look at him when I felt him staring at me.

"Kenai was right. You do have good advice."

"Kenai said that?"

He snorted again. "His says it all the time, and we make fun of him for it."

I poked him in the ribs again.

When we stopped for the midday meal, Kenai and I sat together under a tree with a natural ease we had both begun to take for granted and were soon joined by Sarai and Chloe.

Chloe talked quickly and seemed to be bouncing as she did so. At ten, she was just as exuberant as she had been at three. It was annoying at times, but it could also make you smile. Sarai, thirteen now, was quiet and I noticed she seemed to become more so while we ate, as if she had something on her mind.

Kenai noticed it too and tried to draw her out.

"Is something the matter Sarai?" he asked her. He tossed me a mischievous glance and snatched her uneaten apple.

She didn't seem to notice the apple, just heaved a sigh and asked him, "Are you going to marry Izz?"

Kenai's gaze shot to mine and held.

"Well? Are you?" Sarai asked again when he didn't respond.

"No!" exclaimed Chloe. "Eliam is going to marry her. He told me." Then she slapped a hand over her mouth, hiding a huge smile and stopping any more secrets from escaping.

Kenai took a big bite of the apple and chucked Sarai on the chin. "Do you want me to marry your sister?" he asked her, but stopped chewing when he saw the pleading in her eyes.

Before she could respond beyond blushing deeply, we all noticed Cana had approached.

I looked up at her. She appeared to be feeling better. In fact, she was flushed and glowing. She looked completely content. But when she spoke, her thin voice held a note of nervousness.

"Girls, may I sit here and talk with Kenai alone?"

"Sure," I said quickly. "Come on girls," I said to Sarai and Chloe.

I felt Kenai's gaze on me as I walked away, and when I glanced back over my shoulder his eyes asked me to stay, begged me not to leave him.

So I lingered near a tree where he could see me but Cana couldn't, and he shot me a grateful glance. I couldn't do anything for him, though, except act as moral support. But if just standing there would help him, I would do it.

"Kenai," I heard my sister say, "I want to tell you I'm sorry."

"For what? You don't owe me an apology."

"I do. I fostered feelings between us, and we both know it."

He shook his head. "That was a long time ago, and it wasn't wrong."

"Maybe not, but when Micah told me you had sought his forgiveness I was so...embarrassed that I had not sought your forgiveness sooner. I hadn't done it first. I hadn't done it at all. Micah said he had talked to you about marrying me, and you had given your blessing."

I glanced at Micah. He was the only one in our small camp who wasn't pretending not to notice the conversation under the tree. He was watching openly, standing rigidly, clearly fighting to keep himself from striding over and whisking his wife away from what she was doing. I didn't think he wholly approved of it. I knew he wanted the apology to come from Kenai.

"He was right. I did," Kenai told her. "That is why you don't owe me an apology."

"Micah said it was something you would come to accept in time, and no one had done wrong so there was no need to apologize. I believed him because I wanted to, but it was wrong

197

of me. I owed you an explanation if nothing else."

Kenai was silent for a moment and when Cana looked down into her lap, he took the opportunity to cast me a distressed look. *Help.*

But I gave my head a slight shake. I couldn't help him. Not this time. Not through this.

He ran a hand through his hair, an action I knew meant he was uncomfortable.

"Cana, it is I who must apologize. When I came home from the war, I wasn't prepared to deal with...with anything." He grimaced. "Certainly not with you and Micah. But I treated you poorly, and I let the treatment go on too long. After a while, I didn't know how to change it." He cleared his throat. "Izz said that if I truly loved you, I wouldn't do anything to make you unhappy. That was when I figured it out. I didn't love you enough—not like that."

I couldn't see Cana's face, but his was filled with tenderness and remorse, and his eyes asked her to forgive him.

I saw her nod, but she said, "Kenai, there is one more thing I have to tell you." She paused, looked down, fingered the hem of her sarong, but she looked suddenly back up at him when she spoke. "I am going to have a baby, Kenai. Micah and I are. I'm very happy about it, and I want you to be happy too."

His eyes widened slightly—I guessed he hadn't noticed the signs like I had—but he did not look overly surprised. It wasn't really a surprise. We had all been expecting it to happen soon. We had actually been expecting it to happen sooner.

He got easily to his feet and held out his hand to her. She took it, and he helped her up. Taking her other hand, he squeezed them both in his.

"I'm going to be an uncle," he said quietly and resolutely as if he had said *everything will be fine now.*

198

She just stared into his face, and if I knew Cana, I knew she was crying. Kenai stepped toward her and wrapped her in his arms. I felt ridiculous, but I knew Micah and I were both watching closely for something neither of us saw—because it wasn't there.

Kenai caught Micah's eye over Cana's head, and after that moment, all three of them began behaving as they should.

CHAPTER 17

Keturah's wedding celebration took place on a lovely evening at Gid's home, and I was surprised when I saw Zeke walking down the long path toward it.

"What are you doing here?" I asked him.

"You thought I wouldn't come?"

"I guess I did."

"Then you don't know me at all."

"That's the truth. You've been gone for half my life."

He coughed, crossed his arms over his chest, and leaned back on his heels as we watched the families gather, converse, laugh, and eat.

"Where is your Eliam?" he asked.

"He is traveling here with his friends. Should be here any time," I said without looking at him.

"Father says you have another suitor." He paused for only a moment before he went on. "Have you seen any more of Zareth?"

"No."

"Do you avoid being alone? Do you take a stripling with you when you walk in the woods?"

"Yes."

"Good. When I first got home from the war, I thought you had grown up with a stubborn streak like Keturah's, but I see that your stubborn streak only works in your favor. You want to be obedient, and your stubbornness keeps you on the straight and narrow path."

I laughed a little. "I have heard Mother say the same thing about you."

His brow raised. "Truly?"

"Yes. Zeke?"

He drew his eyes away from the crowd to look at me.

"Tell me about Eliza."

"Who?"

"Eliza, that girl in Zarahemla. Who is she?"

He shifted his weight. "Helaman's niece."

"Do you like her?"

He barked out a laugh. "No. I can't stand her."

Like Jarom couldn't stand Eve, I'd bet. What was with my brothers when it came to women?

I didn't press him.

We were both staring at Keturah as she went from person to person greeting them and talking for a moment with each of them. After a while I asked, "Zeke, how would you have felt if Ket married you because Micah made her? I mean, you know she loves you, but she loves Gid too."

He didn't answer for a time, but I knew he was thinking about it. Finally he said, "Maybe you should ask Gid. He would have a better understanding of it than me."

I let my gaze slide to Gid.

No. There was no way I could ask him a question like that. Not that evening. Not ever.

Zeke laughed at the face I made. But then he sobered and said, "We would have dealt with it."

Dealt with it. That didn't sound very romantic. Letting Father choose my husband wasn't exactly romantic either. But romantic was just another word for irresponsible, wasn't it?

Kenai walked past us. "You two want to play ball?"

Zeke nodded and followed him. I guessed he'd had enough of watching Keturah.

"At a wedding celebration?" I asked.

"We're going way out there." Kenai stopped and pointed to a place in the distance. I could see a group of young men already moving in that direction. Then he leaned down and said in a conspiring tone, "There are too many striplings here. We're kind of in the way."

"I can come?" I asked.

"Sure." Kenai held out his hand. I took it just as I caught sight of Eliam in a small group of men approaching on the long road that led to the farm. Our eyes met, and I flushed guiltily.

How had Keturah ever done this? I was not old enough or experienced enough to deal with this—this multiple suitors business. The emotions were too strong, too confusing.

I knew I would hurt one of them. And I knew, of the three of us, I would hurt the most.

Kenai followed my gaze.

"Hey! Eliam's here, and Mahonri and Jonas."

He led me on a direct path toward them, and I stood uncomfortably between Kenai and Zeke as they all greeted one another.

"Keturah and Gid are there by the house," Kenai said and pointed. "After you've greeted them, come play ball."

I looked around at them, all of them over twenty, some closer to twenty-five, and I wondered that they were all so eager to play this game that was, in my opinion, kind of childish. They had about two hours left of light in which to play, and it appeared as though they intended to make the most of every second.

"Sure," said Jonas. "We'll be out there in a few minutes."

But we noticed then that Keturah was walking toward us in a large group of men.

"Her unit," Kenai informed me. "That's Lib and Ethanim flanking her. Josh, Noah, Zach on her left. Nice to see Zach's wife let him off his leash." He winked at me. "Her name is Beth. She waited years for him while he was away in the army. The short one is Reb. And the cousins, Mathoni, Corban, and Cyrus. I think they all live nearby."

When the group reached us, Keturah stepped away from them and gave me a sisterly hug. "You're coming out to play, right?"

I nodded.

"Good." She left her arm around me as she greeted her guests, and we all continued together toward the far end of the field. She seemed to be falling back, and sure enough, soon I noticed that we were several lengths behind Lib and Ethanim.

She leaned in close and asked me, "How are things going with Kenai?"

I glanced at Lib and Ethanim.

"My guards," she laughed. "They can't seem to let it go. Ever since they found out I was here, they come guard me when Gideon is working in Zarahemla. I really think the habit is so entrenched they can't help themselves."

"You mean it's true? You never went anywhere alone?"

"Not for one single, solitary second."

I didn't believe it, and it must have showed on my face.

"Well, that's exaggerated, but true for the most part."

"Zeke didn't lie about that then."

She laughed. "I've never known Zeke to lie. He doesn't. He wouldn't. I'm not sure if he could."

"I didn't know that. I barely knew him when he got back from the war."

"No, I suppose not." She paused. Looking ahead to the men, she slowed her pace even more. "So, tell me about Kenai. I've been dying to know. Mother's letters barely say anything."

"Kenai is doing so well—eating heartily, helping others, laughing with friends."

"No. I mean *you* and Kenai," she pressed playfully.

My eyes found him instantly in a circle of men.

"Isabel?"

I sighed. "Father introduced me to Eliam. He wants me to like him. And I do."

"Oh. But you still love Kenai." I could feel her searching my face for the answer though she hadn't posed it as a question.

I glanced at her, then away. "It's getting difficult."

She bit her lip.

"Any advice?" I said on a sigh.

"Well, for just this moment, don't stand by either one of them in the game. Beyond that..." She gave me a small smile and shrugged.

"Okay." That had been my plan anyway. "Keturah?"

"Yes?"

"You look beautiful today. I'm really glad you're happy."

"Thanks, Izz. You will be, too," she said genuinely. She held my gaze for a moment, as if trying to make me believe it. "I'm going over there with my old unit. You could go stand between Zeke and Darius. Completely neutral."

I saw a hint of pain in her eyes when she looked at Zeke.

"You still love him," I said.

"More now than ever," she replied. "But different from the way I love Gideon."

"What is the difference?"

She turned to me and we stopped walking altogether. "Oh, Izz, I wish I knew exactly. I wish I could give you one right answer that would magically make things clear for you." Her eyes looked beyond my shoulder, and I turned to see who she waved at.

Gid was walking alone toward us.

I looked back to Keturah and noticed her eyes were shining with love and happiness as she looked toward her Gid.

Her voice was soft. "When I was with Gideon, I thought of Zeke with feelings of guilt and confusion. I wanted to do the right thing, do as Micah requested. I wanted to fulfill both our families' expectations. And most of all, I didn't want to hurt Zeke. Just the idea of it was abhorrent to me. But when I was with Zeke, I couldn't keep thoughts of Gideon from my mind, and I thought of him with feelings of hope."

I didn't have time to respond before Gid joined us and put his arm around Keturah. It seemed so natural for them. They were both comfortable and sure.

I thought of what Zeke had said only moments before. Could I really ask Gid?

I licked my lips. "Gid? Could I ask you a question?"

"Sure," he said.

I noticed he had a thin scar that curved around one of his eyebrows. His brown hair fell nearly to his shoulders and his eyes were the color of damp earth. His shoulders were broad and strong. Keturah looked so fragile next to him, and I wondered if she could still win a pairing with him.

I spoke more boldly, but I spoke to Keturah. "Could I speak with him alone?"

She looked to him. "Okay?"

His brow rose slightly, but he nodded and then watched her as she walked toward her unit.

Then he turned back to me.

I licked my lips again. "I am Isabel. Zeke's sister."

His face softened instantly. "What is your question, Isabel?"

All of a sudden it seemed very stupid.

He waited patiently. He didn't let his gaze slide to the men who shouted and laughed behind him. "It's alright," he said. "You can ask it."

I cleared my throat, which had gone dry. "You know Keturah still loves Zeke." I didn't think it was a secret she kept from him.

He nodded. "I wouldn't want a woman whose love could fade so quickly."

That was a response I hadn't expected.

"What does it...I mean, how do you feel...How will you react to this as her husband?"

He was thoughtful, seriously considering it. "The answer is important to you—that is easy to see. But you must realize, Isabel, that my new brother-in-law may not respond the same way as I do. In fact, we have often differed of opinion in the past."

I was mortified when I realized Keturah had already discussed Kenai and me with Gid. But of course she would. Kenai was her brother, and she worried about him.

I nodded. My ears were hot, but I looked him in the eye.

"Do you believe in God?" he asked me.

"Of course!"

"In the Holy Ghost?"

"Gid...yes, of course."

He shifted his weight and hooked his thumbs into his belt. "I have the comfort of the Holy Ghost. It reaffirms to me that taking Keturah unto myself is right and good. I have never doubted her feelings for me—even when she chose Zeke, I understood why. He was a part of her life, a big part, and he influenced the woman she has become today. He always treated her with respect and love. He taught her how to be in a relationship. So when she grieves for him, for the loss of his excellent friendship and love, I let her. And I comfort her if I can."

I blinked. "You're not angry or jealous?"

"No."

His voice was so sure, I had no choice but to believe him.

He placed his hand on my shoulder.

"It was very nice to meet you, Isabel. I hope our paths will cross again in the future. Is that all you wanted to know?"

I swallowed. Nodded. "I wish you the best in your marriage," I said.

"Thank you," he replied with heart-felt sincerity, and then he turned and walked toward Keturah.

I made my way to Zeke who readily made room for me next to him.

"You know how to play?" he inquired.

"She knows," Darius said from my other side.

"Good. In this circle," Zeke instructed, "we each get one hit. You have to hit the ball to someone else with your turn. In that circle," he indicated one next to us that included both Kenai and Eliam. "They each get three hits. Also, you'll notice they are playing a more advanced version of the game."

I watched for a moment as Kenai hit the ball with his chest, his elbow, and then stood on his hands and hit it with his foot to the next man."

"Is he showing off for me?" I asked in surprise.

Zeke laughed. "No. Well, maybe a little."

"Izz," Darius called me back to our game.

I turned back to him just as he hit the ball to me. I easily got it with the outside of my ankle and lobbed it to Zeke.

We played until it got too dark to see the ball and I noticed the men were breaking out bedrolls.

I looked around for Keturah, but I didn't see her anywhere.

"I'll walk you back," Zeke said when the game broke up.

"Ezekiel."

We turned to see Eliam.

"Please allow me to walk your sister back to the house."

Zeke took a step away from me. "She's all yours."

"Giving away another gorgeous girl?" someone called from the gathering darkness.

Zeke gave a self-deprecating laugh. "This one's too much for me to handle," he called.

"Yeah, so was the last one!"

I heard laughter and ribbing from the men, and I wondered that they could be so thoughtless. Didn't they know his heart was breaking?

I stomped off, tears stinging my eyes. I didn't want to hear any more.

"Whoa! Wait up," Eliam said as he caught up to me, his hand grasping my shoulder.

I slowed and let my posture slump. "Sorry," I said.

"What's the matter?"

"Nothing."

He just waited for me to tell him. He knew I would.

I sighed. "It's just, those men—they were saying such unkind things."

"It's better for Zeke to be teased than to pretend it doesn't exist."

I reached for his hand, something I had never done before. It was warm and moist with sweat from the exertion of the game. It felt especially warm in the cooling night air.

"I trust you, Eliam." I paused. "But I still want to scratch all their eyes out."

He chuckled. "Your protective nature is very sweet, Izz."

"Protective nature?"

"Sure. Yours is very strong. You want to protect everyone."

I thought about that for a moment.

Eliam went on quietly. "I think you're even trying to protect me from what is happening."

My heart sped up. "What do you mean?"

"Are you going to make me say it? You're falling in love with the captain, Izz."

He didn't sound angry or hurt or even disappointed. Just matter-of-fact.

"Eliam."

"I want you to protect the captain. I do. But sweetheart, I'm falling in love, too." He pulled me to a stop and looked into my eyes. "If I thought you could get over Kenai, if you said you could, I'd go talk to your father right now."

His gaze burned into mine. It was so intense, so filled with desire and understanding. He would always be patient and generous. Like Gid. Would he comfort me when I grieved for the friendship I had shared with Kenai? When my heart grieved for the love we had shared?

Should I just say it? It was inevitable anyway.

"I told Father..." My voice broke and I cleared my throat and started over in a whisper. "I told Father I would marry you."

Well, I had implied it.

Eliam's smile started in his eyes and spread to his entire handsome face.

"He wants to wait until after Jarom's wedding to make it official." I said this shyly but with a smile I had caught from his contagious one.

"Isabel," he said, his emotion evident in his voice.

He bent and kissed me, but he didn't have to bend far because I stood on my toes and rose up to meet him. It started like his other kisses, kisses I was familiar with, comfortable with, but it intensified as he let his satisfaction and excitement show. I wrapped my arms around his neck, and I was thinking that we were out in the middle of a barley field and though it was dark, anyone could come upon us. But I lost myself, I let myself be lost, in Eliam's embrace, in his kiss, in his excitement about the imminent betrothal.

And I knew that in time I would let myself feel excitement too.

When Eliam finally ended the kiss, he stepped back. He took a deep breath and ran a hand through his dark hair.

"Sorry. Sorry, Izz. I got carried away."

"So did I," I said, noticing how my lips felt tingly from the roughness of his short whiskers. Just the thought of that made me blush fiercely, and I looked down at my sandaled feet.

But not before I saw Kenai scowling at me from the darkness behind Eliam.

I quickly looked back up, but he wasn't there any longer. He had disappeared in a second, or I had imagined him.

I thought of what Keturah had said about feeling guilt when she was with Zeke. I thought of Gid's firm answer when I asked him if he was jealous. I knew that Kenai would be a maelstrom of jealously.

"But I don't care," Eliam was saying. "When you give your word, I know you mean it."

I let him take my hand once more and walk me back to my father's tent where I laid awake most of the night not crying, but feeling like I should.

But the next morning, Kenai was not a maelstrom of jealousy.

211

Kenai had not camped in the field with the other striplings, but near the house with his family. Near my family. When I entered the yard for the morning meal, he already had a dish of food prepared for me.

"Thank you," I said as he passed it into my hands.

"You're most welcome, Isabel," he replied with a smile.

I narrowed my eyes at him. Had my conscience only imagined him last night?

I spent the day watching the younger children so the women could prepare Keturah for the ceremony. Everything was ready, from the food to the canopy. Leah and Gid's mother had done an excellent job preparing for this day. All there was for the rest of us to do was enjoy it.

Everything was beautiful—the day, the ceremony, the celebration that followed. I had such a good time that I was eager for Jarom's wedding in a few weeks. I just tried not to think of what would happen after that.

My dreams would end, and my life would begin.

"Why are you crying?"

I was sitting alone at the edge of the firelight. Lamech had appeared silently at my side and taken a knee next to me.

"Don't tell me you didn't realize you were crying again."

I laughed. "I didn't," I said as I reached up to feel tears on my face.

"And don't tell me you're crying over some boy," he said. I thought I detected mild hostility in his tone, but Lamech was like that—brooding and moody at the strangest times.

"Have you ever been in love?" I asked him lightly. He was sixteen, maybe seventeen by now. Surely he had fallen in love more than once.

"No way. A complete waste of time. And I doubt you have either."

212

I laughed again and wiped the remnants of my tears away with the knuckles of my thumbs. "Take your hair out of the braids," I said.

He turned his whole torso to look at me. "What?"

"You heard me. Do it."

"No."

"Then I will."

"No."

"I want to see it down. I'll help you braid it back up."

He shook his head.

"It's dark. No one will see. I did that stupid war dance. Take your hair out."

He didn't respond, just kept staring at me, which I took as permission. I reached over and took the end of one of his braids. He stiffened but didn't stop me from slipping off the rawhide thong that held it secure.

He faced rigidly forward as I quickly loosed the long braid. His hair was thick, but it was smooth and silky when I expected it to be coarse. It shone in the flickering firelight that reached us.

He shot me a glance but wouldn't look at me fully.

Quickly, before he could change his mind, I moved around so I knelt in front of him. I loosed the other braid and then moved back a bit to regard my handiwork.

He continued to avoid my eyes.

"You should cut it to here," I said and drew a line just below his collar bone. "And wear it straight down with no restraints."

Finally he looked at me, eyeing me with curiosity. "Why?"

"Lamech," I said. "You've got to know you're the most handsome man here."

He huffed, but he wasn't as disinterested as he tried to appear.

"Handsome isn't even a strong enough word," I said, and it wasn't. I brushed his hair over his shoulders so it hung long behind his back. His dark eyes and sharp cheekbones stood out to a much better advantage than they had with a heavy braid on each side. "I mean it. No one else even comes close. Honestly, Lamech, you'd have girls following you around giggling behind their hands."

He huffed again. "And why would I want that?"

"You could completely waste all kinds of time."

A half a smile cut its way to his lips.

"You knew Sarai was taken with you when you were in Melek."

"No."

I studied him for a moment, the red appearing on his cheekbones, the hard swallow, the schooled expression. He'd known.

He looked far away into a place I couldn't see, perhaps to his vision of his future. The look in his eyes was distant and full of a longing I was sure he thought the darkness hid from me. But it didn't.

"I'm not good enough for your family. Sarai is...she's too pure. I could never think of that."

I snorted. "Why? Because of your father? Don't be an idiot." I yawned. "I'm going to bed. Here, I'll help you braid your hair back up."

He jerked back slightly. "That's alright."

I shrugged, secretly pleased. "Whatever." I got up, and walked away from him. "Oh." I turned back. "Sarai is almost fourteen, so don't wait too long before you speak to Father."

"What if I love you?" he challenged.

"You don't."

"How do you know?"

214

I thought for a moment. I was almost sure he didn't. I had seen the way he looked at Sarai from the side of his eyes, even when he was talking to me. He couldn't love us both. And he wouldn't have been able to talk so easily to me if he did.

"You look at me like Jarom does. Goodnight, Lamech."

I had only gone a few steps into the darkness when Gid gently grabbed a hold of my arm. He stood with Jashon in the shadows.

"Thank you," he mouthed silently.

I looked between them, gathering that they had overheard my conversation with their younger brother—their younger, half-Lamanite brother. I gave them a small smile, looked at the ground, and continued on past.

CHAPTER 18

A fortnight had passed since we had returned from Keturah's wedding. Jarom was ready for his own wedding, but I could tell he was anxious, probably to have it over and done with. A year was a long time to plan on and wait for something.

I was lying under our tree—mine and Kenai's. My eyes were closed, and I was listening to the sound of the breeze in the treetops. The sound of the large leaves of the maize stalks added their own timbre to the music. It all sounded like a rushing river, only quieter, softer, more conducive to the kind of thinking I was doing.

Kenai wasn't there. I had seen him finishing up his gift for Jarom's home, a set of chairs he would carry there before the wedding ceremony.

He had winked at me when I admired his workmanship, which was exceedingly fine. I had no idea where he had learned to work wood that way—certainly not here in the village.

"I'll make a set for your home," he had said as I ran my hand across the back of one chair.

I hadn't known how to respond to that, so I'd only asked "Where did you learn to make them?"

"I picked it up from a tradesman in Manti."

In our village, too small to even have a name, we mostly used stools. Chairs were unusual here, though not unheard of. He hadn't learned it here but had perfected the art here in the village when he had returned.

After I had gotten him to start eating again. After he had accepted the Spirit and the words of Christ back into his heart.

That was what I was thinking about as I listened to the evidence of the wind in the trees.

I remembered the first time I had brought the midday meal here and eaten it under this tree with Kenai. He had been hungry. Perhaps not fully aware of it, perhaps unwilling to admit it to himself, but he had been hungry.

One thought had been going through my mind over and over, crowding out thoughts of my own betrothal, of a time that should have been one of the happiest of my life. I was letting it crowd out those thoughts, and I let my mind roam over the meaning of one phrase I had read in the words of the long ago prophet, Nephi.

Feast upon the words of Christ. The words of Christ will tell you all things what ye should do.

The words of Christ would tell me how to get back to heaven, surely, but would they tell me what to do about my feelings for Kenai?

Angles spoke the words of Christ by the power of the Holy Ghost.

I remembered Gid asking me if I believed in the Holy Ghost. I remembered Keturah telling me about two kinds of obedience. One kind required me to follow the commandments, the instructions of my parents, the words of Christ with exactness. The other kind required me to heed the direction of the Holy Ghost in my heart.

I thought of how Kenai had shunned food just as he had shunned the Holy Ghost for so long, how he had refused a priesthood blessing, how he had refused to repent and forgive,

218

how he had refused to let God's love heal him and wash his guilt and pain away—like water washed dirt away.

I wondered if he had begun partaking of spiritual food when he had taken my apple from me under this tree.

As I lay with my eyes closed, I saw myself so young, so innocent, sitting here with my hair pulled over my shoulder, hoping I could coax him to eat. Just a little. With my innocence.

And yet, I hadn't been innocent. I had known.

I had walked here with that piece of fruit, knowing he must eat it, and knowing I was the only one who could persuade him to do it.

I thought of eating the pitaya together, its beautiful white fruit inside so sweet to the taste. We had shared the fruit his mother had given us while my father watched us eat it.

Had he been pleased? I just didn't know.

None of it was making sense, but it was starting to.

I heard someone approach, and my heart began to pound. Kenai was silent wherever he went.

But, to my relief, it was his voice that said, "You shouldn't be out here alone."

"It's not your job to protect me," I said.

"When Zeke's not here, it is."

"You're not my brother."

"And you're not making any sense. What are you doing out here alone? Did Zeke not insist you have a stripling with you?"

I smiled because none of the men were striplings anymore, with the possible exception of the very youngest ones like Lamech. It was just a word now that everyone used to refer to those who had gone with Helaman to the war.

"He did."

"Isabel, open your eyes." He sounded angry.

So I squeezed my eyes shut tighter.

He huffed. "Izz." He sounded...less angry.

I opened one eye and found him on his heels next to me.

"Izz," he said again and pinched me in the ribs over my heart. "Izz, open your eyes."

"Ow!" I put a hand over my ribs and sat up, turning to see his smile.

"You left your heart vulnerable," he said.

I looked into his green eyes. They made me think of the leaves I had been listening to.

"So I did," I said. "What do you want, Kenai."

"I want to know what you're doing here."

"I'm thinking."

"You can't wander off alone to think."

"Why not? Everyone else can."

"Zareth didn't follow everyone else home from the market."

I didn't have it in me to be truly disobedient to Zeke's wishes—at least not obstinate about it. "Alright, you may walk me home."

"You can't just fix it like that," Kenai insisted.

"What do you mean?"

"I walked right up to you, and you didn't even notice. You're not even trying to be cautious!"

It was true. "Alright, I'll be more cautious."

"You're not getting it."

"Getting what? Have you no faith in the skills you taught me? Or is it me you have no faith in?"

"You're not getting that your safety matters. You're not getting that you're in danger."

"So you have no faith in me."

"Not when I see you lying under a tree having a daydream

with none of your senses attuned to the possible dangers around you."

"Are you a danger to me?"

His only reply was an annoyed snort.

He was fighting what he felt for me. It was as clear to me as the sun over our heads.

"Kenai, tell me about when the army was starving in Cumeni."

His eyes widened slightly at the abrupt change in subject. "How do you know about that?"

I shrugged. "It's not exactly a secret."

"It's not exactly something any of us like talking about either."

"So you won't tell me?"

"What do you want to know?"

"I was thinking about the words of Nephi. How he said 'Feast upon the words of Christ.'"

"'For behold, the words of Christ will tell you all things what ye should do,'" he quoted.

I nodded slowly. "Do you think that's true?"

"I know it is."

"But...what does it mean?"

He shifted so he was sitting too. "Exactly what it says, Izz. Here." He rummaged in his satchel and pulled out lunch for both of us. Something pricked my heart as I watched him prepare the simple fare.

"The words of Christ can be food to our souls and the love of God, like we talked about before, can be life-giving water to our souls."

He handed me a corn cake filled with a spicy stew his mother made. My mother never made it because she didn't like it. But I did, and I knew Kenai did. I wondered if Leah would teach me how to make it. Perhaps I could manage a stew.

"And you want to know what it is to hunger?"

I shrugged.

Kenai was quiet for a time, but the silence between us was comfortable. There had been a lot of silences between us in the past year. Kenai didn't always need words to speak, and I had found that I did not always need words to understand.

"The men were only allowed to hunt game when they were assigned to a hunting detail," Kenai told me quietly as we ate, speaking suddenly into the silence. "They had to bring everything back to camp. It was a great test of honesty."

I turned my head to look at him.

"It didn't affect my men and me as much as the others because we were outside of the city a lot and we ate off the land."

"You were lucky."

He winced. "The others became sluggish, dull-eyed, stopped laughing. Keturah..." He cleared his throat. "Keturah mixed half her rations back in with her unit's food so they could have more. She figured she was so much smaller than the men that she needed less food than they did."

"What happened?"

"Well...she didn't die."

"Was it as bad as that?"

"Yes."

"And when food finally arrived—it did, didn't it?"

He nodded.

"When food arrived, how did the men react?"

"Can't you imagine? But we had order in the army. Whatever Helaman commanded, we did without question. Whatever our chief captains commanded, we did without complaint. So when the rations were still small, even after the men had watched the provisions being carried in by two thousand men from Zarahemla, the men accepted it."

"Why were the rations still small?"

"Well, there were two thousand more men to share them with for one thing. And when you are hungry for so long, your stomach doesn't accept food the way it once did."

"What do you mean?"

"You have to ease it back into accepting food."

I bit my lip. "Like when you came home and you wouldn't eat?"

"Yeah. Izz, what are you getting at?"

"Nothing. I wish I knew."

He reached over and rubbed his thumb along my wrist. "I know."

I closed my eyes again and tried to concentrate on the wind in the leaves instead of the sensation of his thumb on my skin.

"When I came home I felt so much guilt, so much unexplainable pain and sadness. I didn't want to feel the Spirit. When I started to, I became confused because I didn't think I deserved it, that wonderful gift. And when I became confused, I became angry, because the Gospel had never confused me before. I didn't have a desire to turn from its precepts, but I couldn't allow the Spirit to work on me."

I wanted to concentrate on the important thing he was saying, but his thumb still rubbed slowly back and forth along my wrist.

"It's funny—I told myself I was fasting, in a way. Because I wanted to be closer to God, but I felt far from Him." He let my wrist go. "Anyway, when you walked down here with your pretend attitude and your extra food—no, before that—I felt the Spirit, but it was in you, and I didn't want to shun you. And every time you came here and sat near me, I felt it and it was okay. And then you'd leave, and I'd fight it again."

"How long before that?"

"I don't know. The night of the kidnapping maybe. Maybe before that." He let out a long breath. "I wish I'd gotten to you sooner that night. I could have—"

"You had your hands full. There was nothing more you could have done."

"I was going to say I could have lost you that night," his voice softened. "Before I'd even found you."

"Oh."

"Isabel." He slipped a finger under my necklace and pulled it out from under my sarong again. "Stop hiding this. I want you to...Isabel—" He broke off and made a sound of frustration.

"What is it you want, Kenai?"

"I want you to take a stripling with you when you wander off to think."

I rolled my eyes. "How can I think with you hovering over me?"

"You mean how can you think about him if I'm here?"

"No, Kenai!"

"Were you daydreaming of him under our tree?"

I gasped. As if I could. "No!"

He got to his feet and started pacing, but he stopped and put his hands on his hips.

"I—" he started, but didn't finish with anything.

"Kenai." I tried to keep my voice calm. "You fought against feeling the Spirit. Now you fight against what you feel for me." He threw me a wary look. "I understand all your reasons for not wanting me. My youth. Your debt to Eliam—of all people." I looked to the sky and allowed myself a sardonic smile, even a small laugh. "Your feelings for Cana," I added. "But you've never once said you wanted me. And while you were not saying it, Eliam was saying it a hundred times in a hundred different ways—"

"Like kissing you out in the open where everyone can see?"

"There was no one...Kenai!"

He looked knowingly at me. He tried to look smug, but it came across more truly—as hurt.

"No! Like...like..."

Then he did look smug because I couldn't think of anything right away.

"Like helping me kill a deer."

His eyes widened.

Good.

"Like helping me skin and tan hides. Like being interested in me and what I enjoy."

"And what about you? What do you tell him? And are you interested in what he enjoys?"

I wasn't even sure I could name something Eliam enjoyed, at least not above other things. I knew the look on my face told Kenai so.

But that didn't matter. I had a lifetime to come to know those things. And I knew enough. I knew he kept widows supplied with meat. I knew he worked hard. I knew he'd been obedient to his parents and he'd been obedient to his captains in the army.

One of whom was staring at me so intently I had to look away.

I looked toward the maize field. Full of food.

"You kissed me once, Kenai. And I liked it. And so did you. But the fact is, we do make a ridiculous pair, and you know it as well as I do."

He was shaking his head slowly.

"I get the feeling you're upset about Eliam, about what is

225

happening, what will happen. But you still are not saying the thing that could stop it, could make me change my mind."

"So you've made up your mind."

It wasn't really a question, which was excellent, because there was no way for me to answer it. I had. I had made up my mind. I just hadn't acted upon it. I'd acted upon a different kind of obedience instead.

I folded my arms over my chest—not defensively, but to hold myself together for just a few more minutes.

"I've made up my mind to do as my father asks of me, to marry the man he chooses for me, because if I chose, if I chose, Kenai, I would marry a man who can't even admit he wants me." I willed the tears not to fall from my eyes, though I couldn't stop them from forming. "Good-bye, Kenai. I'm going to the tannery. And I'll be traveling without a stripling."

I left him alone under the tree and walked to the tannery alone, but when I drew near, I heard voices. I almost rolled my eyes at Kenai's ridiculous comments about exercising caution as I first hid myself behind a tree to listen for a moment before walking into the clearing. It was Father and Eliam. I peered around the tree and saw them standing together under the awning. Both of them had their arms folded across their chests. They were talking quietly, and I couldn't make out any of the words they said. But these two men had only one reason to be having a conversation.

Me.

I didn't want to interrupt—well, I did, but I didn't want to be involved in the conversation, I didn't want to hinder its progress, and I didn't want them to ask me what I wanted—so I stayed hidden behind the tree. After a while, they left together in the direction of Melek. After I peered around the tree again to be sure they were gone, I stepped out into the clearing.

ARROW TO HIS HEART

We had finished everything a few days ago, and Father hadn't taken on any new work in expectation that he would be completely free for all the celebrations associated with the wedding. But I was able to find a skin that needed grinding to soften it, so I set about doing that.

I had heard of some who actually chewed their buckskin to make it soft and pliable, but I had never found that necessary, and I considered myself an expert when it came to buckskin. If all the other steps were done correctly and with precision—which ours always were—grinding it between two rocks always worked perfectly for me.

I had been working the skin an hour or so before Kenai showed up, walking into the clearing with an odd mix of bewildered determination on his face. I sighed. He still didn't know what he was about.

But for not knowing what he was about, he didn't waste any words.

"You love me," he said as he marched up to me.

I just stared at him. I'd as much as said so, hadn't I?

"Say it," he demanded with authority in his voice I was sure came from being a captain in the army. But he didn't have any authority over me.

Apparently, to him, as much as saying so was not the same thing as actually saying so.

"Kenai."

He reached out and snatched the necklace from under my sarong. He held it in his hand for a moment, squeezing it in his fist before he let it fall heavy and hard against my chest. He spoke slowly. "Don't hide this."

"You did."

"What?"

"You did. You were home for months before I knew what

was on the rawhide you wore around your neck." And I couldn't help but emphasize, "Under your tunic."

His hands were on his hips and he reared back a little, looking away to scoff. "That's not the same."

"It's exactly the same."

"Well, when I took it out, you're the only one I showed it to."

"Okay," I said. "And you are the only one I am showing it to. Look, Kenai." I gentled my voice. "Father is talking to Eliam right now. I shouldn't even be wearing this." My hand went to the pendent, but I couldn't bring myself to take it off. I fingered the barb.

Kenai stepped to me and put his hands to my waist.

"Kenai," I protested.

He looked into my eyes. "You love me."

I rolled them. "And?"

"And I love you. I love you. Isabel. Say you love me." He pulled me closer to him. "Say it," he repeated softly.

I shook my head. "It's too late." I really thought it was too late. "I've already talked to Father." Saying it would only make things worse. If that was even possible.

Kenai showed me it was indeed possible to make things worse when he leaned down and kissed me as if it were his right.

I pulled away from him, though I didn't want to.

He studied my face. He hadn't expected me to pull away from him. "Say you love me. You do. Admit it, Isabel."

Admit it? Wasn't that what I had been trying to make him do? Was it I who couldn't say it? Couldn't admit it? But it hardly made a difference how I felt. I hadn't said it because, well, he was the man, and his was the opinion that mattered when it came to marriage.

I only made a strangled sound with no meaning behind it,

full of panic. Why was he doing this?

He kissed me again, harder, more insistent. "Say you love me." He was demanding. He was begging.

What was he trying to accomplish? Saying I loved him wouldn't change anything. I had thought if he said it, things could change, but then I had seen Father and Eliam.

No, things couldn't change.

They couldn't.

"Fine!" I exclaimed. "I love you! I love you more than any person on this earth! I love you, I love you, Kenai!" I punctuated each declaration with the stomp of my foot, as I gulped in air and tears pricked at my eyes. He started to look satisfied with himself, so I quickly insisted, "But I love him too. So much."

He kissed me again.

"Just stop this," I begged. "I am marrying Eliam. Father wishes it, and I will honor my father."

He kissed me again. "You're letting your father decide this for you because you're afraid—afraid that if you make the wrong choice, you will be at fault."

"At fault for what?"

He bent his head toward me and caught my gaze, held it. "At fault for hurting one of us. You're afraid that if you hurt me, I'll stop eating again and you don't want to be responsible for that."

He was right, and it was too big of a burden.

I started to cry in earnest, and he kissed me again.

"No. Stop this," I implored him, but I was kissing him back, and soon I was pounding on his chest, trying to push him away, trying to distance myself, but kissing him feverishly too.

I knew what he was doing. The same thing I had done to him, only in a different way. Why hadn't I realized he would do something like this? Why hadn't I realized he would retaliate, that retreating was not in his nature? Eliam had explained it to me. When Kenai struck, he struck hard and fast. But why was I so powerless to stop it?

Or was I?

I wrenched my lips from his and turned my face away. "Let me go," I demanded.

His chest rose and fell. "I'm not holding you."

I looked down, aghast to see that he was right. I was hitting him and kissing him and held to him only by my own inability to draw away. And this made me angry.

I could strike hard and fast too.

I threw the heel of my hand up and struck him in the nose, and I executed his last instruction to me with precision.

His hand went to his face, and I turned and ran. It only took me a second to see Father and Eliam standing at the edge of the trees watching us. Without thought, I changed my direction and ran into Eliam's arms.

I hadn't realized I was scared that they would not be receptive to me until his strong arms came around me and held me close to him. I could feel his heart beating as I felt him staring at Kenai over my head. I was sobbing, and I couldn't stop. I didn't want to stop. Didn't want to ever stop.

After a few moments where all three men communicated silently, I heard Father step toward the tannery and Eliam said, "Come on, sweetheart. I'll take you home."

CHAPTER 19

Eliam kept me in the protective curve of his arm as he walked me home. When we got there, he passed through the yard and said, "There's a stream behind your house. Take me to it."

He didn't sound angry, just serious.

"Due north," I said and let him lead the way instead.

"Sit down," he said when we got there.

Eliam went to his heels and let out a breath. He got right to the point. "I saw what happened with Kenai."

I cringed. "I guess it's too much to hope we could talk about something else. Which part did you witness?"

"Izz...all of it."

It figured.

"How long were you going to go before you told me? Forever? Because that's how long marriage lasts, Izz."

"You mean about Kenai? You knew he was courting me." I wanted to insert accusation into my tone, but I only achieved defensiveness. "You knew how I felt."

He shook his head. "Not about the captain. I thought I made it clear that I didn't want an arranged marriage. I thought you, of all people, would understand that."

I rolled up onto my knees, clasping my hands in my lap. "But it is not arranged. We know each other. We like each other. Eliam, we love each other."

"If you marry me because your father wants it, then it's arranged, whether the love comes before the documents are signed or not."

"But..." I still felt the confusion on my face. "Why were you arranging it with my father, then?"

"When? Just now at the tannery?"

I nodded.

He smiled for the first time. "We weren't arranging anything. Very much the opposite."

My voice came out in a whisper. "What?"

"Oh, Izz." He took a deliberate hold of my hand, reaching over to hold it where it rested on my own lap. But he didn't say any more.

And I couldn't because of the painful lump in my throat.

I watched the stream flow past us. It wasn't large, but it was steady, and it had always met my family's needs.

I thought of sitting by the larger river at the falls, of removing my sandals, and Kenai's, and putting our feet into it. I thought of its depth, its strength, its beauty.

"I've been wrestling so much with this, and you don't even want me."

"Izz—"

"You told Father no," I said quietly.

"I don't think I *could* tell him no." He paused. "But he didn't offer anything, and I didn't request anything of him. We were speaking of you and the captain."

I sighed in frustration. "Nobody tells me anything. You weren't arranging anything for yourself, only for me."

"I'm telling you now." He squinted into the distance, and I waited for him to go on. "Your father and I both feel—we felt it even before we saw you at the tannery today—that the greater part of your heart is engaged elsewhere."

When I didn't respond he clarified unnecessarily. "With Kenai."

"But..."

He released my hand and his attention shifted to the barbed arrowhead. He lifted it from where it lay against my chest and fingered the edges, testing their sharpness. "I wondered about this," he said with a sardonic huff. He had never shown that side of himself to me before, the side that could be upset, that could let something bother him, the side that could be hurt and accusing.

"Kenai gave it to me."

"And you felt you had to hide it."

"It doesn't mean any..." I didn't bother finishing when I saw the reprimanding look on his face.

"I intend to withdraw from my courtship of you, Isabel. I *have* withdrawn it."

"No! Eliam, no. I don't want you to do that."

He looked at me, dejection in his eyes. "I really think it's for the best to just do it before my heart gets more involved— before yours gets more involved. Because in the end, I know you'll choose him. And I want you to."

"Are you saying you don't love me?"

His eyes dropped to the ground and he plucked a blade of grass. He was slowly shaking his head. "I'm saying I love you enough to let you be happy."

Zeke had told me the same thing about Keturah. I had repeated it to Kenai. How much easier it was to say than to experience for myself.

"I think I understand. But what about in the barley field? Did you not mean that?" I still shivered when I thought of it, and I couldn't hide my embarrassed blush.

"You know I did. But you know I want more than just one

incredible kiss and half your heart. I want my wife's whole heart. Her whole heart, Isabel. And I deserve it. Do you love me enough to let me find happiness, too?"

I bit my lip. "I do Eliam. You're right. You do deserve it, and I can't give it," I admitted. "Not right now."

"If things change for you..." he began, but shook his head. His voice broke—and the sound of it broke my heart—when he said, "Treat the captain well, okay?"

"Eliam," I entreated, but really, there was nothing left to say.

He got to his feet and held out a hand to me. I took it and allowed him to assist me to my feet. He pulled me up, straight into his arms, and held me loosely with my head tucked under his chin. I couldn't think about it all yet. I just held him too, feeling both miserable and relieved. And that made me feel guilty and dishonest.

When we finally turned together to leave the stream, Eliam said, "That was a really great shot to the nose." A smile turned up the corner of his mouth. "But there was one way it could have been better."

"If you'd gotten to do it yourself?"

He smiled. "I hate to admit it, but yeah. Where'd you learn to do that?"

I allowed myself a small smile too. "Kenai taught me."

We both burst into laughter. Our eyes caught and as they held, the laughter faded. He turned me to face him and reached out to smooth my hair away from my face but stopped himself.

"I hope you find what you seek," I said. "I wish I could...I wish things were..." I shook my head. "I wish you well, Eliam."

He bent as if he might kiss me again, but he didn't. He no longer had my father's permission.

"Come on, let's get you home."

234

When we got there, Kenai sat in the yard, looking for all the world like he was waiting for me. I evaded his eyes, walked around him, and avoided him completely.

I glanced up at Eliam. I had trusted him for the past year with my heart. I had trusted him to protect me, to teach me, to lead me, to be careful with me. I would trust him this one last time to deal with this situation.

Because I didn't know how to.

Eliam left me near the side door of my home and strode over to his captain. He stopped in front of him, and Kenai stood.

"Is it broken?" Eliam asked after a moment.

I couldn't stop my eyes from darting to Kenai. His nose was swollen, bloody, and starting to discolor. My hand covered my mouth. But it was covering a small smile I just couldn't help.

Kenai shook his head, and then grimaced.

"You're going to have two black eyes, too," Eliam said. He wasn't even trying to hide his smile. He glanced at me over his shoulder. Then he turned back to Kenai and held out his arm to him—in respect, and honor.

Kenai looked him in the eye and grasped it.

"I love you, brother," Eliam said. "Be happy."

Suddenly, I had the eerie feeling that this whole courtship had been contrived. It started as a mere idea, but as the moments went on, it intensified until I was sure, just sure, Father and Eliam had some kind of arrangement—not for me, but for Kenai.

Was Father using me? Did he intend to offer me to Kenai as some kind of consolation for what he had done by marrying Cana to Micah? Did he intend to assuage his guilt—for I knew he felt it deeply—by...by...*giving* me to Kenai?

And what had he offered Eliam in exchange? To coax him into courting me all this time? To be so convincing?

I shut my eyes against the sheer humiliation of it all, but

235

it didn't go away. It was too much.

Mother had come to stand by me in the doorway, and she watched Eliam and Kenai in the courtyard.

I turned to her. "Where is Father?"

She was surprised at my tone. I wondered if she knew. Father had kept Zeke and Jarom's estrangement a secret from her. Perhaps he had kept this from her too.

"Getting things prepared at Jarom's, I assume. That is where he's supposed to be."

I wouldn't find Father at Jarom's, but I couldn't stay in the courtyard either. Couldn't be near Eliam for one more second. Couldn't look at what I had done to Kenai's face. My mind searched for a place to go.

"I'll be back later," I told Mother.

"Where are you going?"

"To sulk."

"Isabel, what is—?"

I didn't wait for her to finish. I just took off running, and I ran until I was in the trees. I couldn't go to the tannery. That was too obvious. I couldn't go to the stream or to the waterfall in the meadow. And I couldn't, just couldn't, go to Kenai's tree at the maize field.

When I emerged from the trees and entered the pasture, I saw Micah sitting on his hill, high enough that he could watch over his sheep. I almost turned around, but he saw me right away and waved me over.

"Hey, Izz," he said when I neared.

"Hi," I said without even trying to hide the glumness from my voice.

He watched me in silence for a moment. "Come on up."

With a heavy sigh, I climbed to the top of the hill and sat, but I kept my distance from him.

"I'd ask why you're here, but I can see why."

I looked over at him.

"You're running away."

I gave an indelicate snort.

"Want to tell me what's wrong?"

"No. You're one of the last people I want to tell. You're probably in on it." Then I sighed. "I wish Zeke were here."

Micah put down the scroll he'd been reading. "He'll be here soon. But I have a sister, too. Maybe I can help." His words were kind, but cautious, and with a sister like Keturah, I didn't blame him one bit. I couldn't help another small smile.

And then I burst into tears.

I put my head into my hands and the next thing I knew, Micah was sitting next to me and he had placed an arm loosely around me.

I didn't want him there. I wanted to be alone. I had assumed he would be with the others, preparing for the wedding celebration. But perhaps a part of me had known he would be in the field and come in spite of it, or even because of it.

But I couldn't tell him what was wrong now—I was crying too hard, choking on it. Everything was hitting me at once. Father's betrayal. Eliam's farce. It had all been a joke, a scam, from the very first minute Eliam had called, "Hey, wait up." And it had all been for Kenai's benefit. Not one of them had given a thought to my feelings—how it might feel to be given in marriage like some subservient slave.

I wanted to throw up.

"Breathe," Micah was saying. "Settle down. It's not as bad as all that. It can't be." His voice was calm and reassuring, but he didn't know, and even if I told him, he wouldn't understand.

I shook my head wildly. This was so embarrassing. I wanted to cry alone. I wanted him to go away.

But instead of going away, he turned me into him and held me tighter. "Just cry it out then."

So I did, and when I was done, just trying to get my breathing under control, Micah began to talk.

"I have a feeling this has something to do with my brother. I don't know what's been going on between the two of you, but I know your friendship is the best thing that could have happened to him."

He couldn't know that was the worst possible thing he could say at the moment, though I would savor it later. I had to forgive him for being clueless if I wasn't going to tell him what was wrong. I didn't want to forgive him, so I started talking.

The whole thing spilled out in a rush—Kenai following me to the tannery, Father and Eliam making plans for my life, Eliam withdrawing his pretend courtship.

"And how are you so sure it was pretend?" Micah asked.

"When he clasped arms with Kenai, I just knew. I can't explain it."

"You think your father had some kind of agreement with Eliam to do this, to give Kenai a false sense of...victory?"

"Actually," I said as I wiped my eyes with the knuckles of my thumbs. "I think Eliam had the agreement with Father."

"To help Kenai heal?"

I nodded. "And to appease him over..." I averted my eyes from him. "Over Cana."

Micah took in a slow, deep breath and let it out.

"That is quite an accusation to put forth without evidence," he said.

But it was so obvious. "Father wanted to ease his own guilt. Anyone can see what it did to Kenai, and Eliam wanted to help his brother."

"Kenai is not his brother," Micah pointed out.

"That's what he called him when he—" I swallowed hard. "When he handed me over." I could see it in my mind, see them clasping arms again. "And he's closer to Kenai than you have been," I retorted.

"Isabel, don't be cruel. It was an impossible situation."

"Why did you marry her?" I asked. It was a question I had wondered about for a long time.

"Impressions of the Holy Ghost."

I thought of the conversation between Zeke and Gid. Was that enough? Was it a valid reason to take a wife?

"Somehow I doubt the Spirit wanted you to hurt your brother," I said.

"We don't know all the ways of the Lord."

"Do you love Cana?"

He frowned at me. "Isabel."

"I'm trying to understand."

He sighed. "I am the eldest, and so is she. Do you love my brother?"

That was the problem.

I huffed. "I resent him at the moment. Father intends to offer me to him like a sacrificial lamb."

Micah actually chuckled. "Did your father tell you that?"

"No."

"I think you'd better talk to him before you start making accusations like that."

I looked Micah in the eye. I knew mine were red and swollen from crying. "He intends to offer me in exchange for Cana."

His face softened. "No he doesn't, Isabel. If he intends to arrange a betrothal to Kenai, it will be because he thinks you suit each other well."

I shook my head. "He doesn't think we suit each other."

"Well, I know Hemni. And you do not know him if you think he could be so callous with your feelings, so careless with your life, your future, your happiness. Seeing to your future is not a responsibility he takes lightly, and not one he would throw over just to appease Kenai. You are his child, not Kenai, no matter how he loves him. I am sure he truly thought Eliam would be a good choice for you. And perhaps if Kenai had not gotten better, he still would be. I myself had the responsibility to see to Keturah's future, and I felt sure Zeke was the right choice for her."

"He was. You should have heeded your feeling."

"He was until Keturah made up her mind that she wouldn't live without Gid. Then Zeke was no longer a good choice. Look there."

I turned my eyes to where he gestured, but I already knew from the tone of his voice. Kenai had entered the pasture.

"What's wrong with his face?" Micah asked, squinting a little to see into the distance.

"I hit him. I didn't tell you that part."

"Maybe this is a little more complicated than you let on." For some reason, I loved the admonishing in his voice.

"No. It's exactly as humiliating as I represented it."

"Izz," he said with affection. "Take a deep breath. Give everyone a chance to explain. Especially the guy with the broken nose."

My eyes shot to Kenai as he walked toward us. "Do you think it's broken? Can you tell from here? He told Eliam it wasn't."

"He lied. That nose is broken."

I sighed. "Sorry to have bothered you." I got up to leave. "Guess I'll go face him."

"Breathe," he said. "And Izz? I'm your brother now, too. You can come out here and bother me any time."

The invitation was little comfort, but I nodded, made my way down the hill, and started toward Kenai.

"How did you find me here?" I demanded when he was close enough to hear. He had probably checked all the other places before finding me with Micah. There was at least some comfort in that. I felt smug just thinking of it.

"I tracked you. It was easy."

My upper lip curled in a snarl. "I'm mad at you," I said.

He put his hands on his hips. "I'm not exactly pleased with you right now, either."

I didn't doubt it. I could see that his face was swollen and discolored.

"What arrangement have you made with my father?" I was tired of being the last to know everything.

"He has agreed to prepare our betrothal contracts."

I closed my eyes. My feelings about it were so mixed up. "I don't know how to feel about that," I admitted.

"I wish it would make you happy."

I nodded, eyes still closed, and I heard him move closer.

"Do you still love me?" he asked.

I opened my eyes and looked at him. "Of course I do," I said softly. As if I could stop it. As if I could help it.

"Then we will work out the rest."

He attempted to pull me closer to him, but I put a hand on his chest to stop him.

"Let's go see to your nose."

"There's nothing that can be done, trust me."

"Because you've been hit hundreds of times? Come on."

We found his mother in the village, putting the final touches on many of the dishes for the celebration. Leah was as close as a sister to my mother. Jarom was as close as a nephew, even as close as a son to her. She was as involved in the wedding

241

as she would have been for any of her own children.

"Leah," I called. "Kenai and I need your expertise."

"It's fine," Kenai insisted under his breath.

When she looked over to us, she gasped. "What happened?" She dropped what she was doing and hurried toward her son.

"A big bear," Kenai told her.

I elbowed him in the ribs. "He was being obnoxious, so I hit him, Leah. I am sorry to both of you."

She only glanced at me as she fingered Kenai's tender face, but I saw the wisp of a smile.

"Hemni came by a little bit ago," she said casually.

"Something you were expecting?" I asked boldly.

"I'd begun to worry," she admitted.

"So you are pleased then?" I cast a glance at Kenai. I couldn't read his stormy gaze, but he stood still and submitted to his mother's ministrations.

Leah turned away from Kenai. She stepped to me and enfolded me in her arms. "More pleased than I can say." She gave me a quick squeeze. "Now, take this boy down to the river and find some algae to apply to his nose. Kenai knows the kind. Set it over the swollen area and when it dries, replace it."

I looked at Kenai's nose, wondering if that would work.

Leah turned to her son. "Kenai, you keep it on until it's time for the evening meal."

Before we left the yard, she brought us a cloth she had wet in a cold water basin and wrung out.

"At least wash the blood off your face," she said to Kenai, but she handed the cloth to me.

CHAPTER 20

We left the village and walked through the forest along the path that led to the beautiful waterfall. As the sun began to fall in the sky, the late afternoon air cooled, but the brisk walk kept me warm. There were no trees in the meadow to block the warm rays of the sun, and I basked in the feel of it as we walked together toward the river.

"Where do we find the algae?" I asked. "Is it a special kind?"

"I don't know. Look around."

I stepped to the water and peered into it. Sure enough, the rocks below the clear water were covered in green algae. I reached in and scooped some out. It hung wet and stringy from my hand.

Kenai looked at the algae and nodded.

"Um...lay down I guess."

He eyed me for a moment and then dropped to his heels. Slowly, he lay back, stretching his long legs out in front of him. Placing his hands behind his head, he looked up at me.

I knelt next to him and wrung the excess water from the algae. "I really am sorry," I said as I gently placed it over his nose and cheekbones, trying to position it so it would not drip into his eyes.

"Don't be. I'm glad that it came so naturally to you when

you were threatened. I worried you would be too kindhearted to ever do it."

"Thanks," I said sarcastically.

He smiled. "No. Kindhearted is good, too. And you are."

Cana was the kindhearted one. I guessed we were interchangeable. He was getting us confused.

I looked down at him. He looked ridiculous, but the heaviness in my heart kept me from feeling amused. "I'm not my sister," I said quietly.

He frowned. "What?"

I cleared my throat a little. "I'm not Cana," I said more loudly. "I'm never going to be like her, no matter how much you want me to."

He tried to sit up, but I pushed his shoulder back down.

"If you can just realize—"

"What are you talking about, Izz? I know who you are."

I stared dolefully at him. "Nothing," I said. "Just, don't expect me to be like her—that's all."

"I don't." He tried to sit up again, and I gently pushed him back down.

"Just rest," I said. "I probably messed up your brains, too."

A hint of a smile touched his lips. He did as I said and lay back and closed his eyes, which was better because they were bloodshot and it was difficult to look into them. How hard had I hit him?

"Do you want to live in the village?" he asked after a moment.

"Why wouldn't we?"

He shrugged. "I could sell my work more easily in the city. But I can go to the market or contract with Kalem—he's already branched out into skins. Perhaps we'll open our own shop and sell my works of wood and your buckskins."

I took in a sudden breath. "You will let me continue working with the skins?"

He opened his eyes and looked into mine. "A condition of your father's. But I have no problem with it."

I felt tears well up—it had been such an emotional day—and one actually slipped down my face.

Of course Kenai reached up to smooth it away.

"Were you worried about that, Isabel?" he asked tenderly.

"Yes."

"Aw, Izz."

"Father said you were more inclined to want a woman who was skilled at domestic tasks. Like Cana."

He didn't say anything to that. A shadow crossed his eyes. I had no idea what he was thinking. It must have been true, or he would have refuted it.

I reached toward a moonflower that was just beginning to open as the sun fell below the tops of the trees that lined the meadow. I touched its soft, still unopened bloom, but I didn't pluck it from its vine.

"How does it look?" Kenai asked.

I moved a little of the algae with my finger. "I think the swelling is going down."

He raised his eyebrows.

"Surprised? Your mother knows her medicine. I bet it's killing her not to be doing this for you herself."

"I bet it's not," he said. "When I told her I wanted to court you, she was ecstatic."

I thought about that. Thought about dancing the war dance with her that night of Keturah's betrothal. Thought of her putting an arm around Lamech and leading him away from me, of her eyes flicking toward where Kenai sat alone at home.

But hadn't she just wanted him to be well?

"Really, Isabel," Kenai said, drawing my attention back. "Thank you for agreeing to the betrothal."

"Agreeing," I said slowly, considering, rolling the word around. "You didn't even ask me. How could I agree?"

"You determined to submit to the wishes of your father. When he agreed, you did as well. I honored you by asking your father. That is what you wanted, was it not?"

"Yes," I admitted. "But you humiliated me in front of him." I could feel my temper rising, and I tried with everything in me to tamp it down. For this man would be my husband, and I would have to live forever with anything I said to him now.

"Isabel, I didn't know he was there."

"Didn't you?" I challenged.

"No. How could I?"

I took a deep breath. Then another. Could I be completely honest with him? Would he be angry, as I was? "It's just..." No, I couldn't. Like Micah had said, it was just an accusation without proof.

"Just what?"

"Nothing. But doesn't it seem strange to you that Eliam withdrew his courtship when he saw that you l-love me?" I stumbled over the word. Love. Could it even be true?

"That's exactly what I would expect from him. Why? Does it trouble you a great deal?"

It did, but I didn't voice the full reason. Instead I confided, "I've come to love him, Kenai. This morning he was courting me. Now he's not. I'm...unsettled."

"You can let it go now. It's all settled."

"I would be a very fickle person indeed if I could let it go," I said. "If I could let love dwindle to nothing in an instant. Do you want a woman like that, Kenai? One who could look at you with love in one moment, and with indifference in the next?"

246

"No," he admitted.

"I don't want to be that kind of woman."

He stayed quiet for a time, and I went to the river to scrape more healing algae from the slick rocks beneath the surface of the water.

"Isabel, Eliam withdrew his courtship because he saw that you love me. That's what Hemni said. I'm sorry...if you prefer Eliam." He tried to sound sorry, but his words came out clipped and hard.

"I don't," I said firmly.

I knew what it would mean to Kenai if I did. Because of the situation with Micah, it would hurt him more than it might hurt another man. With another man, I might have accepted the apology. Another man might have meant it.

Besides, it was the truth. But I finally understood what Zeke meant when he said that sometimes love wasn't all that mattered, and what he meant when he said that you could love a person but not enough. I was starting to get a better idea about how much was enough.

He let out a relieved breath as I removed the nearly dried algae from his face to replace it.

"Oh!" I said.

"What is it?"

"It looks better already. Substantially."

"I will not be too ugly for our betrothal then?"

I laughed as he intended me to and placed the wet algae over the bridge of his nose. I didn't remove my hand, but let my fingers comb lightly through the wavy hair above his brow.

"I'm still mad at you," I said.

He sighed contentedly. "And I'm still mad at you. You broke my nose."

"You told Eliam it wasn't broken."

"Like I was going to give him the satisfaction."

I grinned. "I bet he knew."

"It would be impossible not to notice," he agreed.

When the position of the sun approached the time for the evening meal, I scraped the algae off Kenai's face. I dipped the cloth Leah had given me into the river and washed all the traces of the remedy away. Kenai continued to lay back and let me. His green eyes watched my face closely. It was calming to sit near the falls and smooth the cloth over his face, and soon my anger and frustration began to fade.

Everyone had gotten what they wanted. Why did it matter how or what other motives had brought it about?

"Are you sure you want to do this?" I asked in a low, quiet voice as I smoothed the cloth over his face.

"Get married?"

"To me."

He reached up and took a hold of my wrist, drew my hand away from his face.

"Can you be so stupid?" he asked, a teasing glint in his eye. "You are young, innocent, obedient, perhaps sweetly naïve. But I never took you for stupid."

My eyes widened.

He smiled—the smile that was all his own, wry and self-deprecating, humorous and confident all at the same time. How I was enamored with that smile.

"You think I'm stupid."

He chuckled and shook his head. "It's me who is stupid, Izz. If I have not shown you my feelings clearly enough, if I have not dispelled your doubts about Cana, if I have not given you as much to hold onto as you have given to me, I am very stupid indeed."

He hesitated as if unsure of my reception, but leaned up

and placed a very soft kiss on my lips, very unlike his kisses earlier that afternoon.

"You deserve better than me. Someone who has not doubted as I have. You deserve a true, honorable stripling warrior. You deserve Eliam." He let that hang in the air, then added, "Yet you marry me," with a note of disbelief, of wonder.

And that right there was the true genius behind Eliam's plan for Kenai.

Or, was it God's plan?

I looked at Kenai with his broken, swollen nose and his purple face, his black eyes. I remembered the broken man he had been. But he would heal from this just as he had healed from that. I saw this strong man who could disappear in the forest, who could and would and did kill his enemies by striking hard and fast, who was tough enough to let me practice hitting him in the nose just so I could get a feel for it. And yet he had lain back willingly, submissively, and allowed me to apply the balm to his wounds.

It was empowering!

And the sudden rush of love that stole through me was overpowering.

"It's time for the evening meal. Everyone will be waiting for us," I said and got hastily to my feet.

Amused, he said, "No one's waiting for us." He didn't move.

"It's my brother's wedding. I'm not going to miss it," I pointed out. "I should be there attending Eve."

"Alright," he agreed. He got up and brushed himself off. "Am I too ugly to steal a kiss from my betrothed?" he asked.

I made a show of looking him over.

"No, but I'm still mad at you, and we are not yet betrothed. Besides, I think you've stolen quite enough kisses for one day."

He ran a hand through his hair. "Perhaps you would consent to kiss my nose better then."

It was so absurd that I laughed. But I reached up, took his head in my hands, brought it down to me, and kissed him on his misshapen nose.

As we began to walk home, hand in hand, I said, "I think Mui will be quite jealous, for she has not been so lucky as to kiss your nose."

"Don't be so sure," he teased.

I scoffed. "Well, I wouldn't put anything past that mean old goat. She *would* kiss my husband before I had a chance to, just to spite me."

Kenai laughed heartily. Everyone knew what a terrible time I had getting milk from that goat. She and Sachemai were the reason Father had taken me to the tannery that first day, after all.

It felt terribly strange to refer to Kenai as my husband. He wasn't, of course, but it was just a matter of a ceremony and signing a few scrolls. If he and Father had agreed, clasped arms over it, then it was done. And I would honor it.

The wedding was very beautiful and the celebration happy. Eve looked radiant. She and Jarom were at ease with each other, so different from the way they had acted that first evening she had walked into the village with Zeke and her family. I remembered how awkward they had been with each other, and it had all been because of a small misunderstanding.

Zeke arrived from Zarahemla with barely minutes to spare before the ceremony began, but he did make it. He stood by Jarom, and I loved to see my brothers getting along.

I loved to see Kenai getting along with Zeke too. Much of what I remembered about Kenai from my youth had been his friendship with Zeke. I had hated to see it diminished when they came home from the war, each one dealing with his own kind of torment.

I watched the happy couple greet all their friends and relatives. Jarom looked older than he was. He looked content—so different from the brooding oversized boy who had come home from the war disillusioned and overburdened with worry for his captain. Eve looked at peace with the surety that a year-long betrothal could give. Jarom had gone often to court her, and I knew they had come to know each other and become great friends over that time. It showed.

"Eve, you look so beautiful!" I said as I hugged her tight. She grinned at me and cast a quick glance toward Jarom who was laughing with some friends from the stripling army.

"Thank you," she said genuinely. "I'm glad we will be living here near you. We will be great friends."

"I know we will be," I agreed.

"Will you and your Kenai live by us?" she asked. But she answered herself. "Oh, but of course you don't know that yet." She put a hand to her mouth and giggled a little.

"I am not even betrothed yet," I said, trying not to blush, probably failing.

"Yes, but...I have a confession." She leaned slightly toward me, her eyes bright and happy. "I overheard your parents talking, and you must know that your father has agreed to betroth you to Kenai."

I looked at the ground, and I did blush then. "Yes, Kenai told me."

I hadn't even had a chance to talk to Father yet. And I wasn't entirely sure what I would say to him. I was still upset with him and Eliam and even Kenai. I had questions for Father, questions that I would probably never ask, for it was my duty to do as he wished without question or complaint.

And I had no complaint about marrying Kenai.

It was strange, but I had determined to marry whoever my father chose for me, and when he had chosen Kenai, my mind began to clear. By the time I had been scraping algae from the river rocks to smear onto Kenai's face, I had known my confusion was not necessary, because the decision was not mine to make. Once it had been made by the proper authority—which I had yielded to—everything had become clear.

When the celebration was drawing to a close, the large bonfire had burned down nearly to embers, the food was cleaned up, and all the young children gone home with their parents to bed, Kenai strode across the clearing to me and took my hand.

"I'll walk you home," he said.

I had bidden Eve and Jarom goodnight an hour before when they left for their new home. I glanced around. There was nothing left to do. "Alright."

"Did you have a nice time?" he asked me as we walked.

"I did. And did you?"

"I didn't stay long. I'm not much for parties, I guess."

"I can understand that."

He looked at me with raised eyebrows. "But you get along so well with others."

I shrugged. I always felt misunderstood with others.

The crickets chirped. An owl hooted in the night. Two laughing children ran past us.

"Kenai," I said. "Did you see Eliam at the celebration?"

"I did."

"Oh," I said with relief. "He and Jarom are good friends, and I thought he might not come—because of me."

"Did you want to see him?"

"To tell the truth, I had hoped not to see him this evening. I just, well, I need some time to think about things."

252

We had come to my gate and Kenai opened it. We went through and stood together in the courtyard.

"Did it hurt you? When he withdrew his courtship?" Kenai asked with no emotion in his voice. He was holding it back.

"A little," I said.

"I'm sorry."

"I understood his reasons."

"What were they—can I ask?"

"Of course you may ask. It is just as you said. He saw that I love you. He desires his wife's whole heart, and I don't blame him. I would expect his whole heart if we married."

"And you would not give it?"

I shook my head. "I *could* not give it. He knew. He saw that I would not stop loving you." I absently put a finger on the barb of the arrowhead, traced its outline.

He didn't say anything.

"I just worry that he has wasted this year courting me."

"Getting to know you is not a waste of time," Kenai said. "Eliam would agree."

The comment pleased me immensely. "You shouldn't compliment me so."

There was humor in his eyes that almost touched his lips. He bent toward me a little. "Who else will compliment you so, if not your betrothed?"

I swallowed. "When will it take place?"

"What is your opinion? When should it take place?"

"My opinion?"

He nodded. "I know you have one."

"As soon as possible, I should think. I've no reservations. Our families are so close, we need not even have all the formal celebrations."

"I think you deserve all the celebrations."

"I am not very interested in them, and you don't care for parties. Why should we waste our time?"

His eyes twinkled. "Would you consider a shortened betrothal then? I know you are still young, but in so many ways you don't seem it."

"Another compliment? I can't tell."

He laughed. "Yes, it is a compliment."

"You will have to build our home large so I will have room for all my dolls to play with, I think."

"Isabel, could you be teasing me?"

I laughed too. "Perhaps."

He stepped close to me and cupped a hand to the side of my neck. "Perhaps," he repeated the word, "we could save your dolls for our daughters."

CHAPTER 21

I helped Kenai harvest the crop of his field and get it ready to plant again. The work was hard, harder than the work at the tannery, but I was glad to have helped him when we stopped to rest in the shade of our tree. As the breeze cooled my neck, Kenai passed me his water skin, and after I drank all the water, he kissed the moisture from my lips.

He gave most of the crop to the Nephite armies, but he retained enough to last us through the year, and Mother and Cana helped me preserve it. Just as he had always traded with my father for leather, he began trading with his brothers for wool, a sign they had all passed into adulthood.

The maize field was a good living, but Kenai's true interest was in woodworking, and in his spare time, he had become unusually good at it. The pieces he made were very striking.

Mother and Father arranged our betrothal ceremony as quickly as possible, but it had become cold before all was said and done. I lived in my home with my parents and my younger sisters. Jarom and Eve lived in their home near Cana and Micah, but Zeke had stopped coming home altogether after Jarom's marriage. He stayed in Zarahemla even during his time off from his work.

Zeke had been helping Gid complete his responsibility to Helaman for over a year and a half, but it was not for Gid's sake.

It was for Keturah. How long would he do this? How long would he stay in love with her? Keturah was special, but I did not think she was worth all the effort my brother put into her happiness. It was not his job to see to her happiness.

I tried not to think about Zeke and what he was doing. It was his business, and it all made me sad. I hoped for him, and I prayed that he would find someone who would make the feelings he had for Keturah dissipate just as mine for Eliam had.

I didn't see Eliam anymore, but Kenai did. They were still good friends, and Kenai said Eliam held no hard feelings for the way things had happened. He wouldn't, I thought, if he had planned for them to happen. Eliam had not intended to court anyone else right away—he was content to wait for the right woman—but one day Kenai told me Eliam had become betrothed to one of the widows in his town.

"One of the widows?" I asked in surprise. "He told me there were three widows that he supplied with venison, but..."

"But he did not tell you all three were young and beautiful?" Kenai laughed at the surprise on my face. "Yes, I can see why he didn't tell you that."

I folded my arms. I didn't know what to say, or even how to feel about it.

"Her name is Sarah, and she has two very young children."

"Children? Really?"

"Yes, and he is fond of them."

"He will be an excellent father. I know he will be. He's patient and faithful, and an excellent teacher."

He had taught me many things.

One day in the early summer when the maize came to my hip, Cana and I walked to the market together. Cana was pleasantly round with Micah's first child, and I knew she eagerly

256

looked forward to delivering the baby. Leah would be there to help her, and when I asked, she insisted she was not even nervous about it.

"Many women do it," she said. "And I trust Leah with everything. She has been a midwife longer than you and I have even been alive. And besides, Izz, that is what I was born for—to give children to my husband."

I frowned but made no comment. There was no point in arguing. This was one of the areas where Cana and I did not exactly agree. I thought women could have other aspirations. But for Cana, all she really wanted in life was to be a mother, to raise children, and to honor her husband. It wasn't that I didn't want those things also or value them equally. I did.

But I wanted more, too.

Was that greedy? Was it selfish? To want something for myself, that was all my own? To work my beautiful hides and feel the pride of producing them, to feel the pride of perfecting a skill that I loved, that was rare, and that God himself had given to me?

I just didn't know.

But I certainly didn't begrudge Cana her beautiful life's work. In just a few weeks' time, she would have her baby in her arms.

We stopped by Kalem's for a visit. Leah helped Cana pack the food she had come for, and I turned to Kalem.

"Do you think the weather will hold?" I asked him.

But before he could answer, Leah said, "We should see many clear days now." She smiled at me, and soon we were saying goodbye. Leah passed me the market basket full of Cana's goods.

"Do you have a few moments to look at tools?" I asked Cana as I slipped her basket over my elbow and we moved into the crowd.

"Do you need new tools?" she asked as we walked to a

shop that sold sturdy, serviceable tools for skinning and working hides.

"The flint on my dry scraper needs to be replaced." I sighed. "But no, I don't. Not really. My tools work fine."

"But you would like new tools?" she asked with a small smile.

I shrugged.

Of course I would like new tools, but I was immensely grateful for the ones I had. I took great care of them and cherished them both as a gift from my father and for the hours of joy they brought me.

I purchased a piece of flint, formed and sharpened, to replace the dull one in my scraper. I could find the materials in the forest, but I was not a tool maker—my interest lay in using the tools, not making them.

"Muloki or Kalem could help you with that," Cana suggested. Kalem had been a great weapon maker in the Land of Nephi. He had put his skills to good use for Helaman's army, making weapons for the striplings and maintaining those of the Nephite soldiers. Muloki had apprenticed with him and was also very skilled in the art.

"I think Kenai can manage to replace the flint," I said. "Besides, I like to ask him to do things for me. It is a way he shows his love. I like to give him the opportunity."

She put her arm around my waist. "You are so intuitive," she said. "No wonder God hand-picked you to help Kenai through his ordeal."

This was perhaps the dearest compliment of my life.

Cana's large belly was pressed into my side and I felt the baby kick me. "Oh!" I said. "I don't think he likes me."

She laughed. "I think he is insisting you quickly get him a cousin."

I blushed fiercely. "I am not even married yet. You must tell him it is an impossibility."

Giggling, she began to weave through the marketplace, past the gates of the city, into the trees, and toward the village.

We were supposed to stay together. Kenai and Jarom and Father still felt it was not safe for a woman to be alone in the forest, specifically me, but no one had seen Zareth around Melek in many months, indeed not since he had followed me home from the market the previous fall. So I told Cana I would come by her home the next day to help her with the wash—she was having trouble bending over far enough—and I slipped away along the path that led toward the maize fields.

Kenai was working on our house in the village. Father, Kalem, Jarom, and even Eliam were helping him build it, along with other men from the village and many of the striplings who showed up to help build their captain's home. But though all the men came to see him and help him, he always stole away from the group at midday and ate his meal with me under our tree.

I was eager to get there, to see Kenai, to let him steal a kiss from me. I loved to see him eat, especially food that I had prepared. And he outlandishly over-praised everything I made. Eliam had been right. It was not a hardship to cook for a man I loved. That was one of the ways I could show my love.

As I walked through the green forest, almost skipping, I felt a very sudden foreboding feeling, and my steps faltered until I could not move forward. I needed to run back to Cana. It was a feeling I could not deny, and I turned and ran as fast as I could. I didn't know why. All I knew was that I would not be in time.

I heard her before I got to the main path. It wasn't a scream. It was much scarier than a scream—a grunt that was followed by moans of pain.

I veered off the path and cut a direct line through the

forest in the direction she had been traveling. Alone. Oh, why had
I left her all alone?

I saw her on the ground and a man was standing over her
with his foot raised to kick her in the abdomen, probably again.

Zareth.

I went berserk, just as I had during the Lamanite
abduction. But before I could jump on his back and start
scratching, biting, and kicking him, I felt a presence I instantly
recognized as the Holy Ghost. It bid me to be calm.

I called out, startling Zareth enough that he put his foot
down. He turned his head to look at me.

I fingered the sharpened flint I had just purchased. It
would not be long enough to reach to his heart.

Kenai had told me not to kill unless my life was in danger.
But I didn't even have to look at Cana—I could hear her
moaning—to know that her life and the life of her baby were both
in danger.

"Turn and look at me," I commanded the evil man who
stood over my sister. I tried to make my voice sound strong and
without fear, but it felt shaky.

He sneered, but he turned.

"You are Zareth," I said.

I did not want to kill a human being. But I would. The
Spirit had directed me to be here, and I knew I would do whatever
it desired of me. Hadn't I always done what Father desired of me?

"You are this harlot's sister," he retorted.

I controlled my reaction to his disgusting accusation, but
inside I was quaking. I wanted to look at Cana, wanted to run to
her and get her to safety, but I couldn't take my eyes off the snake
in front of me. He would surely strike if I did.

I took a step backward.

He stepped toward me.

Good.

I took another step and so did he.

"You're just a little girl," he said softly. He almost sounded normal, like a normal, rational human being. "Why don't you run along? Your sister gave herself to another man and she must pay the price. But you needn't be here to see it." He gave his head a nod to the side, beckoning me to go. "Go on."

Oh yes. I would kill him.

I stepped toward him quickly and only registered that his eyebrows went up before I applied Kenai's four-count drop to him with hard, fast, precise movements. By the time I counted four, I had him to the ground and my sharpened flint was at his throat.

I really should have found a more accessible place for my knife, I thought a little ridiculously.

He was shocked for a moment, but then he looked with malice-filled eyes into mine. We both knew he could easily throw me off of him, and when he did, I would be on the ground and he would be up kicking me too before I could scramble away.

I pressed my blade deeper into his skin. I felt his blood as it slowly trickled over my fingers.

"You can't do it," he said smugly. "You're nothing but a gutless Ammonite. You don't have the courage."

"But I do."

Kenai.

"Isabel, back away please."

He was panting. He had been running. Had he felt the same impression I had?

I did as he instructed quickly so I was out of Zareth's reach, and I barely spared either man a glance before I scrambled to my sister. I registered Micah running up the path. I could hear Kenai giving commands to Zareth behind me.

261

"Get up. Now."

Cana looked at me with frightened eyes.

"Don't watch," I told her. "Look here. Just at me."

I could hear Kenai and Zareth fighting behind me. I could hear the sound of scuffling in the dirt, of their fists landing on each other, grunts, insults.

I held Cana's face in my hands. "Right here at me," I repeated. I held her gaze. I didn't need to look down. I'd seen already the blood on her skirts.

"I've got her, Izz," Micah said. He eased me away from her and gently took his wife into his arms. "Run to my mother," he told me. "Tell her what has happened."

"She's in the market."

"Tell her I will take Cana to her home. She'll have her remedies and tools there."

I swallowed hard, but nodded—not that he took his eyes from Cana to see it—got up, and turned to go. I watched for a moment as Kenai pummeled Zareth with his fists. I thought of that long ago day when Kenai had first come home from the war, of Kalem commanding Kenai to control himself. It had been almost two years since he had thrown that punch at Muloki. I thought of Kenai instantly obeying, even in mid-swing. He had done it, but he hadn't been in control of himself.

He was in complete control of himself now.

And I wouldn't have dreamed of telling him to stand down.

I ran as fast as I could to the market. I annoyed people as I pushed them aside in my rush to get to Leah. I saw her sitting at the shop with Melia. Muloki was standing near them, teasing them both and making them both blush in laughter.

"Leah!" I called.

All their merriment fell away instantly when they saw me.

"It's Cana," I panted out. "She's been attacked. The baby."

"Attacked?" Melia exclaimed, but Leah was up and moving toward me quickly.

I looked to Muloki. "Kenai could use some help with her attacker. If he doesn't kill him. I think he might. They're on the path to the village."

A look passed between Muloki and Melia. She nodded, and he took off ahead of us, running much faster than we could.

"Micah is taking her to your house," I said to Leah as we pushed our way out of the market.

"Good. How bad is it? What happened?"

"I think he kicked her in the stomach. There was blood."

"How much?"

"I don't know. I was busy with Zareth."

I thought she might ask more questions, but she didn't, just put her effort into running home.

We approached the men on the path. Kenai looked as bloody as Cana, but he was alive and so was Zareth. Kenai stood back catching his breath while Muloki tied Zareth's elbows behind his back. It did not look comfortable. I heard Zareth cry out, but I did not feel bad for him.

"You go on ahead," I called to Leah. "I need to rest."

She gave a quick nod in response, acknowledging that she heard me, and hurried toward home. I wouldn't be any help to her at home. Mother would be there by now and any number of women from the village. Micah would have sent the village men to help Kenai, and they would likely be here in moments. They would take Zareth to the magistrate. I couldn't help at home, but there was one more thing I could do here.

I hadn't had a long enough knife in my hand to reach Zareth's heart. And he'd been right—I hadn't had the guts to slit his throat. But I had successfully lured him away from my sister, employed Kenai's drop, taken Zareth to the ground. There was just one skill remaining that Kenai had taught me to use in the case of an attack, and though I hadn't had any practice at it, I managed to do it quite well.

I noticed Kenai and Muloki exchange a glance, identical winces, satisfied smiles, as Zareth fell to the ground and moaned.

I didn't feel smug. I didn't feel better. But in a small way, I did feel justice.

Men from the village came, and Muloki went with them to the magistrates. He would explain it all. They would want to see Kenai later, but for the time being, I took him to my home and cleaned his wounds. I applied healing balms, to which he succumbed without complaint.

Mother was at Leah's, Sarai and Chloe darting about fetching things for them. Kenai and I had the house to ourselves.

"Your nose is broken again," I said as I wiped the blood away from it.

His knuckles and hands were red and swelling. His lip was cut and bleeding. Bruises were starting to form on his face and arms, probably his chest and ribs as well, though I wouldn't check there unless he said he was cut.

When I had his wounds cleaned, Leah's salve applied, and he was bandaged everywhere that needed a bandage, I said, "Wait here. I'll go get some algae from the stream."

He nodded and sat quietly as I ducked out the door.

I saw Micah pacing Leah's yard, Darius pacing right along with him, so I ventured that way first.

"What is happening? Is she going to be okay?"

Micah only cast me a glance, so Darius spoke up. "They have to deliver the baby, but it might not be born alive. Cana has lost a lot of blood."

I heard Cana cry out from inside the hut. Micah paled and bolted for the door, but Darius beat him to it and held him at bay.

"There's nothing you can do. You'll only be in the way," Darius said calmly. Micah pushed him off but went back to pacing.

"Have you administered a blessing?" I asked.

Darius nodded. "How is Kenai?"

"Cut and bruised."

"You can attend to him?"

I nodded, then turned and hurried toward the stream.

"How is she?" Kenai asked immediately when I returned to the house. He was still sitting in the same position, lightly rubbing a hand over his sore knuckles.

"They're delivering the baby. They still don't know if either one will—" My voice broke. I couldn't finish. It was too terrible, too unthinkable to say.

Kenai got to his feet and took me into his arms. He tried to comfort me, but I was stiff and couldn't relax into him.

"She'll be alright," he said. "She's tough."

"No she's not. She sweet, and delicate, and trusting, and you still love her!"

I burst into tears before I could get out the door.

CHAPTER 22

I ran toward the falls. I heard Kenai behind me, but he didn't catch up—though he easily could have—until I got there, until I slowed and walked through the meadow. There was no place I could go he couldn't find me. I had long ago accepted that, and usually it gave me comfort.

I walked to the river and stood on the bank looking into it. He stayed a few paces behind me, and I just knew he had his hands on his hips.

He spoke quietly. "What did you mean back there?"

I shook my head.

"Tell me!"

I jumped. I'd never heard him raise his voice to anyone, least of all to me.

He took a deep breath, but his voice was still harsh. "I'm tired of you accusing me of this. I'm tired of you thinking of me as a liar. I'm not a liar, Isabel. It's insulting, and you're better than that."

I turned my head slightly, listening to him.

"What kind of proof do you want that I don't love her? What can I do that would make you believe it? Should I not care if she is back there dying? Because I can't do that. I do care. She is your sister and my sister-in-law, and I care about her because you do, because Micah does. Because she is my friend."

"You broke your nose for her," I forced out in a squeaky whisper. "You nearly killed that man for her."

He didn't speak until he had come up behind me and placed his hands on my shoulders. "You really are stupid," he said.

I swung to look at him. "What?"

"I just have to face it—I'm marrying a stupid woman. Your father pulled a fast one on me, and—"

"What?" He couldn't just call me stupid! My hand came up to slap his face, but he caught it by the wrist and before I knew what he was doing, I was on my back on the bank of the river staring up into his face.

"Listen to me," he said in a low voice that rumbled from his chest, which I could feel on mine. "I have loved you since the night you were kidnapped, from the moment I dropped you to the ground, just like this, and took your knife from you. I knew it then. I know it now."

I remembered the moment. I would never forget it.

"But," I whispered, feeling so foolish but still so unsure. "You fought so fiercely for her."

He slowly shook his head, holding my gaze. "I was working on the frame of the door of our home—*ours*, Isabel—when I felt the strongest prompting to run toward the market to find you. I knew you were in danger. I knew I had to get there. I dropped my tools and ran for you. I didn't know Cana was with you. I wasn't thinking of her for one second in my panic to reach you. Not one second."

I studied his face. So bruised, so ugly. I thought of how he had shunned the Spirit for so long, and yet today he had felt it and obeyed its promptings, saved my life.

Just as I had once followed the promptings and saved his.

"When I saw that man turn to face you," he continued, "I

knew I couldn't get to you in time. I don't know what I would have done."

I'd have killed him, his eyes said. *I'd have torn him apart piece by piece.*

"I saw you take him to the ground. I was so proud. You gave me time to get there, to get to you."

I felt tears slip from the corners of my eyes. "Is that true, Kenai?" But I knew it was.

"What does your heart tell you?"

"I can hardly trust my heart."

"Then trust mine."

I ran my fingers slowly up both sides of his ribcage counting each rib as I went in a whisper so soft it was little more than the movement of my lips. If he asked, I would say I was checking for broken ones. But he didn't, so I just let my fingers rest over the narrow area that covered his heart.

"You've left your heart vulnerable," I said.

He didn't reply, just kissed me.

And as he did, I knew in my heart, just knew, he was telling the truth. He loved me. For some crazy reason, he loved me.

His kiss was soft and awkward because his nose was broken. His lips were salty with sweat and blood. But it was the most wonderful kiss.

After a time, I said, "I feel guilty being so happy, kissing here in the meadow, while Cana suffers."

He nodded and pulled away, shifting back onto his heels so I could sit up. I did, but I moved to the stream and found the algae that would take his swelling down.

"Lean back," I said.

"It hardly seems important," he said. "With Cana and the baby in such real danger. This is just a scrape."

I knew what he meant. "Still," I said.

And so he lay back and let me take care of him again.

We were quietly talking, waiting for the algae to work, when Darius came into the meadow. His face was still shadowed with worry, but fortunately not with grief.

"The baby is small but okay," he said instead of a greeting. "Cana is...well, she lost a lot of blood."

A look passed between the brothers. I remembered how Zeke had lost much blood during the battle for Cumeni, and he had made it. Cana would too. I had to believe that.

Kenai squinted up at Dare. "Was Mother able to stop the bleeding?"

They were both well-acquainted with wounds and blood and healing. I was sure they had both seen more terrible, ghastly wounds than they could describe to me in a hundred years—not that I would want them to. Besides this, their mother had been a midwife for their entire lives. They were bound to have heard many things, and both likely knew more about childbearing than I did.

Darius nodded. "Yes. She's asleep now. Dinah is caring for the baby and Mother won't leave Cana's side. You know how she is with a patient."

"How is Micah?" Kenai asked.

Darius sighed deeply. "You can't even imagine."

Kenai looked at me. "I think I can."

Back away please, Isabel. How calm he had sounded! How in control! But he had been crazy with worry.

Darius looked around the meadow, stretched, and looked down at Kenai, still lying back with the algae on his face.

"You look ridiculous," he said.

"Izz, get the algae off so Dare can straighten my nose."

I looked between them.

"He's done it before. Many times. But if you have any extra cloths in your satchel, you might get one wet and cold. It will start to bleed again."

I knew I paled, but I reached into my satchel and retrieved another cloth. I turned to the river and cringed when I heard Darius move toward Kenai. I heard Kenai's intake of breath, his good-natured grunt of pain.

"You can turn around now," Darius teased me.

I realized I had been standing still as a stone.

"I didn't hurt him." He laughed. "Much."

Kenai grunted his disagreement, but he came up behind me and took the cloth from my hand, kneeling to wet it in the river himself.

"It's better than the alternative," Darius went on.

I turned to look at him, a brow raised in question.

"An ugly bridegroom."

I couldn't help a small smile.

Cana slept for three days while we all worried. Mother took the baby, a beautiful tiny boy, to Cana many times a day so he could nurse while she slept. I worried that it would take too much of Cana's strength from her, but Leah insisted it would only help.

Micah hardly left her side, and I started bringing his food to him. It took him two days to notice it did not taste good.

"Izz," he said as he gagged it down. "Really?"

"Kenai likes it," I protested.

He actually laughed, and that was when Cana opened her eyes for the first time.

I quickly left him alone with his wife and went to tell Leah she was awake. But she didn't stay awake very long that first time.

"Cana ordered me to thank you a thousand times," Micah said after she had fallen back to sleep. He hugged me and kissed

271

me on the top of my head. "Thank you, Isabel," he said. "Thank you for being there, for what you did."

"Kenai makes it sound braver than it was," I said. "Every time he tells the story, I think he embellishes it a little more."

"The Spirit can make us brave," he said.

"As a soldier, you would know," I replied.

He shook his head. "The Spirit helps all men and women. All who are worthy of his help."

Cana was going to make it. The baby was fine. Zareth was in prison. Everything was going to be okay.

The following week, my father would hand me over to Kenai like a little lamb to the slaughter, and I had never been happier about anything in my life.

Until I saw Zeke walk into the village a week early escorting a beautiful, really beautiful, brown-haired girl who was trying to keep a scowl on her face.

Kenai was walking me home from the tannery, where he had spent all day building a woodshop on the corner of the property where he would work in the days while I worked my hides. It had been Father's idea.

"Because I want you to be happy," he had said.

I had long since given up my anger over, and even the idea of Father offering me to Kenai in exchange for my sister. Micah had been right. It was absurd.

In the past six months—Kenai had truly arranged a short betrothal—Micah had spent extra time and care reassuring me. I had hardly known him before, but he became my friend, my older brother, and I loved him for his mentoring and advice.

But my true older brother was home for my wedding, home for the first time in six months, since my betrothal, and he was walking toward me on the main road of the village.

"Zeke!" I exclaimed and ran to him.

I hugged him, even with all his gear on, though it was awkward, and I started telling him everything there was to tell.

"Whoa," he said sternly. "How is Cana?"

"She's well. The baby is well too. Oh, you have to see him! He is beautiful! They have named him Naham."

His relief showed as the concern melted from his face.

I remembered the girl then and turned to her. "Forgive me. I've been so rude. I am Isabel." I placed a hand on her shoulder.

She did the same and looked between Zeke and me. "I can see that you are Ezekiel's sister." She smiled, and I thought it was perhaps the most beautiful smile I had ever seen. "You look so much alike."

I grinned. "Yes, my betrothed thinks Zeke is very pretty."

She laughed. "He is right."

"And you are Eliza," I ventured. How embarrassing if she wasn't. But she had to be.

She stole a look at Zeke, her eyes wide.

That's right, I thought, *he's been talking about you.*

Zeke actually blushed to the roots of his dark hair. I raised an eyebrow at him with a little challenge in it. There was no way he had brought this girl to his village and had no feelings for her.

But Kenai approached then. I introduced him, and soon Zeke and Eliza were lost in the crowd of people who had come to greet them.

Kenai tugged me by the hand toward the maize field. The corn stalks came to my waist, and I skimmed my hand over the tops as we passed along the rows. Soon it would be time to harvest again. Then the land would lie dormant until it was time to plant once more. And we would. There would be new starts, there would be food for us, and there would be food we could share with others who hungered.

When we were standing under our tree, where I had brought the fruit and Kenai had eaten of it, he turned me toward him with the slight pressure of his hand. The breeze ruffled the leaves in the trees above us, all around us. A lock of hair blew across my face and Kenai tucked it back with one finger.

"Your hair is soft like the silk of the maize," he said.

"Is that a compliment?"

He shrugged but didn't hide a small smile.

"I'm glad Zeke is home," I said.

"He will be home for good soon, and with a wife."

"That's what I think too. Did you see the way Eliza looked at him?"

"Nah. Too busy noticing the way he looked at her. It was the way I looked at you—that night, with the Lamanites. When I had you pressed to the ground like an enemy."

"Bewildered?"

He laughed. "Panicked."

"Well, they will never be as happy as us," I said softly.

"Impossible," he agreed. He paused for a moment. "Isabel, I have a gift for you."

He reached into his satchel and withdrew a roll of father's leather that was tied closed with a length of rawhide. I took it from his hands. It was heavy, and I already knew what it was.

"Open it," he said when I hesitated.

I glanced up at his face, watching me with veiled anticipation.

When I untied the rawhide, the bundle unrolled. Inside, I found a set of tools. Each tool was in its own pocket, sewn neatly into the leather. I slid a scraper from its pocket to reveal its exquisitely carved handle.

My hand shook a little as I slipped the scraper back under the leather.

274

"Don't you like them?" Kenai asked. I could hear a smile in his voice.

I looked up at him. "I like them very much, Kenai." I cleared the emotion from my throat. "I have something for you, too." I slipped my hand inside my own satchel and pulled out my gift to him.

His fingers brushed mine when he reached for the apple I held. He didn't take it from me, but held it between us. We both looked down at it, considering it, remembering all it had meant to us.

I remembered walking down into the maize field that first day, Kenai gesturing to the tree, pulling my apple closer to myself, subtly goading him into taking it.

I remembered the sound of him biting into it.

I thought of all that it had started, that bite—Kenai beginning to eat again, accepting food, just a little at a time. I thought of him accepting the Spirit into his heart again to teach him—line upon line. To lead him—precept upon precept. To feed him.

Until at last he could truly feast upon the bread of life.

Finally, he took the apple in his hand, and he took me in his arms. But instead of kissing me, he bit into the apple with a grin. Its juice dripped down his chin, and instead of wiping it away with the brush of a finger, I kissed it away.

Our own wedding was more beautiful than any of the weddings I had been to, though my husband was ugly. But I thought of the Spirit that had guided him to me that day on the path with Zareth, I thought of how he had trained and was prepared to protect me from harm, and he was the most handsome man on earth to me. His bruising would fade, and when it did, I didn't see how anyone would be able to disagree with me.

At last, when the celebration was over, Kenai and I walked hand in hand to our new home. He opened our own gate for me, and we stood in our own courtyard.

But before he could take me beyond the door, I dropped him to the ground in four swift movements.

He looked up into my eyes, and his were filled with laughter and hope. "You love me, little girl," he said. "Admit it."

"I do," I replied. "And you love me."

PLEASE ENJOY THE FIRST CHAPTER OF

THE CAPTAIN'S GUARD
A STRIPLING WARRIOR NOVEL

Chapter 1

I had seen the guard on my uncle's estate before, but usually from a distance. If possible, he was even more handsome up close, but I disregarded that and said, "The garden is not big enough for you? Get out of my way."

I could see he was torn between his impeccably good manners, which I had noticed on previous occasions, and doing something childish like pulling my hair or dropping a snake down my sarong. But his mother would have been so proud—he opted for manners.

"Excuse me," he said and stepped to the side with the clipped movements of the soldier he was, but he couldn't push aside the irritation in his sharp, cocoa-colored eyes.

After we had passed each other, I turned to watch him continue along the garden path alone. Strong shoulders, assessing eyes, long strides—he was hardly out for a pleasurable stroll through the gardens. Most probably he was doing a security check of the grounds, I thought. But then I noticed he held a missive in his hand, and I figured he was headed to the stream to read it in private.

I thought of the irritation in his eyes.

Well, I consoled myself, irritation was better than the complete indifference he had shown me yesterday and the outright ignoring me of the day before. All things considered, I thought irritation was a promising sign.

I paused next to a hedge that intersected a tall rock wall. When I saw the guard slow uncertainly, turn his face a little, and then stop and turn all the way around to catch me watching him, I quickly ducked behind the wall.

So he was not indifferent to me after all.

My face heated, but I smiled.

I had been watching him for a while. I didn't know his name, but I knew he was lonely too.

He never looked at me if he could help it, and when he did, he avoided my eyes. So lately I had been trying to get his attention.

When the guard walked with Uncle in the hallways, I would stride up and ask Uncle for something outrageous from the market—a jade and copper necklace, a little pot filled with expensive perfume, bags of cocoa, new sarongs, belts, scarves, head-dressings, bangles—anything to make the guard notice I existed. Uncle always looked at me with kind eyes and said I could have whatever it was I wanted.

When the guard was standing watch at the estate gates, I would glide past him without a look, but not before I had dropped whatever I was carrying and waited for him to pick it up and return it to me with his cool, polite manner.

And just now, I had accosted him in the beautiful gardens that bordered the estate.

I hurried away and took the flowers I had gathered from the gardens into the house.

I loved living here on the estate with my Uncle Helaman and my cousins and their families. I especially loved to play with their little children. It was so different from living in my small home in Noah.

Though I had once loved that too.

But my cousins were all much older than me, their life situations very different, so I often felt lonely for someone to talk to.

Even speaking so rudely to the guard had been a kind of relief—just to talk to someone.

I felt pathetic as I thought about the encounter, as I removed the old flowers from the vases in the long hall and replaced them with the fresh ones—pink today. The seasons were changing and these would be some of the last—maybe another few weeks of blooms—but they were certainly some of the prettiest, I thought as I stroked a silken petal.

I made my way to the end of the hall where Uncle's office was located, where he conducted his church business and coordinated with the men of the government and military.

In truth, I didn't even know all the great and important things he did. I only knew he was busy, much too busy to overly concern himself with entertaining a poor, orphaned niece.

I placed the last of the flowers in the large vase outside Uncle's office. Then I swept my hair with its large, outrageous curls over my shoulder and held it back as I bent down to smell them.

Hurried footfalls sounded behind me, coming quickly down the hall, and I straightened as the guard from the garden swept past me through the door of the office, hardly sparing me a glance, though he must have seen me or else he would have run me down.

It wasn't good of me, but I lingered near the door to listen.

"Ezekiel," Helaman greeted cheerily.

"Captain," he responded.

"You're troubled. What is it, son?"

"I've just had a letter from home. It's Cana...and the baby.

They've...had an accident. I'd like to request leave to go early. I was planning to go home for the wedding next week anyway. I'd like to leave sooner than planned so I can be there with my family in case..."

His name was Ezekiel. And he had a family—a wife, a baby.

"Of course, of course you must!" Uncle said with great compassion in his voice. "I'll summon Aaron to come early to replace you. And you know he can stay as long as needed. You must stay in Melek as long as necessary." He paused. "In fact, I wonder if you might do me a favor that would detain you even longer."

"Of course, Sir, it would be my honor to do so."

"Excellent. Eliza needs to visit her family too."

No I didn't.

"I would like you to escort her to Noah."

"Captain?"

"Melek is on the way. You can stop there first. Complete your business, and then escort her on."

"But, Captain..."

"Hmm?"

"You wish us to travel...alone?"

Uncle Helaman chuckled. "That won't be a problem for you, will it Ezekiel?"

"No, Sir," came the firm answer.

"Good. If you could, would you find her now and escort her to me here?"

"Of course, Sir."

"But before you go, there is something I have been meaning to bring up with you, Ezekiel. I would like you to consider..."

But I didn't hear any more. I skittered down to the end of

the hallway and pretended to arrange some flowers until I sensed Ezekiel behind me. I hadn't even heard his footfalls. But I heard him breathing.

"Eliza?"

I stilled.

"Your uncle wishes to see you in his office."

"Uncle?" I said with too much surprise as I whirled to face him. He could surely see right through it. I swallowed. "Alright."

When I chanced a quick glance up at his face, he was looking at···my neck? My shoulder? Certainly not at my face. And he was clenching his jaw.

Was I that distasteful to look at? Usually men liked to look at me.

His wife must have been very beautiful indeed if I paled in comparison.

I raised my chin. "What does he want?"

"I don't know."

I glowered at him. Of course he knew. We both did.

"Or rather..." He cleared his throat. "It is not for me to say."

So he had a hard time lying. A slight flush crept up his neck. I looked more closely at him and noticed that his doleful brown eyes were looking back at...the bridge of my nose? My cheek?

I sighed and turned on my heel to flounce down the hall.

He followed me and stood at the front of the large table where Uncle Helaman sat reading scrolls. I passed the table and stood beside my uncle.

He looked up from his work. "Good afternoon, Eliza," he said with a warm smile.

"A beautiful one," I agreed.

He looked back down at his desk and moved some scrolls

around. "Eliza," he began. "I want you to prepare for a journey."

"A journey? You wish me to leave, Uncle?"

"No, no. Nothing like that. I think only that it is time you visited your sister."

I said nothing. I didn't think Helaman truly understood, but he did know how things were between my sister and me. Visiting her would not be pleasant.

Definitely not worth the journey.

I turned and walked to the window which looked out over the city. Go to Noah. But why? I looked back to the two men. Ezekiel's eyes flicked to me, caught for a bare moment, then flicked back to a spot on the wall above Helaman's head.

"Ezekiel will escort you. You'll be making a stop at his home for his sister's wedding. Please be ready to leave at dawn."

And that was that. That was how much power my uncle had over my life. It seemed abrupt, even harsh—though his manner was kind—but Helaman had to act with abruptness. He had so many important things to do and to divide his attention between. Transferring the responsibility for me to one of his most trusted guards, even for this small time, would likely be a relief to him.

Uncle turned back to Ezekiel. "You are dismissed to make your preparations."

Ezekiel cast me another sidelong glance, turned on his heel, and left the office without another word.

Uncle turned to me. He held out an arm, and I immediately went to him and knelt near his chair.

"Do I really have to go?" I asked him. "You know how Nelia is. She will not welcome me, as you have."

Helaman placed a hand on my head and smoothed it down my hair. But as soon as he removed his hand, the large curls sprung back up, and he chuckled.

"Just like your mother's curls," he said, sadness showing in his eyes. He cleared his throat. "It is wisdom that you go, my dear. A wise purpose of the Lord."

I looked at him skeptically. But I agreed, sighed, and got up to leave.

"Be kind to Ezekiel," Helaman said as I moved around the table.

"But that, Uncle, would not be any fun."

"Nevertheless, he's just received some bad news. He needs your kindness, not your clever insults."

"I am always kind," I said, inserting an extra note of innocence into my tone.

He sighed. "You are too much alone here."

"I find plenty to do," I insisted, hoping he would not send me away for good, because the only other place to go was to Noah with Nelia and her bitter family.

"There is not any work here to occupy you. My cook and my servants keep everything done."

"I read. And I sew. I visit the women of the church, watch their children for them while they go to the market."

"Well," he said. "It is time you got married and had children of your own."

It was much past time.

We had never much discussed my marriage except once when I had first moved here he had informed me he would see to it. But I had been here over a year, and he never had.

"Perhaps," I hedged.

"You do not want to marry?"

I shrugged. "That's not it, exactly." I couldn't stop my eyes from going to the door.

The man I wanted to marry was apparently already married.

He grunted, stood up. "I have to go into the city. We will discuss your marriage when you return from Noah." He came to me, kissed me on the top of my head, and gave me a quick hug.

"Do you have someone in mind?" I asked, surprised, for that is what his tone implied.

"I think of nothing else," he said, not really answering the question.

I laughed, though the thought unnerved me, because he had a thousand other things to think about. If this was on top of his list, it would be done directly.

"Will you see me off in the morning?" I asked.

He shook his head, but said, "I will try. I've got to be at the government building very early on the morrow."

"It's alright," I told him. "Don't trouble yourself. I will just kiss you now." I did, and I left.

I was melancholy as I prepared my things for the journey, laying flat each sarong, smoothing the wrinkles out, and rolling it very tightly to fit into my large travel pack. I looked wistfully out into the garden. I was bored. I was dying to get out of the busy city. I was lonely. A journey would be, well, at least something different.

But after some deluding myself, I admitted the lonely guard was the cause of my melancholy. He was married. I hadn't realized I had put so much hope into the idea of coming to know him, of being friends, of pushing our loneliness away together. It was a disappointment.

But the dawn was beautiful.

I stood in the large courtyard of Uncle's estate and watched dawn rise with its wisps of pink shooting through the sky. No one was about—no laughing children, no patrolling guards. It was as if dawn were rising only for me.

"Nice day for a siege," said a voice behind me.

I jumped in surprise and whirled. "What?"

Ezekiel shook his head. His eyes were sad, as if he were remembering something.

"Nothing," he said quietly. Then his demeanor changed and he clipped out, "Are you ready? I want to leave immediately."

Confused at his sudden change in temper, I snipped, "I wouldn't be standing here if I wasn't."

He openly scoffed and looked down to my belongings at my feet. He was so rude.

"At least you're packed appropriately."

"That sounds like an insult hidden in a compliment," I said.

I caught the fleeting smile on his lips before he turned his head from me. He gazed at the gate.

"Well, gear up," he said.

I stared at him for a moment, then looked down at the huge pack which included provisions, food, and my bedroll and tent.

"I can't get that on myself," I protested.

He sighed heavily, reached down and with one strong arm hoisted it up. "Turn," he commanded.

I did, and he helped me get the pack strapped onto my back. I swayed a little under its weight.

I heard him sigh deliberately and then felt him rifling through my belongings. I whirled, almost losing my balance.

"What are you doing? You're going to steal from me right under my nose?"

He gripped my arms to steady me. "I'm not stealing from you. What I thought was appropriate appears to be over-prepared. Your pack is too heavy. You have to leave something."

"No. I need it all."

"You don't need the food. We can eat from the forest."

"I'm not going to depend on you for my food. You'd probably starve me."

He glared at me, but he had the hint of a smile in his eye, as if he were considering the prospect of starving me.

"You don't need the tent, either," he added.

"Yes I do."

"No you don't."

I returned his glare. "I suppose you think I'm going to sleep under the stars with you?"

I guess he hadn't thought of it that way because he colored and let it go.

"Don't say I didn't warn you," he said.

"I won't."

He started toward the gate. "Can you walk with that on?" he threw over his shoulder.

"I don't know how you ever got anyone to marry you," I called as I started after him. "At least not anyone with any self-respect."

I wanted a hole to open up in the ground so I could fall into it, but there it was. I had said it, and I couldn't recall the words.

He turned back to me, confused, probably at the jealousy in my tone. "I'm not..." He looked at me closely for a moment, considering, debating whether or not to tell me something. "I'm not going to talk about that," he said finally and turned back around.

I wanted so badly to say *I'm not going to talk about that* in a low mimic of his voice, but I remembered the words of my uncle and restrained myself. Ezekiel had received a worrisome letter from home. What had he said? *It's Cana and the baby.* But why did he never go home to see them?

I knew that he had a small hut here on the grounds of the

estate where he stayed by himself. And I knew he alternated schedules with another guard, only working two weeks of every month. The other guard, Gid, was really nice, but when he was with Ezekiel, he seemed guarded. They were friends, I thought, but perhaps not very close ones.

I followed Ezekiel down the road that led to the main square of the city, but he bypassed the square and led me down a side road that led out the north gate. We were hailed by the guard there, and my escort stopped to talk.

They obviously knew each other. "Where are you headed?" the guard asked as his eyes flicked to me. "Melek?"

Ezekiel nodded. "It's Kenai's wedding."

"To your sister, right?"

"Don't remind me."

They both laughed. I stared at Ezekiel. I had seldom seen him so much as smile.

"Introduce me to your traveling companion," said the guard as he turned to me, a smile still in his eyes.

I returned his smile sweetly, because his smile was a nice change from Ezekiel's constant frown.

"Uh, this is Eliza, Captain Helaman's niece. Eliza, this is Kimner. He was one of Helaman's chief captains."

"When you boys were playing war, you mean?"

They exchanged a glance, but Kimner continued to smile at me. "Yeah," he said easily. "It was a fun game."

He, at least, I could tease.

"We've got to get going," Ezekiel said quickly, giving my arm a nudge to get me moving.

"I won't detain you then. When can we expect you two back in Zarahemla?"

"A fortnight. Maybe two."

Kimner gave me another long look and whistled, and

Ezekiel grunted and hurried me away from him.

"Why are you being so rude?" I asked him.

"I'm not."

"You are."

He sighed. "It's going to be a long journey if you contradict everything I say."

"You are the one who is contradicting everything I say."

He barked out a laugh. "Proving my point, Eliza. Proving my point."

"No I'm not," I said on a giggle.

I wanted to laugh with him, to say things that would make him smile. He was so sad. Sometimes he looked so morose that I couldn't help but desire to make him glad again.

But of course, that was for his wife to do—not for me.

Still, I remembered Uncle Helaman's charge to be nice to Ezekiel, so I tried.

But he made it so difficult.

Ezekiel had been right, my pack was too heavy, and it only got heavier as the minutes turned into hours. The air was cool, the seasons on the cusp of changing, but I was breathing heavily and, to my embarrassment, sweating by the time we stopped at midday. But I had the sneaking suspicion Ezekiel was testing me, and I wouldn't fail. I wouldn't give him the satisfaction.

At least not this early on, I thought as I drained the water from my water skin.

I caught him regarding me with a sidelong glance.

"What?" I said.

I thought he actually rolled his eyes. "Nothing."

I tried to stretch my back without removing the pack, but it was impossible. I knew if I took the pack off, though, I would never get it back on. I wouldn't be able to on my own, and I wouldn't want to either.

Helaman had sent a whole band of men to escort me to Zarahemla when I had asked for his aid. I hadn't had to carry a thing, though I had insisted on carrying the very most basic of items—my satchel, some food, a change of clothing. Ezekiel probably knew it. He had probably carried some of my things.

I grimaced when I thought of how helpless I must appear to him, what with all my demands of Helaman for necklaces and bangles and new sarongs. It was no wonder Ezekiel regarded me in very poor esteem. I had done that to myself. I had only wanted him to notice me, but I hadn't given much thought to what about me he would be noticing.

"When will we stop for the night?" I asked as I wiped my forehead.

"When it's night."

That was it. "Ezekiel, do you have a problem with me?"

"No."

Right. He had a big problem with me.

Or just a big problem.

About the Author

Misty Moncur wanted to be Indiana Jones when she grew up. Instead, she became an author and has her adventures at home. In her jammies. With her imagination. And pens that she keeps running dry.

Misty is the author of *Daughter of Helaman, Fight For You, In All Places,* and other novels in The Stripling Warrior series. Her stories are filled with tenderness and humor, and her characters are real, endearing, and memorable. Her LDS fiction titles will inspire you.

Misty loves to read anything with a romance in it, edit, type, stare out the window, and hang with her family. She lives in the wild west where she has yet to see a stagecoach or a gunfight, and is, frankly, rather disappointed about it.

73976667R00181

Made in the USA
Columbia, SC
21 July 2017